THE
SURFACING

CLAIRE ACKROYD

THE SURFACING

CLAIRE ACKROYD

LAKE UNION
PUBLISHING

Text copyright © 2025 by Claire Ackroyd
All rights reserved.

Published by Lake Union Publishing, Seattle

www.apub.com

Amazon, the Amazon logo, and Lake Union Publishing are trademarks of Amazon.com, Inc., or its affiliates.

ISBN-13: 9781662525872
eISBN: 9781662525865

Cover design by Liron Gilenberg
Cover image: ©[Credit] / [Stock House]; ©[Credit] / [Stock House]

Printed in the United States of America

No one was meant to die. It was my sister's wedding, after all, and my mother didn't want to spoil the day with a corpse. All we had to do was have a discussion, maybe even offer a bribe, as crazy as that sounds, but most of all make sure the past wasn't in danger of surfacing.

Or at least that was what my mother's letter suggested. I was keen to avoid the wedding altogether, had already circled 'Sorry I can't make it' on my RSVP with a big fat Sharpie. I hadn't seen my sister, Aurelie, in five years, and was hoping for at least another five without her preening, puffed-up presence – taking the view that the best way to stop the past from coming to light was to avoid those people with whom it was buried. But the letter had arrived before I'd had a chance to post my RSVP (a casualty of living in a remote area of the Scottish Highlands). And, as I watched the letter's corner burn bright in the flame of a match, my mother's rounded script curling into black tongues which disintegrated and dropped away into ash, I found myself beginning to agree with her.

Perhaps the wedding wasn't such a terrible idea after all. Perhaps it actually presented an opportunity. To get answers. Closure. Because, in order to truly leave the past behind, I needed to know who was responsible for what had happened to Jennifer twelve years before, in the summer of 2005. And if Sarah (or my mother) actually knew what had happened to Peter that very same summer – well, I needed to know that too.

When psychologists unpick the mind of a murderer, they always debate the role of nature versus nurture. Which is pointless when you think about it, given the murderer's family is responsible for both.

Still, no one was meant to die at the wedding. But, unfortunately, they did. On the Saturday night, after the ceremony, when the festivities were in full swing.

And, even more unfortunately: I killed them.

SEPTEMBER 2017

THURSDAY, 9 A.M.

I must be the only twenty-seven-year-old in existence who's been given a packing list by her landlady. I snort when I see the A5 page on my bedside table, a tick box next to each item and a smiley face in the corner. Ridiculous. But now I have it, it would be even more ridiculous not to use it. *Dress for Friday night's dinner*: tick. *Wash bag, pyjamas, underwear*: tick, tick, tick. *Dress for wedding (not black)*: only my green tunic fits the criterion, so I bundle it into the rucksack. *Wedding present?* Cross. I visited Aurelie and Alistair's website yesterday and bought them a silver toilet brush – which, price aside, seemed appropriate. Another instance of dealing with my sister's shit.

To be fair, I don't have a standard tenancy agreement with my landlady, Kirsty. I'm part of her artist residency programme, which means I get to live almost rent-free in a tiny cottage next to her larger one, and to paint every day, taking inspiration from the countryside around me. Doing my best to capture the magnificence of the glens and shimmering lochs, the gnarled mountains and buttresses of rock, the heather and wind-soaked moorland. Then, on Sundays, I go to her and Rob's house for lunch; discuss my weekly progress with them over lamb and roast potatoes (or sometimes steak-and-kidney pie). If there's sticky toffee pudding for dessert, we might discuss Scottish art more broadly too: how the Romanticism of the early nineteenth century gave way to the Naturalist movement, for instance.

Yet Kirsty and I don't just share an interest in art and food; we're also united by suffering. Because, twelve years ago, in the summer of 2005, both of us suffered a terrible loss. I lost Jennifer – my best friend, my only friend – and she lost her son, Peter. Jennifer was taken from her home in Bristol, while Peter disappeared a mere four weeks later, from the shores of Loch Ness. Less than a mile from where my family and I were camping at the time.

Neither has been seen or heard from since.

I pull open the bottom drawer of the wardrobe and extract my shortbread tin from under a box of tampons. Take off the lid, unfold the old piece of newspaper inside, and take out the pot of nail varnish it protects. A small cuboid of plastic, with a caked-on lid and reservoir of pale blue lacquer. An ugly, unusable thing, but also infinitely precious, because it's the only item of Jennifer's I own. I squeeze it tightly in my hand, bring it close to my chest, where it nestles against my ribs.

Then, one-handed, I smooth out the creases in the protective newspaper to gaze once more upon Peter's face: his wide smile and chipped front tooth. His mass of wavy hair. To read the headline I've read so many times that even the curves of the font are imprinted on my brain – *Man goes missing in Loch Ness storm* – and the text underneath, which gives all the details, or as much as the journalists knew. That Peter was nineteen when he disappeared, and working at the North Ness Hotel. That he was last seen by a hotel guest, on the banks of the loch, minutes before the storm began. That the only thing found in the loch after the storm was an old canoe.

I refold the article around the nail varnish and put it back in the tin. Return the tin to the drawer before changing my mind and packing it in my rucksack instead. I want it with me this

6

weekend, not because I'm planning to paint my nails, and certainly not because I need access to the details of Peter's disappearance (I memorised those years ago), but because having it will keep me focused. It will remind me of the trauma of that summer, and how justice has yet to be served.

I zip up my rucksack and take one last look at the view: across the slate waters of Loch Broom to the mountain of Beinn nam Ban. I could look at this view forever without growing bored – at the way it changes with the weather, the seasons, the light. The crystalline blue of a summer's morning; the pink-white sky of winter when snow is on its way. The dolphins which perform a running stitch through the waves, and the auks which sit on the crags above the bay.

It was this view that convinced me to stay when I first arrived and saw the photos of Peter. There are about thirty of them in Kirsty's living room, taken from throughout his (brief) life: Peter as a baby, Peter as a schoolboy, Peter as a teenager. Peter on the beach with his parents, Peter climbing a mountain with his aunt, Peter eating an ice cream with his cousins. An overwhelming quantum of Peter for even the most indifferent of observers, but a downright disturbing quantum of Peter for someone who was there, at Loch Ness, on the very night he disappeared. Who can't shake the memory of her tent bucking in the storm as the rain impaled the earth around it; of wild winds and chattering teeth and unfathomable loneliness. Of her sense of dread when the police arrived at the campsite the next day and went from tent to tent, asking questions. *Have any of you seen this man?* So even though I came to White Croft knowing I would meet Peter's mother, I was unprepared for the sight of his round, freckled face looking at me thirty times over, as if he were reaching across time and through glass to grab me by the throat. My breath went jumpy when I first saw them, and my legs buckled, necessitating a lunge for the mantelpiece. *A mistake*, I thought. *A terrible, awful mistake.* I was turning to leave, muttering apologies at the window, unable to look at Kirsty, when I caught sight of a white-tailed eagle flying above the bay. And as I watched it, dipping and gliding, my lungs began to regulate. I continued to watch it, giant and unworldly in the fading orange of the evening sky, and engaged my diaphragm; picked up on the smell of pastry baking in the kitchen. My limbs became stronger and I realised there was no cause for panic. That I'd been drawn to this place for a reason – like a salmon pulled to its spawning ground, or a monarch butterfly tracing the route of its forebears. By the strange currents humans don't understand.

So I kept looking at the view: at the eagle and the sky and the mountains.

And I stayed.

No sooner have I dumped my rucksack into the boot of my car than Kirsty comes running out from her cottage, a plastic tub in her hands. 'Provisions for the journey,' she says, pressing the tub upon me.

'Thank you.' I know better than to protest.

'Have you got something to drink?'

I point to the bottle of water in the passenger footwell and she tuts. 'I meant something caffeinated. I could get you a thermos of tea?'

'No. Thank you.'

'Coffee, then? Or hot chocolate?'

I shake my head. 'I can always get something at the services.'

'All-righty.' She knots her hands together, separates them again, pulls me into a hug. 'You don't have to go, you know.'

'I do.' A deliberately vague response.

She squeezes me harder, and I can see the line of her parting from above. The brown-grey hair emerging from her scalp, the colour of water-stained wood. 'Well. I hope it all goes smoothly for you. Or as smoothly as it can.'

'Thank you.' She knows about my strained relationship with Aurelie; how the two of us have barely spoken since secondary school.

'And I hope your mam's doing all right.' Pulling away, she tries to catch my line of sight. 'That she feels well enough to enjoy the wedding.'

I nod and kick a piece of dirt loose from one of the car's tyres, thinking about our recent conversation by Loch Broom. When I didn't turn up for Sunday lunch and Kirsty came to find me on the shore, throwing pebbles into the water. When I explained my mother's cancer had spread from lung to bone. She held me in her arms, then, said she was glad I'd told her. That I should feel able to tell her anything and everything.

It was a nice sentiment, and I thanked her for it. But it was also wrong. If I actually told Kirsty everything, she'd know me for what I really am.

And then she wouldn't want to know me at all.

FRIDAY, 2 P.M.

Day two of driving, and the first day of seeing my family again. It's difficult to process this fact, what is to come, while sitting in roadworks on the M6, but I don't suppose paying to use the toll road would make it any easier. I switch stations, from Radio 1 to Classic FM, and turn up the volume. The violin's notes are familiar: full and quivering. The same notes I heard at a concert long ago, when the soloist was too good for the orchestra. When my mother sobbed, and Aurelie glared from above her flute, lips pursed. Our father wasn't there.

But then, he rarely was.

The music is in 4/4, otherwise known as Common Time. A misnomer, in my view, because there's nothing common about it. Even the sayings can't agree: time flies; time is money; time is both killed and saved. The only consensus: it is malleable, shifting, slippery. We can be taken back across the years by the scent of lavender or the strains of Elgar. We can be pulled forward by ambition, by dread, by forgetting to notice. We can live, as I am doing now, in a moment that is both infinite and fleeting.

A point of no return.

The wedding is to be held in Berkshire, close to Aurelie and Alistair's home and six hundred miles away from mine. I did the first half of the driving yesterday, stayed overnight in a B&B near

Carlisle. A nice enough place, if functional, with glossy white walls and modern bathrooms. Certainly in better condition than the North Ness Hotel ever was, with its high, cracked ceilings and worn carpets. With its cold, crumbling dining room, where Aurelie first met Alistair. With its rudimentary campsite, where we spent all those long, drawn-out summers, and its rundown boathouse—

Peter's face flashes into my mind, then, round and smiling, followed by a snapshot of my mother's letter. *Sarah says she knows something about his disappearance.*

I look out at the tarmac. It's been five years since I was last in England, and I haven't missed it. Or perhaps it's just the memories I haven't missed. Memories which seep from the stench of petrol, from the itch of sweat upon my skin.

I shut my eyes, try to block them out.

A horn sounds, and I open my eyes to see the man in the car behind waving his fist, his face puce. A few metres of space has opened up between me and the car in front.

I release the clutch and inch forwards. I release the middle finger of my left hand too, raising it to the rear-view mirror so the puce-faced man can't miss it.

I see the towers above the trees. Four of them, tall and crenellated, like rooks on a chessboard. My first glimpse of Goreton Manor Hotel. After receiving Aurelie's invitation (thick card, tied with ivory ribbon), I went straight to the hotel's website to check it out. Built in the nineteenth century by a rich landowner and collector of exotic animals, it's considered a fine example of the neo-Gothic style, apparently, with a proliferation of follies, steeples, towers and gargoyles, and a famous aviary once visited by Queen Victoria.

As I turn the last corner of the driveway, the hotel's main frontage comes into view. Every surface fussy and twisted, a paean to embellishment.

The perfect wedding venue for my sister.

The car park is surrounded on all sides by a tall yew hedge, which cuts off much of the daylight; I switch on my headlamps to avoid scraping any BMWs or Audis. The top of the hedge has been trimmed into a series of shapes – spheres, pyramids, spirals – which resemble tiny tombstones. There are only two gaps in the hedge: the one I entered through, which leads to the front of the hotel, and a much narrower gap, which leads directly into the hotel gardens. I park my car by the latter, look through it to a paved path with pink and white roses behind.

Then I turn off the engine and breathe deeply, in through my nose and out through my mouth, like my mother taught me. Slowly, slowly, from the depths of my abdomen. A way of coping with the coils of anxiety; of stopping them from pulling tight. Sitting up straighter, I let my lungs inflate. Hold the air for as long as I can. Exhale.

Maybe I should just reverse the car and go back. Back along the driveway. Back along the Berkshire lanes. Back along the A-roads and the motorways to Scotland, and then further; back past Edinburgh, Inverness and Ullapool to the blessed solitude of my cottage.

But if I go back now, I'll never move forward.

I've come here with a plan – we both have, my mother and I – and I can't return to Scotland without answers. Is Sarah responsible for what happened to Jennifer? And has she actually learned anything about Peter's disappearance? My mother says we need to find out what she knows, and if necessary, bribe her into silence.

The truth is dangerous for our family, she wrote in her letter. *If it ever got out, it could be misunderstood. Misconstrued.*

I think my mother's wrong about Sarah. She might be cruel and deceitful (as well as my sister's matron of honour: a badge of dishonour if ever there was one), but I can't believe she knows anything about Peter. She's almost certainly just been gossiping – trying to stir things up. Wanting to feel important; to generate excitement in her tedious existence.

But my mother's right about one thing: if the truth comes out, it could damage our family.

Because we all lied about that night, about where we were when Peter disappeared.

The hotel lobby is grand, with wood-panelled walls and vast oil paintings of hunting dogs and pompous men in breeches. There are floor-length red curtains, tied back with gold rope, and an enormous fireplace with a grate of unlit logs.

And Aurelie. She is standing in the centre of the room, wearing tight jeans and a white T-shirt and talking to a woman holding a bunch of flowers. There is a momentary flinch when she sees me, before she stretches her face into a smile. 'Stephie! You've made it! How lovely!'

I hate being called Stephie. I walk toward my sister and she embraces me, but only lightly and from a distance – the way one might comfort the unwashed.

She draws back. 'Stephie, this is my wonderful florist, Hannah. Hannah, Stephie.'

'Hi,' the woman says. 'Sorry I can't shake your hand – occupational hazard. Lilies!'

'Stargazer lilies,' my sister adds. 'We're having them all around the room at tonight's pre-wedding dinner. Aren't they beautiful?'

'I thought lilies were meant to symbolise death?' The words are out of my mouth before I can stop them.

Aurelie's lips – bubble-gum pink, too shiny – pucker. 'Please, Stephanie,' she says. At least I'm Stephanie again now. 'It's my *wedding*. You don't need to question everything.'

There is a pause, during which Hannah fiddles with the lily stems. 'Better get these in water!' she says. 'It's always hot in hotels. See you later!' She hurries away.

'Yes, see you later!' my sister calls after her, one manicured hand raised in the air. She turns and looks me up and down, takes in my tracksuit bottoms and trainers before returning to my face. 'So,' she says.

'So?'

'It's been a long time.'

'Yes.'

'Four years?'

'Five.'

'Five?' She lets out a low whistle. 'Goodness. Half a decade.'

'Mmm.'

'Incredible. Doesn't time fly! And you haven't met Ally yet, have you? I mean, not properly?'

'I suppose not.' The last time I saw her husband-to-be was twelve years ago, in the summer of 2005. Back when he was still just a waiter at the North Ness Hotel. Before Jennifer and Peter disappeared.

'Well, he's lovely. Really good for me.'

If someone were actually good for Aurelie, they would explain to her that life is not a West End show with her in the starring role. That it's not even the Edinburgh Fringe. That she just exists, along with the rest of us, in a universe of ever-increasing entropy.

But I don't think she means that. 'Right,' I say. 'That's great.'

'Isn't it? I feel so lucky. He has such a similar outlook to mine. So many similar interests. Loves films! And, being a lawyer too, he gets my job. He understands that I have to work long hours to close deals.'

'Right,' I say again.

'And our new house is lovely, overlooking the river. Ally's a keen rower, you know.'

'Yes, Mum said.'

Aurelie raises her eyebrows. 'Did she? What else did she say about him?'

That he's stinking rich and likes to make a spectacle of his largesse. That he speaks too loudly and his hair contains too much product. That he doesn't like to talk about his past.

'Oh, you know,' I say.

'I don't, actually.'

'Just that . . . he seems to make you happy.'

She smiles widely, so I must have said the right thing. For once. 'He does make me happy. And it makes him happy to make me happy. So hopefully we should be happy together!'

'Yes.'

'And we both *love* London, love the city life. In fact, it's one of the things we first bonded over: how much we prefer it to Scotland. All that cold, wild emptiness! I don't know how you put up with it.'

'I like the cold, wild emptiness.'

She taps her fingernails together. The sound is like rain on hard earth. 'When did you last see Mum?'

'Five years ago, at her birthday party. The one at the Italian restaurant.'

'Ah.' The tapping becomes more pronounced. 'Well, in that case, I should probably warn you, so you're prepared: she looks awful.'

My insides tighten. 'Oh.'

'She's thin. Really thin. I tried to buy her a new outfit for the wedding, one that would fit better, but she wouldn't let me.'

'Right.'

'And her breathing's become laboured. She coughs a lot.'

'Yes.' I have heard this, over the phone. The way our mother's voice sometimes snags, forcing her to pause. The way her lungs betray her.

'I'm just glad I can do this.'

'Do what?'

'Get married. She said if she can see me married, she can die happy. It's all she wants. That, and having her children together, one last time.'

If only that were true. But Aurelie never saw the letter our mother sent to me six months ago. The one she insisted I burn after reading. The one which led to my being here, this weekend.

After all, I'm sure as hell not here just to see Aurelie get married.

And nor is our mother.

I ignore the signs for the lifts; make my way to the stairs instead. If Hell were a place on Earth, it'd be a lift: a small, windowless box where thoughts are inescapable. I once had a panic attack going up to the third floor of a Premier Inn, and sank to the floor, curling into a foetal position and staring at the wall, smooth and coffin-like, until my mother managed to coax me out.

The stairwell is a couple of degrees colder than the rest of the hotel, and not so well maintained. Clean, yes, but the steps are scuffed, and there is flaking paint on the window frames. There's also next to no decoration, just a series of alcoves with glass display cases. The first houses a stuffed raven, its glassy eyes staring, and the second a collection of tortoiseshell combs. In the third is an old hunting knife, with a wooden handle and a silver blade.

Exiting the stairwell on the third floor, I am once more surrounded by grandeur. The walls are painted a deep red, lit by sconces, and there is thick carpet underfoot. I test how silently I can walk: one foot placed on to the ground, then the next, and repeat. There is the occasional creak, but nothing more.

I am only a couple of doors away from Room 318 when I hear voices behind me. Keen to avoid the possibility of further conversation, I consider running the last few metres, but check myself. Now, more than ever, I must try to be normal. *Nor-mal, nor-mal, nor-mal* (in time to my gait): a state I journey toward but never reach. Normality is not something you can learn (I have learned); you are either born into it or you are not. I have spent hours watching people, trying to emulate their body language and verbal tics. The way they nod slightly when others are speaking, or mirror their stance. Their use of filler words – *mmm, ah, right* – to glue conversations together. Yet when I try to put these things into practice myself, the words seem misshapen, my posture stiff.

'Stephanie? Stephanie! Is that you?'

It's too late to run. I turn to see my aunt Jane filling the corridor with her broad, bosomy body and even broader (but less bosomy) hat. It is made of felt and flops around her ears, like a fedora that's given up.

'Stephanie!' she calls again, rushing toward me, her wheelie case lurching from one side to the other. 'Stephanie!'

'Hello,' I manage, as she abandons her case and pulls me to her in a hot, sickly smelling embrace, her hat pressing against my cheek.

17

'Oh, it's so good to see you.'

'Right.'

'How is life?' She pulls away.

'Okay.' This isn't a time for truths. 'Thank you.' Over her shoulder I can see my uncle Grant approaching. He has lost a lot of hair but not his moustache, which still sits in two distinct sections above his lips, like fallen eyebrows.

'Isn't it exciting?' she goes on. 'Aurelie. Getting married!'

'Yes,' I say, just as Grant reaches us. He puts down the bags he's been carrying and leans in to kiss me on both cheeks. He smells strongly too, but astringent, vinegary. The sort of smell that can strip skin.

'Stephanie,' he says, drawing back and observing me. His lips rise on one side, in an expression that might denote amusement. 'Good to see you.'

'Hello.'

'Isn't it wonderful!' Jane says. 'The whole family back together again! Even your father!'

I opt not to reply.

'So what do you know about your future brother-in-law?' she asks.

'Not much.' This *is* true; beyond the occasional word of thanks, I never spoke to Alistair at the North Ness Hotel, and I've barely spoken to my sister since. In fact, until this weekend, I've success-fully avoided all of the hideous-sounding events she (or they, but almost certainly she) has organised over the past decade: various birthday parties, her hen do, their housewarming.

'Oh, don't be coy. I hear he's quite the catch!'

I shrug. 'He used to serve us pancakes. When we went on holiday to Scotland.'

'Not anymore though!' Jane winks. 'I hear he's very rich these days.'

She says this as a statement, not a question, but smiles and waits. 'Apparently so,' I say.

'A lawyer!'

'Yes.'

Grant snorts. 'Just what the world needs. *Another* lawyer.'

Jane ignores him. 'And handsome,' she says.

I shrug again.

'Oh, go on, Stephanie.' She clutches at my arm. 'You must be able to tell us something about him.'

She waits again, her hand still squeezing. 'He speaks too loudly,' I say. 'And puts too much product in his hair.'

This makes her shriek with laughter. She loosens her grip on my arm, only to clasp on to her husband instead. 'You're hilarious!' she says. 'Isn't she funny, Grant?'

He wrinkles his nose. 'Funny ha-ha or funny peculiar?'

'I hope Aurelie's asked you to do a speech.'

'No.'

'That's a shame. I do like a funny speech. At my wedding to Grant, the best man did a hilarious speech. Everyone was crying by the end.'

Crying has always struck me as a pointless activity; it's been years since I've bothered. A teacher once told me crying cleans the eyes, but when I asked if that meant happy people had dirty eyes, she told me to go to my next lesson.

'So,' Jane continues. 'How are things with you, Stephanie?'

'Okay.'

'Still in Scotland?'

'Yes.'

'Any nice Scottish men up there?'

Here we go. Jane has always been obsessed with my love life, or lack of it, asking questions which she knows I have no desire to answer. 'Rob's all right,' I say, hoping to deflect her.

'Rob. Oooh. How do you know him?'

'He and his wife, Kirsty, are my closest neighbours. We eat lunch together every Sunday.' Not this one, though. This Sunday they'll be alone with their lamb, potatoes and carrots; the third chair at their table empty once again. 'Nearly every Sunday,' I correct myself. 'We tend to have a roast.'

But Jane isn't interested in my dietary habits. 'Any *special* Scottish men?' She leans in closer and I step back. 'Or has Aurelie already cornered that market? Perhaps she's like me: partial to a man in a kilt.'

I look across to Grant – to his long, skinny legs in blue chinos – and try not to picture him in a kilt.

He taps one hand on her wheelie case. 'Instead of talking about your fetish for tartan skirts, shall we get our luggage into our room?'

'Or woman?' Jane lets out a giggle.

'Oh, for crying out loud.' Grant picks up his bags and walks off.

'What?' she calls after him. And then, to me, 'He doesn't understand that lesbianism is fashionable these days.'

I look at my feet.

Jane clutches my arm again. 'I'm sorry. Have I embarrassed you?'

'You're embarrassing yourself!' shouts Grant, without turning. 'It's clear she doesn't have a partner.'

'It's not clear at all!' Jane shouts back. 'We haven't seen Stephanie for years! People change!'

Even though Grant is now some distance away, I can see he is shaking his head. 'Some people don't,' he says.

Jane releases my arm and gives it a pat. 'Don't listen to him.'

I nod, despite agreeing with Grant for once. Some people don't change.

He and my aunt are as awful as ever.

◆ ◆ ◆

When Jane finally leaves, I enter my room. It is large, with more red carpet and a four-poster bed with gold draping. There is a surfeit of pillows and cushions in a variety of shapes and colours. I put down my rucksack and sort through them. I like a firm, standard-shaped pillow, but the only options here are velvet triangles, tiny gold squares, and a couple of oversized pillows which seem designed for suffocation.

The rest of the room isn't much better. A pair of red and gold armchairs sit in front of a window adorned with more gold fabric, and a chandelier with fake candles dangles off-centre from the ceiling. Dark wood furniture adds to the dismal effect. As well as a wardrobe, there is a desk with three drawers; I open the first to find a ballpoint pen and a pad of writing paper, both with *Goreton Manor Hotel* inscribed across them in cursive lettering. The second drawer is empty, while the third is much larger, containing a kettle, two cups and a handful of fancy teabags. At least there isn't a bible.

I inspect the rest of the room – television, hairdryer, telephone; a poorly rendered painting of a naked woman, arms contorted to cover her breasts and groin; pocket-sized bathroom – and unpack. It doesn't take long. Afterwards, I remove the cushions and pillows from the bed and stack them at the bottom of the wardrobe. Then I take off my trainers and lie down. I look up at the ceiling. There is a patch which is whiter than the rest, clearly newer paint, and I can see Peter's features in its brush strokes. The slant of his eyebrows; the loose waves of his hair.

Sitting up again, I roll back my sleeve to look at my watch. Sunday morning will be a write-off, as everyone will be sleeping off hangovers. Which means, realistically, I only have until 11 p.m.

tomorrow – just over twenty-nine hours from now – to draw a line under the past once and for all.

The clock is ticking.

FRIDAY, 6.15 P.M.

My mother's room is on the fifth floor, and is considerably more luxurious than mine. She has a coffee machine, for a start, plus a sofa and a balcony. And the decor is calmer: less red and gold, more grey and neutral tones. The paintings are equally bad, though; one provides a close-up of a horse's head, teeth bared, while another shows a woman in a too-big hat by a window. The artist was perhaps hoping to channel Vermeer, but seems to have come closer to channelling Aunt Jane when she snoops on her neighbours and wonders out loud when the Ocado man will come.

I see all of this before I see my mother. She said she was going to jump in the shower, but would prop open her bedroom door and I should come up when ready. So here I am, perched on her sofa next to a copy of *Country Gardens* magazine, listening to the sounds from the bathroom. Running water and repeated coughing. I try to distract myself by looking at pergolas, and then by turning on the television, but there's nothing on. I watch snooker for long enough to see a red ball being sunk. Maggie, a counsellor from my sixth-form days, once suggested I might like snooker – might enjoy the structured order in which the colours have to be potted – but she clearly didn't understand that a penchant for orderliness is not the same thing as a desire to be bored.

My mother emerges a couple of minutes after the shower is switched off. I force myself to look directly at her, and it's not as bad as I'd feared: she is slender, yes, but smiling, and her movements are slow but stable. Her wig is on straight. Although her quilted dressing gown has perhaps given false reassurance – as she walks toward me, I can see just how thin her legs have become.

But maybe that is actually better. For her illness to be so obvious that it cannot be ignored, nor wished away. For there to be no choice but to confront it.

'Hello, my angel.' She smiles and opens her arms to take me in. It seems the wrong way round, for the frail to embrace the healthy, but I let it happen.

'Hi Mum.' I keep my arms limp by my sides, not wanting to knock her. I've read that people undergoing chemotherapy can bruise easily. 'How are you feeling?'

She pulls back. 'Oh, I'm fine, all things considered. How are you?' Her tone is level, as if this is a normal weekend. As if we last saw each other five days, not years, ago. As if she has summoned me here simply to catch up, and not to ensure another guest's silence.

'Okay.'

'How is Scotland?'

'Good.'

'Still enjoying the painting?'

I nod.

'And it's not too lonely?'

'No. I've got Kirsty and Rob for company.'

'Kirsty and Rob. Of course.' Her smile fades, and I wish I hadn't mentioned them. She doesn't like the fact I'm living next door to Peter's parents; thinks our closeness is remiss given everything that happened.

'They're good people, Mum. They really are.'

'I'm sure they are. It's just . . .'

24

She doesn't need to finish her sentence, because we've had this conversation before over the phone. Many times. And I can see that, on surface inspection, it *is* unsettling – my life having nudged against Peter's on multiple occasions. The night he disappeared from Loch Ness, when we were camping on its shores. The fact he and Alistair, and two of Alistair's groomsmen, all worked together at the North Ness Hotel. And of course now my artist residency near Ullapool, living next door to his parents. Except, when considered carefully, these connections feel more inevitable than odd; a product of unavoidable symmetries. Because both Kirsty and I have suffered loss. Both of us appreciate art, and the beauty of the Scottish Highlands. Both of us are searching for closure, and can recognise something of that yearning – something of *ourselves* – in the other. And when you think of it that way, it seems entirely reasonable we should be drawn together.

'They're very kind to me,' I say, thinking of the shortbread tin in my room. Of the old pot of nail varnish, and its protective wrapping of newspaper. Of Peter's face forever smiling, and Jennifer's face forever out of reach. 'In fact, they're kind to everyone. Kirsty was asking after you before I left.'

'Me?' She toys with the sleeve of her dressing gown. 'Why would she ask after me?'

I stare at her, wonder if she's being deliberately obtuse. 'Because you've got lung cancer?'

'Right.' She pauses, turns away to cough into a tissue.

I look at her more closely: the set angle of her mouth; the slight twitch of her jaw. 'Mum, you do realise it's all nonsense?' I say. 'Sarah claiming to know anything?'

She sighs. 'Maybe. But you didn't *hear* her. She sounded earnest. She sounded . . . convincing.'

She said this in her letter too. That she'd overheard Sarah whispering to Aurelie in the changing room at the bridal shop, claiming

25

she'd learned some facts about Peter's disappearance. Saying she was thinking of telling the police. *She sounded like she really meant it*, my mother wrote. *If it hadn't been for your sister – who pleaded with her not to say anything, not until after the wedding at least – I think she'd have done it.*

'But how could she possibly know anything?' I say. 'She wasn't there.'

'I'm not sure.' My mother shuffles her way to the front of the sofa, uses an arm to lever herself into a seated position. 'But she has lots of friends, doesn't she? Lots of acquaintances.'

I shrug. 'Perhaps. But I don't see what any of them would know either. Besides, even if Sarah has somehow miraculously . . . inexplicably . . . learned something, I don't see how it would impact us.'

'Don't you?' My mother looks at me with a long, searching expression.

'No.' I come round to sit beside her. We've had this conversation before too, but it seems worth repeating. 'I mean, I'm aware we weren't one hundred per cent truthful with the police about that night, but they've no reason to go back through our statements. Because we didn't *know* Peter—'

'He worked at the North Ness Hotel, along with Alistair and the others—'

'Right, but we never met him there, did we? Or at least I don't remember doing so.' I think back to the decrepit dining room: all faded grandeur and scurrying waiters in tartan. I can easily picture Alistair, tall and oily, and can vaguely remember Mike and Lewis, who will be acting as two of his groomsmen this weekend. Mike was quiet, pale, while Lewis was the opposite: loud and ruddy-cheeked. But I can't picture Peter in that room, can't recall his messy hair and chip-toothed smile in among the olde-worlde furniture and (generally) olde-worlde customers. 'Do you?'

'No, but—'

'So even if the case of Peter's disappearance gets reopened, we won't be of any interest to the police, will we, because we had no motive?'

I want her to agree with me, to smile and tell me I'm right. That's she's just being paranoid. But instead she narrows her eyes, looks down at her hands. 'Does there always need to be a motive?'

I'm not sure if it's what she's saying, or the fact she's speaking in a hushed, portentous tone, but I feel a flicker of fear, deep inside my abdomen. 'Is there something you're not telling me?' I ask.

'Of course not! I've told you everything.' But she's given away by the red lines across her cheeks. The same ones which used to appear whenever she claimed she'd only had a couple of drinks. 'How about you?'

'How about me what?'

'Is there anything you want to tell *me*?'

'No.' There is a pause, which extends into a silence, and I return my gaze to the red lines, which are spreading to her neck. A sign she's lying, or at least not disclosing everything she knows.

The silence is becoming thicker, curdling the air around us. 'So,' I say. 'Your plan?'

'What about it?'

'Are we still—'

'Yes.'

She doesn't even let me finish my question. Just assumes that I want to go over the arrangements once again. She repeats them all now: how she's going to talk to Sarah tomorrow evening, by the quiet of the lake. How she'll ask what she knows and explain that, in the fear of the moment, we panicked and said some silly things to the police. That, in the unlikely event of the case being reopened, we don't want our original statements to be undermined. And perhaps that, if necessary, we've got the money to keep things quiet.

Yet this is very much my mother's plan, not mine. I'm with her on talking to Sarah, but offering a bribe at any point seems ridiculous. Not just because it was years ago and I don't believe Sarah knows anything anyway, but also because I can't countenance giving money to someone who made my teenage years a misery. Who single-handedly turned the rest of the school, including my very own sister, against me. Who mocked and taunted and bullied, and worse – far, far worse – was almost certainly responsible for Jennifer being taken away all those years ago.

But I don't tell Mum any of this. Instead, I simply nod, and she nods back, in what feels more like a temporary truce than a meeting of minds.

Another silence unfolds.

Time to change the subject. I think through my usual conversation starters – the weather, clothes, travel – and decide the last of these is probably best. The weather is warm, but not remarkably so for late summer, and clothes at a wedding are a thorny issue. Especially if Aurelie tried to buy our mother a new outfit and was rebuffed. But travel is a safe topic. Which roads we took to get here, what the traffic was like, whether and where we had to fill up with petrol. I am about to mention the roadworks on the M6 when my mother speaks again. 'Apparently your father has already arrived.'

I am suddenly conscious of the workings of my stomach: its digestion of the crackers and cream cheese I ate for lunch. Or possibly its failure to digest; it feels as if the cream cheese has formed a solid lump at the base of my throat.

'Are you all right, my angel?' Her tone is sweet again; her capacity for sympathy at its greatest when it comes to my father's shortcomings. She takes my hand. 'He got here a couple of hours ago, apparently, on the train; Aurelie messaged to tell me. And he'll be at the dinner tonight.'

The thought of having dinner in the same room as my father makes me want to retch. I can't contemplate picking up a fork and using it to convey food to mouth, when my muscles know better, when they twitch with the urge to thrust it into the side of his head. To literally prick his conscience.

But thinking of his conscience just leads me to mine. To the memories which have formed me, for good and ill. Jagged pieces of time, lodged like shrapnel in my brain.

And my father left the first piece.

◆ ◆ ◆

February 1997

I pick my way over the kitchen floor, stepping in the gaps between the shards of porcelain, turning my feet to fit. Feel a rush of nausea when my toes make contact with a flap of chicken skin, puckered like a deflated balloon. Look back as I reach the door to see my mother take hold of the dish of potatoes – raise it to chest height, extend her arms – but escape before it comes crashing down, splintering across the tiles. A single potato rolls out into the hall and comes to rest upon the doormat.

My sister says nothing. Just grabs my hand and leads me up the stairs to the landing where we sit, knees hugged to chests, faces pressed against the banisters. Not wanting to hear but also needing to. I'm only seven, but old enough to sense the cusp. Aware this moment will serve as a marker between the past and everything to follow.

Our mother screams. Our father tells her to calm down, which makes her scream more. There is the dink and hiss of something else breaking. 'How could you fucking do this?'

'Mummy used the f-word,' Aurelie says. Her eyes are wide.
'What's the f-word?'

Aurelie turns, solemn, her face framed by moonlight from the window. 'It's what people say when they're really angry.'

'Why is Mummy really angry?'

'I don't know.'

'Is it because—'

'Shh.' Our father has come out into the hall. He stops by the front door and the solitary potato; looks back toward the kitchen.

'Get out!' our mother screams.

He turns round, as if searching for something. 'I didn't . . .' he says. 'I mean, I tried to—'

'Get out!'

'But I just—'

'If I have to look at you for one more second, I swear I'll kill you.'

'Okay, okay! I'm going.' He takes his coat from the peg and opens the front door. Glances back over his shoulder at the landing – for one second, two – and is gone into the night.

My mother squeezes my hand. 'I know it's hard. But at least the rest of his family are only evening guests tomorrow.'

'We're his family.'

'Yes of course.' She traces one finger in a circular motion on my palm. 'I didn't mean . . . It's just that it'll be easier. Not having Lucille and the twins here for the wedding itself.'

Lucille and the twins. Grandma used to have a photo of the three of them with my father, standing by a pool with palm trees in the background. They were all in swimwear – my father in knee-length trunks, Lucille in a bikini, and Sebastian and Imogen in matching sunsuits – with their arms draped around one another and wide grins on their faces. Gappy ones too, in the case of the twins. They looked how a family is supposed to look: a balanced unit, smiling and smiled upon. In sharp contrast to the photo of Aurelie and me, which sat further along Grandma's mantelpiece, showing us both in school uniform: our shirts too small, buttons straining for release. Aurelie attempting to look happy, and not quite succeeding, while I wasn't even trying.

I don't know what happened to those photos after Grandma died. Sebastian and Imogen are at secondary school now but I still visualise them as five-year-olds. As beaming, sun-kissed five-year-olds.

As stealers of the smiles that should have been ours.

Aurelie's weekend schedule states that Friday's pre-wedding drinks and dinner will begin at 20.00 in the Cadbury Chamber, with an after-dinner digestif at 22.30 in the Rowntree Room. The unifying theme is not chocolate, however, but famous Victorians, with further festivities planned in the Darwin Hall, Dickens Room and Nightingale Suite.

At 19.20 I enter the Barnardo Bar. A visit here isn't part of the schedule; it's my own personal add-on, because I need a drink. Two, actually. Unlike my mother, I don't have an unhealthy relationship with alcohol; I simply have a good understanding of my body's response to it, and what's required to make the best of a bad situation. One unit has no effect, two reduces my anxiety, three makes me relatively relaxed, and four is optimal. Beyond that, however, I start to get clumsy and more anxious again. So, four units it is. Two double measures of gin.

Gin is my drink of choice because it tends to be measured with precision. Wine, on the other hand, varies enormously in terms of both alcohol content and quantity poured. I am adept at converting percentages to units, but this only works if people adhere to stated measures, and don't judge a 'small' or 'large' glass by eye. It also relies on being allowed to finish a drink before being topped up, which I have found to be a near impossibility in most social situations. Even Kirsty and Rob used to try to refill my glass at our Sunday lunches, back when I drank wine. Whereas now that I bring gin with me – pre-measured into a thermos flask, and decanted – they leave my glass alone. After everything they went through with Peter, they respect my preferences. Kirsty says I'm like him, in that I 'know my own mind'. Which I suppose is a compliment, although I'm hard-pressed to think what else I could know.

But the barman is unwilling to accept I want my drink straight. He reels off the names of five different types of tonic, and when I say no to all of them he offers soda water, lemonade or juice. I say no to all these too, at which point he finally hands the glasses over, but not before dropping a chunk of cucumber in each. I fish it out and discard it in the tips tray. It never fails to amaze me that humans are capable of gene editing and quantum computing, yet can't leave a drink ungarnished.

I take my drinks over to a table in the corner and sit with my back to the wall. This allows me to survey the entire room, which is painted an intense shade of burgundy and filled with mahogany furniture. The effect is oppressive, or perhaps that's just my mood. One thing I do like is the ceiling, which is covered in a lattice of gold fretwork. It reminds me of the ceiling of Bristol's Old Vic – where I worked for a time – which I used to observe at length in preference to checking tickets or directing people to the toilets. I was eventually fired because I didn't do enough to 'connect with the customers', but I reckon I could still draw the ceiling from memory. The great circle at its centre, like a cross between the sun and a collection of ferns, sending out creepers into each corner, and the golden lattice around its perimeter, with four twisting vines inside.

'Have you got any Moët?' Her voice is instantly recognisable: high and wheedling. 'We need Moët!'

I knew this moment would come, but am still unprepared for it. Unprepared for the adrenaline that pulses through my body and gives my brain an overdose of lucidity. Too clear, too sharp.

Sarah.

I look away from the ceiling and there she is, with her back to me, talking to the barman. She is wearing a short-sleeved dress with enormous puffs of material upon the shoulders which she pats periodically, as if worried they might come loose. Her legs are layered in fake tan and elongated by a pair of high heels, and her hair comes down to her waist. Still blonde. She reaches a hand down to smooth it almost as often as she pats her ludicrous puffs.

Extracting a huge phone from a tiny bag, like some sort of modern-day Mary Poppins (albeit not one you'd leave with your children), she turns side-on to look at its screen. Her nose is the same, and her chin: both exaggeratedly rounded. She taps at her phone with long violet fingernails.

The barman places a bottle in the bucket. It has a yellow label, so isn't Moët – maybe Veuve Clicquot? Or Heidsieck Monopole? Back when I worked at The Clifton Cask, I could identify several brands of champagne and wine from just a glance at the bottle, even though people rarely ordered anything other than cider. Or perhaps because people rarely ordered anything other than cider, as it meant the same bottles sat for weeks at the front of the fridges, and I didn't have much to do other than look at them. I certainly didn't want to talk to the old men who leaned on the bar, smelling of smoke, telling me to cheer up.

Sarah turns now, and sees me. There is a brief moment when her eyes narrow and her forehead creases but she is quick to plaster on a smile. She walks over, still smiling, the bucket clasped to her chest. I don't smile back.

'Stephanie!' she says. 'I can't believe it!'

I'm not sure what she can't believe. Whether she's shocked I might attend my sister's wedding, or shocked I still exist. Or perhaps it's more than that; perhaps my presence takes her back in time too.

'Hello Sarah,' I say.

'Oh gosh, you . . .' She hugs the bucket more tightly to her. 'You look amazing!'

There are several things this could mean. It could mean I now look like a twenty-seven-year-old woman, not a fifteen-year-old girl. That I've grown curves and tamed my teeth. It could be mere conversation-filler. Or maybe, just maybe, I should take the comment at face value (so to speak).

I know I'm not unattractive. My forehead is a little high, but I have neat features and shoulder-length brown hair which matches my eyes and which Kirsty tells me is 'thick and lustrous'. I also have a narrow waist and perfectly passable breasts. But I'm still suspicious of being told I look good. And I'm particularly suspicious of being told this by Sarah, whose hand I wouldn't grasp even if I were hanging from a precipice and she and I were the last people on Earth. Although that's a bad analogy. If she and I were actually the last people on Earth, I would launch myself from the precipice willingly.

But of course there is another possibility. That she has said I look amazing simply to detract from the past. From thoughts of what she and my sister did.

'How are you?' she asks.

The memories begin to creep back: the graffiti etched on to my school locker, the mocking laughter. The chemical cherry smell of the taxi. The way she watched and did nothing when the men came to take Jennifer away.

I blink – once, twice, three times – to stop them in their tracks.

34

'It's so amazing to see you again!' she says. 'After all these years. Aurelie wasn't sure if you'd be able to make it. She says you live a long way away now. Near where you and she used to go on those awful camping trips. Edinburgh, is it?'

'Ullapool.'

'Oh, gosh! I expect that's cold!'

I take a mouthful of gin.

'I live in Woking these days,' she says. 'Much warmer!'

I take another mouthful of gin; refuse to let my mind wander.

'I'm so excited to be your sister's maid of honour,' she says. 'I was so honoured when she asked me. Which I suppose is appropriate! I've so enjoyed helping her with all of the wedding planning. And the hen – oh, gosh! – that was hilarious. Such a pity you couldn't make it. Aurelie in a vintage ballgown, with a wig and fan and everything, in a club!'

I've finished my first drink already. Too quick, much too quick.

'And there was a' – she lowers her voice conspiratorially – '*stripper*. In the back room of the club. Dressed in full Regency attire. Until he wasn't! Although he had a disappointingly small . . .'

She giggles, and it strikes me just how little she has changed. The same meanness. The same desire to gossip at others' expense. But perhaps I can use this to my advantage. Rather than enduring the complexity and hassle of my mother's plan tomorrow – the lake trip and possible bribe and goodness knows what else – perhaps I can get the truth from Sarah right now. 'What exactly happened at the dress fitting?' I ask.

'What dress fitting? Is that a euphemism for the stripper?' She giggles again. 'Although I guess that should be *un*fitting.'

'No, I'm talking about the actual dress fitting. When you went to try on dresses with Aurelie and my mother, in London. Six months ago.'

'Oh!' Her nose wrinkles. 'Aurelie's dress had to be taken in quite a bit, because she'd lost a lot of weight. She'd been doing that diet – you know, the cabbage one?'

'No. Anything else?'

'Oh gosh, I can't remember. I had a stinking hangover from Aurelie and Ally's housewarming the night before. Oh, we picked out a garter! A blue lacy one. Quite raunchy.'

This is worse than useless. I need to be more direct. 'Did you discuss Peter?' I ask.

'Who?'

'A boy – well, a man – who drowned in Scotland twelve years ago.'

She taps at the puffs on her shoulders. 'Why are you asking about that?' She sounds a little jittery.

'I just thought you might know something?' I hold her gaze, refuse to break eye contact.

'What?' Her voice falters, and I realise this won't be as easy as I'd hoped. 'Why would I know anything?'

'I don't know. That's why I'm asking.'

She looks away. When she looks back, she is smiling again. 'Have you seen the dress?' she asks.

'What dress?'

'The *wedding* dress.'

I shake my head while inhaling gin fumes from my second glass. Forced to accept I can't get anything out of her just yet. That I'll have to bide my time.

'It's stunning, it really is. Modern, but classy at the same time. A touch of old-school elegance.'

Old-school elegance. An oxymoron if ever I heard one. There was nothing elegant about Waldenborough High. Nothing elegant about the cruelty, or pretence. And Sarah and my sister were the worst: pretending they weren't responsible for Jennifer being sent away after taunting us both for months.

'Talking of your sister, she's going to wonder what's happened to me. I promised champagne.' Sarah nods at the bucket. 'To soothe the pre-wedding nerves!'

She says something else then, something about seeing me later, but I am no longer listening. Instead I am thinking about Aurelie. About the fact she is nervous.

And for the first time this evening, I smile.

FRIDAY, 8 P.M.

The Cadbury Chamber is so crammed with stargazer lilies that I nearly gag upon entering. They are everywhere – in vases down the length of the dining table, in jam jars upon sideboards, in a vast bouquet on top of the piano – and their fetid sweetness is overwhelming. There is even a single lily tucked into each napkin ring, in case we were thinking of tying napkins across our noses to block out the stench.

It doesn't help that the room is already crowded. Everywhere I look there are people clustered together, drinking and braying. And Aurelie is right at their centre, in a silver dress, along with Alistair. He hasn't changed much in the last twelve years. Still tall, still slim, still obsequious: just like he was when he served us pancakes at the North Ness Hotel. All smile and slime (dreadful even in anagrammatic terms). The scene in front of me, with him and Aurelie holding court, is reminiscent of a Hogarth engraving I once saw at the Royal Academy of Arts, in which bewigged, frock-coated individuals gather round a corpse. Its title, fittingly: *The Reward of Cruelty.*

There are name cards upon the table, and as I ponder whether to travel in a clockwise or anti-clockwise direction to search for mine, someone calls to me. I turn – ninety degrees, one-eighty, two-seventy – and there he is.

My father.

The first thing I notice: he is now bald. The second: he has developed jowls. And yet his clothes, if anything, have become younger in style: he is wearing skinny jeans and some kind of diamond-patterned neckerchief. For an awful moment I think I see a nose piercing too, before realising it's just a trick of the light.

'Stephanie. Hello.' He steps forward, arms unfolding as if to hug me, but I step back and he stops. His hands are left dangling, redundant, so he clasps them together and presses, like an atheist resorting to prayer.

'It's good to see you,' he says. 'How are things? I mean . . . are you all right?'

'I've been better.'

He fails to take the hint. 'Your aunt has told me things are . . .' He doesn't finish his sentence. 'You look well, though.'

His gall in telling me how well I look makes me feel the opposite. There is a familiar twinge in my pelvis; a low-level tightening.

'Lucille's looking forward to seeing you too.'

The tightening becomes more acute. I place one hand on my abdomen and cast around for an escape. But there isn't one. Not unless I'm willing to push my way through a group of second cousins who are currently blocking the doorway and who, if disturbed, will no doubt want to 'catch up'. I know from past experience that the pointy-eared one, Stanley, considers himself something of a careers adviser.

A waiter approaches us with a tray of champagne flutes. I have already consumed four units and know any more will make things worse. But it could also, in the short term, provide some relief. I am nothing if not rational – if a plane crashes, I will take advantage of the cheap travel offers the next day, and I always walk under ladders in preference to stepping out into busy roads – but even

I am occasionally susceptible to prioritising immediate gain. To discounting the future too heavily.

I take a glass of champagne, down it, and take a second.

My father's eyes widen. But he forfeited his right to concern a long time ago. A monthly allowance and an annual birthday card do not a parent make. Nor do his other postal offerings: usually a cutting of one of his newspaper articles accompanied by a scrawled, handwritten message. *Thought this would appeal to you* or *Thinking of you* or similar. He always gets it wrong. If he were really thinking of me, as opposed to himself in relation to me, he would send an article in line with my interests. Scottish wildlife, perhaps, or patricide. Not some self-indulgent crap about fathers' rights or families reconnecting.

'It'd be great if I could talk to you this weekend,' he says.

'You are.'

'No, I mean: properly talk. Sit down together with no distractions.'

I curl my toes inside my shoes. 'Aurelie's getting married. There will be nothing but distractions all weekend.'

He smiles. 'I'm sure we can find some time. A quiet moment between drinks or whatever. There's some things I need to talk to you about.'

'Then tell me now.'

'It's not the right place to discuss it.'

'Why?'

He sighs. 'It's about my will.'

The room suddenly seems colder, the smell of lilies stronger. 'What about your will?'

'It's just . . . I'm thinking of making some changes.'

'What do you mean?'

He runs one hand across his shiny head, returns it to the stem of his glass. 'Like I say, Stephanie, this isn't the place to discuss it.'

A photographer approaches me. 'You look just like the bride!' It's a good job Aurelie isn't in earshot.

'A close relative, I presume?'

'Her sister.'

'Wonderful.' He taps one hand on his camera. 'Could I get a couple of photos, please? Maybe in front of these beautiful flowers?'

'We were actually just in the middle of a conversation.'

'Is this gentleman part of the family too?' The photographer steers me into the centre of the room.

'Yes. He's . . . he's my . . .' I can't bring myself to say 'dad' or 'father' in his presence. I toy with the idea of calling him 'my sperm provider', but even I can see how that could be horribly misinterpreted.

'I'm the father of the bride.'

Of course. Here I was wondering how our relationship could be defined, when it didn't need to be defined at all. Not when everything can be defined in relation to Aurelie. Self-centred, self-righteous Aurelie. Our rotten family's lodestar.

'Lovely. In that case, let's have you here, and here, please. That's it. And if you could lean together.'

I don't lean, but I can sense my father's increased proximity in the way dogs sense an impending thunderstorm. I resist the temptation to run off and hide under the table.

'And big smiles please.' The photographer starts fiddling with his camera, turning dials and peering through the viewfinder and turning dials again. I wish he'd just use the autofocus function. The more he turns, the more I feel as if my insides are turning too.

'Go on: big smiles!'

I can't do it.

'Say cheese!'

I focus on a clock on the wall, watch the second hand ticking round. More turning. Everything turning.

'Cheese!' says my father.

'Breathe,' I whisper to myself.

'Lovely,' says the photographer.

A couple more photos, and then the clink of metal on glass, as two men on a dais demand our attention. I don't really remember them, as these are two men I haven't seen for years, not since they were skinny twenty-somethings wearing the black trousers, white shirts and tartan waistcoats that comprised the waiters' uniforms at the North Ness Hotel. Now it seems both of them have filled out: one muscle-wise, and one stomach-wise. Muscle-wise is dressed in a pale blue shirt and jeans, while Stomach-wise is wearing a bright red jacket, as if he's about to go on a hunt. 'Ladies and gentlemen!'

The room falls quiet.

'On behalf of Alistair and Aurelie, we're delighted to welcome you here tonight,' Stomach-wise says in a loud Scottish lilt. 'I'm Lewis, your Master of Ceremonies for the weekend. Aka the one in charge of making you drink!'

A couple of people laugh and raise their glasses in the air. My champagne glass was halfway to my mouth but I lower it again.

'And I'm Mike,' says Muscle-wise. He is softly spoken compared to Lewis but his Scottish accent is stronger. 'The *best* man. Aka the one who's going to give Alistair hell.'

This receives more laughter, including a high-pitched peal which I recognise as Aurelie's.

'Which means I have an easy job,' Mike continues, jiggling his right leg. 'As I have so much material to work with.'

More laughter, and a couple of cheers. Someone shouts, 'What goes on the stag stays on the stag!'

Lewis smiles. 'He has plenty of material without needing to go anywhere near the stag. No need to mention ping-pong balls or . . . whoops!'

There are huge guffaws now, but only from one section of the room. Aurelie's eyes narrow, her smile beginning to slip. I locate my mother in the crowd too, watching the two men on the dais with an odd, crumpled look on her face, as if she's about to cry. I hope she hasn't been drinking.

'Our delicious dinner is to be served in, I am reliably informed, two minutes,' Lewis says. 'So, Mike, can you whet our appetite with a hint at what's coming tomorrow?'

Mike scratches at his shoulder. 'Er . . . okay. Brighton Pier. The Swedish twins. Janie.' His delivery is flat but he still gets a cheer after each one.

'Don't forget Loch Ness.' A voice – female, Scottish – calls this from the back of the room, and everyone turns to see who has spoken. The crowd peels back to reveal a petite red-haired woman who is smiling broadly, as if she's just told a joke. I feel like I know her from somewhere, and wonder if she's a distant relative. One of Great-Aunt Maureen's numerous offspring, perhaps.

Then I realise the atmosphere in the room has changed. Mike stutters something until he is overridden by Lewis, who says, 'Ladies and gentlemen, please charge your glasses, and find your seats! Dinner is about to begin!'

There is a swarm of movement around me. But I stay still, observing. My mother is helped to the table by a man in a suit. My father looks for his name card while simultaneously chatting to an attractive woman in a polka-dot dress. Aurelie gesticulates to a waiter. Sarah rushes to her side. Mike gulps a beer. My aunt and uncle barge their way through a circle of people. The red-haired woman sidles from the room.

And Alistair? Alistair is the most interesting of all. For, like me, he remains still, watchful. But, unlike me, his eyes are wide, almost bulging, and his skin is deathly pale.

I have seen enough emotion charts over the years to know what this means.

He is afraid.

No, that's not quite right.

He is terrified.

As I walk to my place at the table, I try to marshal my thoughts. Try to determine who the red-haired woman was, and why she mentioned Loch Ness. And, more pertinently, why Alistair seemed so frightened.

She can't be one of Great-Aunt Maureen's brood after all, because she's not stayed for dinner. Yet I'm certain I've seen her before, and I'm guessing it must have been in Scotland, given her accent and the fact she mentioned Loch Ness. Although that does little to narrow it down. Our family camped at Loch Ness every summer between 2000 and 2005: the years when my mother accepted my father back into the fold (after kicking him out for being unfaithful) before he left of his own accord (after being unfaithful again). A period I sometimes refer to as the VOMIT years, where VOMIT stands for 'Volatile Oppressive Merger with an Inevitable Terminus' ('marriage' would be a better 'M' but my parents never got that far). Our father drove us up to Scotland in his beaten-up Volvo, to camp in a tent with a small communal area and two even-smaller sleeping compartments: one for him and my mother, the other for me and Aurelie. When we weren't attempting to pitch the tent – my father swearing and my mother watching on with an armful of disarticulated poles – or to sleep on thin foam mats which only served to emphasise the uneven ground beneath us, we were usually out walking. Scrambling over rocks and moorland paths, surrounded by swathes of purple-red heather, or squelching through green, mossy forests. Our shoes damp, our feet blistered, and Aurelie complaining almost constantly about the indignity of being in Scotland while her friends were basking by swimming pools in France and Spain. We drank flat cola and ate cheese sandwiches made with cheap white bread. And sometimes, for a treat, pancakes at the North Ness Hotel, which is, of course, where Aurelie met Alistair. Where she toyed with her hair as he took our orders; as he competed with Mike and Lewis to see who could carry the most plates at once.

'White or red?'

A waiter hovers beside me, holding two bottles. I instinctively place a hand across my glass. 'No, neither. Thank you.'

'Would you like some water?'

This comes from the person at the table on my right: a man with a narrow face and large ears. He picks up a jug, poised to pour.

'Oh. Yes please.'

'Great. Great.' He fills my glass and passes it back to me, watches with approval as I take a mouthful.

The very second that my glass is back on the table, his hand is extended. 'Hi, I'm Mitchell.'

I hate shaking people's hands. Not just because of the germs – although I once read that a single hand can harbour ten million bacteria – but because it's so intimate. Fingertips are full of nerve endings; as receptive to heat as lips. It's weird, if not downright perverse, that we welcome strangers by press-ing sensitive body parts together. If someone suggested greet-ing with groins, there would be an outcry.

However, the downsides of social conformity must be weighed against the upsides. Or, more accurately, against the lack of other downsides. When I refuse to shake somebody's hand, it almost always leads to upset. And so I hold out my hand, let Mitchell clutch it in his own. His fingers are hot and slippery. And I can't help but do what I always do in these situations: compare his clasp to Jennifer's. Her fingers were long and cool, her palms soft. After placing my hand in hers, it would be laced with the scent of lavender.

◆ ◆ ◆

September 2003

The new girl has been sent the wrong way: toward Music and Drama instead of the Science block. A few minutes ago, I saw her in the middle of the corridor, looking down at her timetable before looking up, scanning the noticeboard and signs. Walking one way and then the other, oblivious to the giggling nearby. Her hair tied in a long plait and her bag worn on both shoulders, instead of slung across one. Her skirt regulation-length, and her shoes shiny, tied with large bows.

A gazelle on the plains of Waldenborough High.

It was Sarah who went over. Who pointed in the wrong direction, to the amusement of those around her. Who watched, eyes gleaming, as the girl set off the way she had pointed.

The bell rings for third period and the corridor empties. Within seconds, I'm alone by the lockers, and need to decide which way to go. Science block or girl.

It's an easy choice: I soon catch her up, but linger a few metres behind, not quite daring to approach. Past Maths, English, Humanities. I draw closer outside the IT suite, and closer still in the Drama corridor. Someone is reciting Hamlet *in a loud monotone nearby.*

She turns. 'Are you following me?'

There's no point in trying to lie. 'Yes.'

'Why?'

'I thought you might need help. Seeing as you've been sent the wrong way.'

She pulls the straps of her backpack tighter. 'I don't need help.'

'But you've gone the wrong way. Everyone in Year 9 has Science now.'

'Apart from you?'

'No, I have Science too.'

'Then why are you here?'

'Because I thought you might need help.' Our conversation is becoming circular. 'I can show you how to get to the Science block.'

She picks her hair away from her shoulders. 'Is this a trick?'

'No.'

'Why should I believe you?'

'Because I don't do tricks. I don't like them.'

An appraising look. From the neighbouring room, louder now: 'To. Die. To. Sleep. To. Sleep.'

She turns her head. 'What is that?'

'Someone trying to recite Shakespeare.'

'He's not very good.'

'He's terrible.'

Her lips part in a semi-smile, revealing two rows of white, even teeth. She unfolds an arm from her body and holds out her hand. 'I'm Jennifer.'

I look at the offered hand: at its tapered fingers with their short, clean nails. Everything in perfect proportion. As if in slow motion, I reach my own hand toward it. 'Stephanie.'

'Nice to meet you, Stephanie. So where is this Science block?'

'I'll show you.'

And this is how it begins.

◆ ◆ ◆

When my mind returns to the Cadbury Chamber, Mitchell is talking at me. Something about wine, I think, because he keeps using the word 'appellation'. I nod and tear off chunks of brioche – the champagne has made me hungry – while looking across the table at the other guests. My mother is animated, talking and waving her water glass around, while my father is having a more earnest conversation. As he speaks, he unfolds and refolds one corner of his napkin, and I find myself wondering what he meant about his will. He's always said the twins, Aurelie and I would receive equal shares of his wealth, that everything would be split four ways. But now it sounds like he might be reneging on that promise. The thought makes my muscles clench – it's not as if I mind about the money, exactly; it's more about the message it sends. *You're worthless.* Or, more precisely: *You're worth less.* Which is somehow worse.

The emcee and best man, Lewis and Mike, are seated either side of a woman with a low-cut dress. Lewis's face is nearly as red as his jacket now, and he seems to be doing all the talking, aimed mainly at the woman's cleavage. Aurelie is flanked by men too: Alistair on her right, and an older man – Alistair's father? – on her left. Yet there are no lustful looks here. In fact, the betrothed couple could almost be strangers; Aurelie has her back to Alistair while she talks to the older man. She smiles occasionally but her shoulders are rigid. When Alistair taps her arm, she doesn't turn. When he taps again, she says something to the older man and gets to her feet. Alistair watches as she walks off but, when she is nearly at the door, he gets up too; runs and grabs her. She tries to shake him away. They start to speak, close together, urgent. I can't hear what they're saying but Aurelie's eyebrows are lowered, her chin thrust forward, while his hand remains tight upon her arm.

'Any more water?' Mitchell thrusts the jug in front of me.

'What? Oh, yes please.' I twist round so he can refill my glass.

'Important to stay hydrated at a wedding. And look: you've got the lemon! That bodes well.'

When I turn back, Aurelie and Alistair have gone. 'What?'

'The lemon. Hindus believe that lemon in water wards off evil energy.'

'I'm not a Hindu.'

'Well, no, but—'

'And it would take a hell of a lot more than a lemon to ward off the evil energy around here.'

I stand up and walk off before he has a chance to respond.

The corridor outside is empty. According to a gold plaque on the wall, one way leads to the hotel lobby, the Barnardo Bar and the Livingstone Restaurant, the other to the toilets and a series of function rooms. I opt for the latter, unsure why I'm out here. It's not as if I care if Aurelie and Alistair are arguing. Perhaps I just need silence, to clear the noise which is building inside my head. There's something about that woman with the red hair – the way she changed the atmosphere in the room simply by mentioning Loch Ness – which has put me on high alert. I walk round a corner and past several paintings of bloodhounds, into a long passageway with double doors at the far end. The toilets are located about halfway down, and there are other doorways too. As I continue to walk, I hear voices.

'I swear I don't know her. Why would I lie?'

'I don't know. Why would you?' I recognise the hard-edged consonants as Aurelie's.

'Are you sure you didn't invite her?'

'I think I know who I invited.'

'But there are loads of people here.' Alistair's voice is pleading. Plummy too; not at all Scottish-sounding. Perhaps a result of all the public schooling my mother says he had. 'Maybe you invited a friend of a friend, or a distant colleague.'

'Why would I do that?'

'I don't know. On a whim?'

I move closer, beyond the women's toilets and past other rooms. More gold plaques provide their names: the Rowntree Room, the Peel Parlour, the Brunel Suite.

'On a whim! You think I've spent months meticulously planning—'

'Or perhaps you found yourself in an awkward social situation?'

'—*months* meticulously planning numbers and seating plans, only to invite someone on a whim? And then not even include her in the seating plan?'

'I don't know. I don't know how these things work. All I know is I didn't invite her.'

Her. Are they talking about the red-haired woman?

'Have you shagged her?'

'What!'

'It's a simple question. Have. You. Shagged. Her.'

'God, no! She must be about fifty.'

'So?'

'So why would I?'

'I don't know.' Aurelie's tone is cutting. 'On a whim, maybe?'

'Jesus, no. Also, I love *you*. You're the one I'm marrying, remember?'

Their voices become louder as I reach a doorway on my left. The Shaftesbury Suite. Peering in carefully, I first see only darkness, but then discern their outlines. Hers: compact, barely moving; his: taller, arms waving about as he speaks.

'Maybe you shagged her before you met me?'

'No.'

There are numerous smaller shapes behind them.

'And now she's got a score to settle?'

'No!'

Chairs, I realise. The room is full of chairs, set out in rows. An invisible audience to this display of marital disharmony (and they're not even married yet).

'But you worked there.'

'What?'

'Loch Ness. She mentioned Loch Ness, and you used to work there.'

His arms become still.

'I've heard the stories from Sarah,' she goes on. 'About the three of you at the hotel during your university holidays, competing to see who you could shag.'

'And how the hell would *Sarah* know what we got up to? She wasn't there.'

'Sarah knows everything about everyone.'

'Look' – he sounds as if he's trying to stop his temper from rising – 'I know Sarah is your friend, but she's also an irrepressible gossip, who says stuff purely for dramatic effect.'

Exactly, I think. If only I could persuade Alistair to make the same point to my mother.

'So you weren't shagging around while you were there?'

'Well, put it this way: I wasn't a celibate monk, but I was also single and in my twenties, so—'

'So you *were* shagging around!'

'Jesus, Aurelie! We've been over this before. Having sex with other women in the past doesn't mean I'm going to have sex with other women now. In fact, I'd argue it means the opposite.' He puts an arm around her. 'Look, I'm not your dad. I love you and I want to be with you. I'm not going anywhere.'

'So what was that woman talking about?'

'I don't know; she's probably just some crackpot who likes to gatecrash weddings.' But the conviction has drained from his voice.

There is a call from behind me. 'Stephanie!'

I turn to see my aunt stumbling along the corridor, one hand against the wall to steady herself, the other clutching a glass of champagne. 'Stephanie!' she repeats. 'Do you know the way to the Ladies?'

I have no choice but to walk over, point out the relevant door – approximately two metres away from her hand – and listen while she regales me with tales of her weak bladder. She breaks off when Aurelie and Alistair emerge from the darkened room. 'Well, well, what have we here?' she whispers, her voice hot and damp in my ear. 'Could it be, young Stephanie, that the bride and groom have engaged in a little pre-wedding hanky-panky? If so, they're following in the finest tradition of your mother, although in her case there was no wedding!'

I pull away and wipe my ear with my sleeve.

'Hi Auntie Jane,' Aurelie says. 'I'd like you to meet' – she smiles more widely, lips stretched to the point of snapping – 'my fiancé, Alistair.'

'Enchanté.' In one fluid movement, he takes Jane's free hand and touches it to his mouth. 'I can see good looks run in the family.'

She beams. 'Delighted to meet you too.'

'And Ally, you might not remember, but this is my sister. She's changed a bit since our pancake days.'

'Oh!' His smoothness seems to desert him for a second; he leans back, ever so slightly, like a tightrope walker losing his footing, before tilting forward again. 'Good to meet you properly.' He doesn't attempt to take my hand or (thank God, or any other higher powers that might exist) kiss me. 'Although I feel I know lots about you already.'

'Really?' I keep my expression level. 'Because I know almost nothing about you.'

'Come on, Ally.' Aurelie glares at me. 'We need to get back to our guests.' She takes his arm and sweeps him off down the corridor.

Jane turns to me with unfocused eyes. 'He *is* handsome,' she says. 'And charming! I see what you mean about the hair, but if I were twenty years younger, I'd definitely be tempted. Now, would you mind holding my glass for me while I visit the Ladies?'

As she pushes open the door, I continue to watch the couple. Alistair glances over his shoulder as they reach the corner, sees me looking and immediately turns away again. I, however, don't break my gaze.

That's right, I think. *I'm watching you.*

FRIDAY, 10.30 P.M.

Back in the Cadbury Chamber, there is flavourless food and conversation to be endured. On, and on, and on. I learn that Mitchell likes talking about suspension bridges. He learns that I don't. When Lewis finally announces dinner is over and invites us all to make our way to the Rowntree Room for a digestif, I jump to my feet.

As the other guests continue to chat, my mother beckons me to her. 'How are you doing, my angel?'

I flick my gaze to the table to check her wine glass. Still dry. 'Glad dinner is over.' I help her up. 'How are you?'

'A bit tired, to be honest.' We walk slowly across the room, our arms interlocked. 'I was sitting next to cousin Mary, and she didn't stop talking. She's going through a bit of a rough patch.'

I've learned enough about conversational etiquette to know I should ask her to elaborate. But I can't bring myself to care about cousin Mary's patches, rough or otherwise. 'Why is Dad changing his will?'

She stops. 'Where did you hear that?'

'He told me.'

'Oh, for goodness' sake.' She moves off again, with renewed pace. 'What's wrong with that man?'

'He abandoned us to start a new family,' I suggest.

'True. But I was actually referring to his crappy timing.' She gets that faraway look in her eyes, and I wonder which particular episode of crappy timing she's remembering. My father getting her pregnant when she was nineteen, perhaps. His cheating on her when she was suffering from a slipped disc. Or just: his cheating. His missing of my only star role in a school play (and I mean that literally as well as figuratively: I was the Star in the Nativity when I was eight) to go to a colleague's book launch. All the nights he worked late while my mother's wine consumption morphed from a habit into a problem. His trip to Edinburgh, ostensibly for work but really because he couldn't keep his penis in his pants. His leaving us for good shortly after; the sense of hopelessness as our mother lay in bed for three months eating nothing but pistachios, their shells piled up on the bedside table like little corpses. Or now, on the eve of his eldest daughter's wedding, his references to his will. A grenade lobbed casually among the grands crus.

'What exactly did your father say?' my mother asks.

'That he wants to talk to me about his will.'

'And that's it?'

'Yes.' I adjust my hold upon her arm. 'I probed him further but he said it wasn't the time or place to discuss it. Even though he was the one who mentioned it in the first place.'

She shakes her head. 'Can't he just let you enjoy Aurelie's day?'

I don't point out the obvious: that Aurelie's nuptials will provide me with about as much enjoyment as an aneurysm. And not one of those good ones that kills its victim quickly. 'Do you know what changes he's planning to make?'

'No.' She looks away from me. 'He and I aren't really on speaking terms.'

I follow her gaze to the bloodhound paintings on the wall. Such ugly dogs, with their wrinkled foreheads and drooping ears. Rather like my father, in fact; sagging under the weight of his ego.

'Do you know who that woman was?' I ask.

'Which woman?'

'The one with the red hair. Who mentioned Loch Ness, before dinner.'

'No.' She looks back at me. 'Why do you ask?'

We are approaching the Rowntree Room now; there are people clustered by its entrance, shrieking and laughing. 'I just wondered,' I say. 'If she might know something. About Peter.'

She gives a little laugh at this, one without any jollity in it. The emotional equivalent of skimmed milk. 'And you tell me I'm worrying too much?'

I am about to say it's different – that she is needlessly worrying about Sarah, whereas I am trying to understand why a petite Scottish woman would say something mysterious about Loch Ness at Aurelie and Alistair's pre-wedding drinks, before disappearing altogether – when the coughing begins. It starts off normally enough – a catch in my mother's throat, a thick-sounding hack into a tissue – but soon turns into something worse: a full-body spasming which causes her to double over, leaning on me, unable to find her breath.

'Mum?' I say. 'Mum!'

All at once there are people beside us, creating a chorus of noise. Someone asks if she needs help, and someone else says they will call an ambulance.

'No,' I say, as fiercely as I can. 'No ambulances. She hates hospitals.'

'But—'

'It's not what she wants, okay?'

My mother is leaning almost horizontally across me now, her chestnut wig gleaming in the overhead light. A pair of arms appears beside me; helps to take her weight. 'I need to get her to the floor,' I say. The arms lower her into a seated position, her back against the wall.

'Like this?'

I recognise the Scottish lilt and look up to see Lewis's chin, so densely stubbled and close to me that I feel like a fingernail about to be scrubbed. I nod, and crouch beside my mother. 'Try to breathe slowly, Mum,' I say. 'In from your abdomen, like you always taught me. And then out, slowly, slowly.'

'Is there anything we can do?' A woman's voice, very close.

'Can you give us a bit of space?'

'Sure.' She doesn't move.

'A bit of space, please!' Lewis bellows.

The woman steps away but I can see a phone in her hand. Her fingers moving toward the nine. 'I really think we should call—'

'No!' I grab the phone and hurl it across the corridor. Its casing splinters against the opposite wall. 'No ambulances.'

The woman stares at me, grievance hardening around her features. Beyond her, another face is staring too. A male face: rigid but for the tiniest movement of his eyes. Mike. The best man.

I turn back to my mother, lock on to her gaze. 'Forget about everything else; it's just you and me here. Just you and me and slow, deep breaths.'

The words she always used. The words she passed to me in times of trouble so I could, one day, pass them back.

But she grips my arm, hard, and I realise these aren't the words she wants. That she's actually thinking of her letter. *We need to act.* And so, as she continues to gasp for air, I put my mouth to her ear and whisper, 'I'll take care of it.' Her rounded script flashes into my mind; the way it curled into black tongues as the paper succumbed to the flame. 'I'll take care of everything.'

Her grip relaxes. Seconds later, breath rushes back into her body.

◆ ◆ ◆

As my mother's breathing returns, I slump back against the wall. Thinking of the suddenness with which life can be taken. Of the fissures which can rip through the flatland of existence without any warning.

The people around us leave. Except for Lewis and Mike, who remain nearby, hands clasped behind their backs like stewards at a cricket match. When Aurelie appears, Lewis tells her what's happened. She comes closer as they talk, twisting the chain of her handbag around her fingers. 'Are you okay, Mum?' she asks.

'I'm fine.'

'That's not what Lewis said.'

Our mother jerks her head up. 'Well, Lewis isn't me.'

'No, he's not, but still . . . can we get you a doctor?'

'No. I'm fine.'

'We could postpone the wedding—'

'No!' Our mother's voice is brusque. And then, more gently: 'Aurelie, darling, that's the last thing I want. You must go ahead. You must. Please . . .'

'I don't know.' More twisting. 'Only if you're sure.'

'I've never been more sure.'

'Really?'

'Yes. And do you know what else I want?'

There is a pause, and I wonder what would happen if I were to intercede. If I were to tell Aurelie about our mother's letter, and her plan for tomorrow. If I were to tell our mother I intend to comply, but only for as long as our objectives align. Because, at the end of the day, she wants silence, and I don't.

I want answers.

'What?'

'I want you to go into that room, get hold of a large whisky, chat to your guests, and not give me another thought.'

Aurelie twists the handbag chain tighter, creating white patches of skin between her knuckles. 'But how can I—'

'You can and you will,' my mother insists. 'And now Stephanie is going to help me to bed.'

There is no choice but to take the lift: my mother can't possibly climb ten flights of stairs. She says she will go on her own but I refuse to leave her, so we step inside together. I close my eyes and she talks to me the whole way up, to distract me, explaining how Aurelie and Alistair have got separate rooms tonight, for tradition's sake. How Aurelie is sleeping in the room next to hers on the fifth floor, while Alistair is sleeping on the fourth floor, by his groomsmen. How, tomorrow night, the newlyweds will have the penthouse on the sixth floor, replete with champagne fridge and jacuzzi bath.

We exit the lift and she goes quiet, the last of her energy expended. I help her to her room, and with undressing. Just like the bad old days. Shoes off, tights peeled down, dress unzipped and removed over her head. I even unhook her bra. I find her nightie and put it on, thread her birdlike arms through its sleeves. She says she is too tired to go to the bathroom so I fetch her toothbrush and brush for her, get her to spit into a glass. Then she lies down and I place the duvet across her. I say goodnight and walk to the door but she asks me to stay. Her voice is the smallest I have ever heard it.

I switch the light off and lie down beside her, listen to her breathing. When her breath begins to slow, I alter my inhalations to match. Let my eyes adjust, so that pieces of the night become objects. The television, the desk, her shoes. After a couple of minutes, I slide off the bed. I am halfway to the door when she mutters something.

'Stephanie?' Her voice is slurred with sleep.

'Yes?'

'Can I ask you a question?'

'Okay.'

'It's something I wouldn't normally ask, but I hope you won't mind, given . . .' She coughs and turns on to her opposite side. 'Given the circumstances.'

My adrenaline spikes at her words, my heart beginning to thud in the dark. But I keep my voice level. 'Ok-ay.'

'Have you ever been in love?'

'What?' This is not what I expected.

'Have you ever been in love?'

I stare at the curtains, at the slice of moonlight where they join. At the way it turns into a silver finger pointing across the bedroom floor.

And, despite myself, I start to remember.

April 2005

Jennifer has applied clear polish to my nails, with a stripe of blue across their tips. I, however, have been more ambitious, attempting to create ten miniature scenes on her hands. I won't let her look until I'm done, have implored her time and time again to wait a couple of minutes more, and now a full hour has passed. A full hour of tiny, painstaking brushstrokes; of spending so long with each nail that I've memorised their angled planes.

'Can I look now?'

'I'm just applying the finishing touches. There.'

She lifts her hands. Her mouth falls open and she lifts her hands further, splays her fingers.

'You don't like them?' The prospect is disorienting, like flying over the Atlantic through a wholly blue sky. Impossible to see where the sky ends and the ocean begins.

'I . . . They're amazing. How can you do that?'

'Do what?'

'Paint in that level of detail. They're like proper works of art.'

'So you do like them?'

'I never want to clean my nails again. Oh wow – is that me?'

I don't need to see where Jennifer's looking. 'Yes.'

'That's incredible. Is it like . . . a little story?'

I suppose it is, except there's nothing little about it. Not to me. I've never had a proper friend before. Nobody to partner with in lessons, to sit with at lunch, to do homework with in the evenings. To accompany me to the park or the shops. To splash with in the pool at the local leisure centre. To make me feel it's not a problem I'm a pariah at school; that my sister no longer speaks to me; that my father is rarely around and my mother rarely sober; because I have someone. But how to phrase all of this without scaring her away? 'Sort of,' I say.

'Can you tell me?' she says. 'Can you tell me the story?'

I take her hand in mine. 'The pictures are ten moments in time: past, present and future. So this first one, on your thumb, is of you as a little girl in China. I based it on that photo at your house. The second, on your index finger, is of you when you first arrived at Waldenborough. You're standing by the lockers.'

'Oh yes, I can see that! The tiny blue lockers behind me – that's so clever!'

'The third one's a bit messy, but it's meant to be you on the tennis court.'

Jennifer nods. 'And this one is me playing the violin?'

'Yes, that's when you played the lead in that concerto and completely stunned everybody.'

'I don't think I stunned anybody.'

'Oh, come on! Everyone was mesmerised by you that night. Even Sarah and my sister, although they wouldn't admit it.'

'But they were even more horrible to me after that.'

'They were just jealous.' I feel a sudden compulsion to run my hand up her arm. To map its contours: the jut of bone at her wrist; the hair follicles, raised from her skin like Braille; the hollow near her elbow. 'Their flute playing was nowhere near as good.'

'It was fine.'

'Fine, yes. Great, no. Your violin playing was – is – great.'

'Um, thank you, I guess. So go on: what are the rest?'

I talk her through them: the birthday cake we made that sagged in the middle; the time she won a prize for a history essay; the picture of her with her mother, Lan, at Weston-super-Mare. An orange balloon in the sky behind them. 'And the eighth picture is of the present: can you see?'

Jennifer peers at the middle nail on her right hand and lets out a squeal of delight. 'It's you painting my nails! That's so meta – I love it. So what are the last two? Is that you and me again? With the Oriental Pearl Tower behind us?'

'Yes, that's us in the future, when you show me round China.'

'I've never been to Shanghai.'

'It doesn't matter; the picture is of the future. We can go together.' I wonder if I've said too much.

'And the last one, the one of the stars.' She gives no indication that *I've overstepped. 'Is that me going to space, or is it supposed to represent death: heaven or something?'*

I stare at the tiny nail with its even tinier stars. A glimpse of another galaxy. 'It can be whatever you want it to be.'

'It's brilliant.' She reaches out to hug me. *'You're brilliant.'*

Have I ever been in love? I am about to say no but something stops me. Maybe it's the darkness, coupled with the moonlight. Maybe it's because I have just undressed my mother; have seen her stripped back, and need to rebuild her with something. Or maybe it's because offering up a piece of my truth might prompt her to do the same.

'Once,' I say.

A pause. 'Recently?'

'No. Years ago.' I press the palms of my hands together. 'At school, in fact.'

'At school? Did I know him?'

'Her,' I say. 'And yes, you did. It was Jennifer.'

A much longer pause. 'Jennifer?'

I nod, even though I doubt my mother can see.

'My God.'

The quiet that follows has a weight to it. My body turns in upon itself like a closing fist.

'I'm so ashamed,' she says, her voice clearer now. And then, rapidly, 'I don't mean I'm ashamed of you. I could never be ashamed of you.'

'Then what are you ashamed of?'

'Myself.'

This makes no sense. When I eventually speak, it comes out as a whisper. 'Why?'

She is quiet, and I think perhaps she hasn't heard. Or, worse, doesn't want to reply. She is lying so still, just a knot of bedclothes. I shut my eyes, seek refuge in the dancing white lines. I open them again and she hasn't moved. And then, as disorientation is kicking in, as I'm starting to imagine things which cannot be there, she responds. Four brief words.

'Because I didn't know.'

◆ ◆ ◆

I leave soon after that, into the corridor where the light is too bright and too yellow. I can hear the thud of music from somewhere lower in the building, and the cry of a child from one of the nearby rooms. Otherwise, I am alone.

Or not: as I walk to the stairwell, I sense I'm being watched. I turn to see a cockatoo, staring out at me from a painting with one tiny black eye. Its feathers are smooth and white but its beak is monstrous, claw-like. I turn away, accelerate my steps, but there is a sound – a click – which makes me look round again. I picture the bird uncaging itself from its frame.

But the noise has come from a woman, not a bird. A small, thin woman with red hair tied in a ponytail. She is moving in the opposite direction to me, walking quickly, her left foot rolling inwards.

The Loch Ness woman.

'Hello!' I call out. 'Excuse me!'

She doesn't turn.

'Excuse me!' I say again. I switch direction, jog a little to try to catch up with her. 'Hello! Hi! Do I know you?'

She must have heard but she still doesn't turn. Instead she reaches the lift and presses the button to summon it. The doors open immediately.

'Hey! Hi!' She steps inside and I begin to run, building up speed until I am beside the lift and its doors are closing, and there is a split second in which I could wedge my foot into the gap to stop her, to give her no choice but to talk to me, but I hesitate. As the doors shut, I see her grey-green eyes staring into mine.

And then she is gone.

SATURDAY, 6.45 A.M.

Contrary to expectation, I sleep deeply in my four-poster bed. I'd been convinced there would be nightmares, visitations. That I'd see Peter, with his chipped tooth and wild hair, staring up at me from the void. Or Jennifer, splashing past with long, lean limbs, laughing as I turned to catch her.

The lack of disturbances makes waking even more unpleasant than usual. I've always disliked that liminal space in the morning, when distortion gives way to reality, but at least a restless night means a gentler reintroduction. Today, by contrast, I am taken from slumber to awareness at a speed that makes my body tremble. And the realisations keep coming, one after another: I'm in a hotel, not my cottage. I'm surrounded by other people. I have only a matter of hours to get to the truth.

I sit up, gasping, and realise I have a crick in my neck from sleeping without a pillow.

It doesn't end there. All at once I remember the cockatoo, the phone splintering against the wall, Sarah's smiles, my father's presence, Aurelie and Alistair arguing, the woman with the grey-green eyes, telling my mother about Jennifer.

I don't normally sleep this late. The wedding schedule says breakfast will be served between 08.00 and 10.00 in the Livingstone Restaurant, but the idea of small talk over bacon and eggs turns my stomach. What I need right now is crag and loch, heather and glowering sky. The pure, cold air of Scotland searing my lungs.

Instead I have Berkshire. Home to Windsor Castle, commuters and cut grass. I open the curtains, hook them into the fabric loops at the sides of the window, and look out at the gardens. A series of square lawns and gravel paths, divided by stone walls and hedges. Everything unnervingly neat.

I take a shower, but only a quick one. The water pressure is weak and the shower drips after I get out, despite my turning the dial as far as it will go. I dress in my sweatshirt, tracksuit bottoms and trainers (drip), grab my sketch pad and pencils (drip, drip-drip), and go.

The corridor is empty. So is the stairwell. In fact, I don't see anyone until I am near reception, and then only hotel staff. Men with gold name badges, women in blue tunics pushing cleaning trolleys, waistcoated staff in the restaurant, preparing breakfast. A man in the first category approaches, asks if he can help. When I tell him I'm off for a morning walk, he launches into a barrage of information about the sun terrace, the kitchen garden, the hotel's farm-to-fork policy, the Gargoyle Trail, the aviary, the award-winning herbaceous borders, the topiary, the wildflower meadow, the lake and the woodland tracks. 'There's also a children's play area,' he says, looking down at my side, 'but perhaps that's not of interest?'

Or perhaps it's none of his goddamned business. 'I'd like to go to the lake.'

He inclines his head. 'An excellent choice. The rose garden is also glorious at this time of year, and you'll have it to yourself if—'

I thank him and walk away before he has a chance to say anything else. Past the restaurant and through a mullioned door, then down a set of steps into the gardens. The air is already warm, suggesting a hot day ahead; the sky a mix of lilac-blues, pinks and greys, stippled with cloud. I follow the path around the perimeter of the hotel and see a sign for the Gargoyle Trail. Looking up at the building, several are immediately obvious: a human face with bulging eyes and extended tongue; a horned bat; a griffin with scaled wings and looping tail. I see more of them as my eyes attune to the stone: coiled serpents, fanged monkeys, a grotesque angel. Some jut out over buttresses and below arched windows that have been divided into multiple tiny panes, while others sit higher, near the crenellations and slim steeples.

I pass the restaurant terrace and the aviary comes into view: a sprawling structure where (according to Aurelie's schedule) wedding photos are to be taken later. It is half pavilion, half prison: a series of green domes laced with iron fretwork and gold roses, held up by iron bars. Inside, pressed against the bars and reaching into the domes, is dense foliage. Plants wrestling one another to find the light. I can't begin to imagine how the photographers will create happy images here, against the dark twisted vines. I suppose they could use the aviary entrance instead, but that's almost worse: a hybrid of faux Greek pillars and Egyptian statues. There are two stone jackals with sharp, pointed ears – reminiscent of second cousin Stanley – and, behind these, a pair of scarab beetles with outstretched antennae.

I come to a fork in the path. The right-hand route leads directly to the jackals and beetles while the left veers off to the rest of the gardens. I go left. As I pass the turning to the car park, I see my car through the gap in the hedge, and wonder again if I could just drive away from all this. If I could work harder to forget. I stop walking and turn my face to the sky, shut my eyes. Focus upon the warm breeze and the scent of vanilla from the rose garden. A sparrow's chirps, the trills of a greenfinch.

According to the hotel website, the aviary used to house birds from across the globe. Balinese hummingbirds, Indian egrets, Australian lorikeets. Birds of all colours and sizes, captured and brought here to satiate the Victorians' desire for spectacle. Held behind bars, allowed to fly only the shortest distances. How must they have felt, these birds, when they spread their wings – their glorious, multi-hued wings – and soared straight into a metal mesh? And how many times did they try again, before dying or refolding their wings in wearied defeat?

An image of the taxi arrives in my head before I can stop it. Those wipe-clean seats and that awful fake-cherry smell. And then Jennifer is in my head too – being escorted by the men out of the library, mute as the ghosts of the birds around me – and I realise that of course I can't forget. I whisper an apology to her for even considering it; intone promises under my breath. *I will find out which one of them sent you away.*

Then I open my eyes and keep walking: past the rose garden with its sweet-scented thorns, past the tentacled leaves of the kitchen garden, and through a series of stone archways to the wildflower meadow. The path is level, with lights at regular intervals on either side, just like the photos on the website suggested. Hopefully easy enough to navigate in the dark. I walk on, through a sea of colour – tall yellow grasses, brick-red poppies and purple-white corncockles – until I reach the shores of the lake.

I sit down by the water's edge, and breathe deeply. So this is where my mother and I will come tonight. The place where she intends to silence the whispers, and I intend to unearth the truth. To hear from Sarah's own mouth why she betrayed Jennifer. My mother has chosen this spot because it's close to the hotel, and yet secluded, safe from onlookers and eavesdroppers. I studied the area for her on the satellite view of Google Maps: the lake, elliptical in shape, with clumps of reeds and a dirt track around its edge. The old wooden jetty a few metres to my right, where the water is darker, deeper. The hide on the opposite bank. And here it all is, just as those images suggested, but brought to life with unfurling plant buds and scurrying insects and jubilant, noisy birds. Coots, moorhens, ringed plovers. I trail one hand in the water, and relish the sharp shock of cold. Watch as a pond skater moves away, long legs skimming across the surface of the lake. Look down into the shallows, where there are rocks amid the weeds and silted light.

I've always found water soothing. Even after what happened at Loch Ness. My mother says I cried a lot as a baby, much more than Aurelie, but that a bath always used to calm me. The same was true of swimming, particularly after Jennifer was taken away. As a fifteen-year-old, I went to the leisure centre in the mornings, early evenings and sometimes even during my lunch break, finding respite in submersion. Coming up only for quick gulps of air. Trying not to think about her absence. My body moves differently underwater, with an ease I can't realise on land. Everything quieter. Simpler.

Water is a large part of what drew me to Scotland. The few green areas in London are full of ball games, dog walkers and sunbathers. People, people, people. Once, when seated in my usual spot by the Round Pond in Hyde Park, watching the geese and swans while eating my cheese and crackers, a group of men appeared with tiny model yachts. The birds hated them (the yachts), and I hated them too (the men and the yachts), partly because the birds did, but mainly because they stripped away all the wonder of being by the water. The equivalent of climbing Everest by clocking 8,849 metres on a step machine.

Shortly after, I moved to Inverness, where I could spend my days by unspoiled water: the Moray Firth, the Cromarty Firth, Loch Duntelchaig. And, of course, Loch Ness.

I find a fresh page in my pad and ready my pencils. I could have done this earlier, but I prefer the process outside. I have a retractable utility knife, which I run along the side of each pencil to expose the graphite within, before using sandpaper to sharpen the tip. It makes the pencils look odd – a bit like swordfish bills – but means they can produce both fine lines and wider, softer textures. I place the shavings into a resealable freezer bag which once contained a portion of Kirsty's shepherd's pie.

I often think of Kirsty when I sketch, not just because of her shepherd's pie but because she understands the power of art, especially when it conveys the splendour of the Northwest Highlands. The sweeping moors, the purple-petalled primrose, the molar-toothed ridge of Stac Pollaidh. She has several Scottish artworks in her cottage, including a vast watercolour of the Isle of Skye as seen from Applecross, which takes up most of her living room wall. As well as a much smaller painting I did of the view across the mountains to Lochinver, which sits above her bedside table.

For my first two years in Scotland, I earned money by painting people's dogs. Border and bearded collies, terriers, spaniels. The dog commissions haven't gone away but I now receive other commissions too: of red squirrels and eagles, stags and seals. Seals are my favourite because painting them provides an excuse to gaze for hours at the sea, capturing the sky and waves as well as the speckled bodies which emerge to flump on the sandbanks. The Moray Firth is my preferred spot to see them, because they're so prolific there; every summer, more than a thousand converge upon its shores.

It was thanks to the Moray Firth, in fact, that I first learned about Kirsty's artist residency. It was a very stormy day – the wind probably a nine or ten on the Beaufort scale – and my coat whipped against my body as I walked from the car to the water. The sky was a dark grey, shot through with indigo; the waves five times their normal size, pitching and foaming. No seals. I didn't attempt to remove my sketch pad from my backpack but I took a few photographs and thought of the paints I would use to recreate the scene. Blue Grey, Mayan Violet, Lamp Black. And then, out of the blue-grey-violet blackness, a figure appeared.

I don't know whether it was just the extreme conditions – the air roaring in my ears, the salt spray misting my lips – but there was something almost magical about the way she materialised from across the rocks, her waterproof jacket sucked tight around her torso while her hair flapped, wild and untameable. About the way she took a camera from her pocket, and pointed it directly at the sky. About the way she took photo after photo of the tumorous clouds, legs braced against the wind, before suddenly lowering her camera and looking at me, and I mean *really* looking at me, seeing me as I don't think anyone had since Jennifer. She asked if I was a photographer too. She had to shout to make herself heard. I shouted that I was more of an artist, which made her smile and ask if I didn't consider photography to be art. I shouted that I wasn't qualified to say what qualified, but that I earned a living from painting dogs, which probably didn't, which made her laugh and ask what I wanted to paint. Which led to a (shouted) discussion about mountains and lochs, and creating art for art's sake, which in turn led her to recommend a website for local arts funding. And as I plugged the web address into my phone, then and there – my fingers cold and clumsy, the screen smeared with the spray of the sea – I felt weirdly buoyed up, like this was the beginning of something important. A friendship, perhaps: the sharing of interests, company, confidences.

But then, scrolling through the list of initiatives, I saw an entry for the 'Peter Ferguson Artist Residency Programme'.

And knew it was the start of something else altogether.

I keep sketching until over an hour has passed. It's normally a relief when this happens – when I become so immersed in line and shade that everything else falls away. Yet not today. The sun has risen too high too quickly, bleaching the landscape around me. I take out my phone.

Kirsty answers after just two rings. 'Hello? Stephanie?'

'Hi, yes. It's me.'

'How's it going?'

'It's . . . what it is. You?'

'I'm grand. Although it feels odd knowing White Croft is empty.'

I picture the little cottage: its thick stone walls and curved fireplace. My single bed under the roof in the upstairs room. 'I'll be back soon.'

'Aye, that you will.' Her voice sounds stiff. 'So.'

'So?'

'How is it? Seeing your family again?'

I run my index finger in a figure of eight through the water. 'It's . . .'

'Difficult?'

She's always been good at finishing my sentences. 'Yes,' I say.

'You poor lamb. It's never easy to go back.'

The understatement of the century.

'How is your mam?'

'Not great.' I tell her about my mother's coughing fit last night, how thin she's become.

'I'm so sorry,' she says. 'And your sister?'

'What about her?'

'Are you two . . . getting on?'

I make a figure of eight in the opposite direction. 'Define "getting on".'

'Oh.' She makes a sad, sighing sound. 'Perhaps you could come back early.'

I look out at the lake, at the moorhens bobbing their heads.

'Stephanie?'

I remove my finger from the water and hold it out in front of me. Watch it dry while I attempt to change the subject. 'What are you and Rob doing this weekend?'

It's a stupid question. Kirsty spends every Saturday in the summer cleaning and readying their holiday cottage for the next set of guests. But she's kind enough not to point this out. Instead, she tells me Rob is mending their garden fence, and she might visit Carol in Ullapool. Carol's cherished dog, Barnacle, has developed a limp.

'So have you spoken to the groom yet?'

It takes me a moment to realise she's no longer talking about Barnacle. 'Briefly,' I say.

'And?'

'And what?'

'Do you like him?'

'No.'

She makes a guttural noise and I try to backtrack. Even though she's told me she doesn't recall ever meeting Alistair at the North Ness Hotel, nor Peter ever mentioning him, she still might not appreciate my badmouthing someone who worked with her son. 'I mean, I don't really know him,' I say. 'He might just be one of those people who creates a bad first impression. Or, strictly speaking, fifth or so impression, if you count the times he served me pancakes at the North Ness Hotel.'

'Initial impressions are important.'

'I thought they shouldn't be trusted?' This was Maggie's first-ever piece of advice to me, at our first-ever counselling session. I'd been perched on a small beige chair in her small beige room at school, looking around at the peeling posters on the walls, when she began to emphasise the importance of adaptability, explaining that sticking to a first impression of another person could irreparably damage relations with them.

But perhaps she just said that because I'd told her I didn't trust counsellors.

'Not always,' Kirsty says. 'But they can be useful. And some people have better instincts than others.'

'You know social skills aren't my strength.'

'Social skills are not the same as instincts. Your instincts are good, Stephanie. What did you not like about him?'

'Alistair? He just seems a bit . . . off.'

'Off?'

'Like he's putting up a front.'

She is silent.

'But I guess I shouldn't be surprised,' I say. 'It's probably what attracted my sister to him in the first place; she likes things to be perfect.'

'Putting up a front isn't perfect.'

'To her it is. Everything has to be stage-managed, all the time. My mother says she's coordinated the napkins with the flower girls' hair ornaments.'

'That sounds . . . intense.'

'I don't even know what hair ornaments are.'

'People can be very particular about weddings,' Kirsty says. 'Put a lot of pressure on themselves.'

Pressure is something I can relate to. Even out here, in the open, the air feels like it's bearing down upon me. I look at my watch. 'I'd better go,' I say.

'All-righty.'

'I'm off to see Mum. Before she disappears with Aurelie for three hours of hair and make-up.' *Three hours.* Concorde could cross the Atlantic in less.

'Are you having yours done too?'

'No. I hate make-up.' Even as I say the words, I remember the scrawl of lipstick on my maths book at school. A girl's body with a shark's head. The other children laughing. 'All that powder and glitter near my eyes, and I wasn't exaggerating when I said they're spending three—'

'Did they offer for you to join them?'

'What? No. They know how much I hate it.'

There is a pause. 'So what will you do?' she says eventually. 'While they're doing that?'

'Oh, I don't know,' I say. 'Maybe read. Or eat. Or do some more sketching.'

'You've been sketching?'

'A little.'

'That's wonderful.'

I look at the paper in front of me. At the dark shading to represent the water in shadow and the lighter lines elsewhere, flat and listless. Nothing like the torrid waters of the Moray Firth when the wind gusts across from the North Sea. 'It's not wonderful,' I say. 'It's mediocre. I'm used to drawing waves; the lake is too still.'

As soon as the words are out of my mouth, I realise my mistake.

'The lake?'

'Mmm.'

'There's a lake there?'

'Yes, in the hotel grounds. A small one, a short walk away from the main hotel building.'

'Are you alone?'

Her words are getting higher in pitch and I scan around, with a view to providing reassurance. Tall grasses, trees, still water. 'Yes, other than the birds. But it's perfectly safe.'

'You should go back to the hotel. Or better yet, come back here.'

'Kirsty, you don't need to worry.' She is unflappable the vast majority of the time, but water is the one thing which makes her agitated. It's because of Peter, of course, because she now conflates all bodies of water with his body. Even though it was never found.

Perhaps because it was never found. The only thing that turned up after the storm was that battered canoe.

'I'm safe here,' I say again.

'Lakes are not safe places.'

'This one is. It's mostly shallow.' I don't tell her about the deeper section, or the rocks amid the weeds.

'That doesn't mean it's safe!'

'Kirsty, it—'

'Stephanie, please! Even a metre of water is enough for an accidental death. And more to the point . . .' She stops.

'More to the point?'

She lowers her voice. 'It's definitely enough for a deliberate one.'

Walking back to the hotel, her warning spins inside my head. And I can't help thinking: she knows. She knows something is happening at the lake tonight.

Except that's impossible. My mother and I haven't told anyone what we've discussed, nor put anything in writing (other than her letter of six months ago, which is now a pile of ash). And whenever we've spoken by phone, I've made sure to walk out on to the moors, with no one else around. Kirsty is simply scared for me because of what happened to Peter. She still sees him everywhere: in the third chair at her kitchen table; on the saddle of his bike, propped against the outhouse wall; in the forests of Drumrunie, where he tramped most weekends. And in water, every type of water: from the smallest of ponds to the largest of lochs.

I see Peter in many places too. Whenever there's a full moon, or a storm, I'm taken back to the night he disappeared. To the lightning which cleaved the sky above Loch Ness and the rain which roiled its depths. To the fat, white moon which illuminated a strip of water below it, like an upside-down exclamation mark. To the sound of our tent flapping wildly in the wind.

To Aurelie's sleeping bag, lying empty beside me.

The hotel terrace is busy by the time I return, full of women wearing oversized sunglasses and men with plates of breakfast meat: sausages, bacon, black pudding. Some of them are drinking Bloody Marys too, red and viscous in the morning sun. My father is sitting at a small table on his own, with a plate of grapefruit and a newspaper. He is wearing aviators and a floral shirt which has too many buttons unfastened, revealing wisps of grey chest hair. I look away when he raises a hand in greeting.

And nearly walk into Sarah, who is coming down the steps in just a bathrobe and slippers.

'Oh gosh, Stephanie!' she says. 'Thank goodness!'

I presume this isn't her standard morning greeting.

'I've been looking all over for you.' Her hair is wet, hanging loose about her shoulders.

'You have?'

'Yes. But you weren't in your room, or—'

'How do you know where my room is?'

'Oh, what? Your mum told me.'

I make a mental note to take this up with my mother later.

'But you weren't there, or with Mike, or at breakfast.' She glances across the terrace at the people eating.

'Why would I be with Mike?'

She looks back at me. 'Sister of the bride. Best man. You know.'

I stare at her. 'No, I don't.'

'Just . . . there's a tradition. And Mike is single. As well as easy on the eye, don't you think? Tall, dark and handsome!'

I continue to stare as I remember what my mother told me about Aurelie's twenty-fifth birthday party. That Sarah had spent all evening sidling up to Mike, and all night making awful noises with him in the room next door. *Like a cat being strangled* were the precise words my mother used.

'Don't you think he's good-looking?' Sarah asks.

I shrug. 'Objectively, perhaps.'

'What's that supposed to mean?'

I shrug again. 'He fulfils a heteronormative tick list.'

'Pardon?'

'Tall, as you said – tick. Square jaw – tick. Broad shoulders – tick.'

'You certainly seem to have noticed a lot about him.'

'I notice a lot about everyone.'

Sarah bunches her hair into her hand and lays it across her shoulder like a sodden rope. 'Anyway, none of that matters right now. The point is: she needs you.'

'Who does?'

Her mouth opens without speaking, and I feel a creep of dread. 'Is it my mother?' I ask. 'Has she had another coughing fit?'

'Big cock,' she says.

'Excuse me?'

'Mike has a big cock too. As I can verify from the night of your sister's housewarming.' She smirks. 'And no, your mum is fine.'

I start to walk away but she catches my arm, forces me to turn. 'It's your sister.'

SATURDAY, 8.40 A.M.

I quickly establish that Aurelie isn't in any immediate danger; she's neither choking on her own self-importance, nor being blistered by her incendiary conceit. Nonetheless, Sarah is unimpressed to learn I'm taking the stairs. 'Your sister's on the *fifth* floor,' she says.

'I'm aware of that.'

'The *fifth* floor,' she says again.

'The one between the fourth and the sixth?' I say. 'Goodness. However will I find it?'

'There's no need to be sarcastic.'

'Of course not. No need at all.'

She glares at me, but I keep my gaze level until she turns and flounces away toward the lift.

Only when she is out of sight do I walk to the stairwell and begin to climb. Past the glassy-eyed raven, the combs, the hunting knife. I don't feel the need to rush. After the events at Waldenborough High, I owe Sarah and my sister nothing.

Or, rather, I owe them nothing good.

◆ ◆ ◆

January 2004

Jennifer is the only one concentrating. Head down, tongue edging from her mouth, she is working through the Year 11 algebra assignment, despite the fact we're only in Year 9. Columns of linear equations take shape in Sarah's exercise book, between ruler-drawn margins.

'Don't forget to make a couple of mistakes,' Sarah says. 'So it's realistic.'

Jennifer writes a series of letters on the page: plump 'a's, tall 'b's, and 'x's which slump to the side like clumsy kisses.

'Did you hear that, Spend-a-Penny Jenny?' says Sarah. *The awful nickname she's using was coined by an annoying, rat-faced boy called Ryan a couple of months ago, after Jennifer bought a sausage roll with nearly a pound's worth of pennies. However, while Ryan was the one who thought it up, it's Sarah and Aurelie who have ensured its longevity. To them, the double meaning of the phrase – the fact it also refers to urination – is the height of hilarious wordplay. And yet, when given a homework assignment on wordplay and double meanings in* Romeo and Juliet *last week, they handed it straight to Jennifer to complete.*

Jennifer looks up now, gives a small nod. 'I heard you,' she says. 'I've made a deliberate mistake here.' *She points to the page.* 'And here.'

'Good,' says Sarah. 'I've got some Physics for you after this.'

'No, it's my turn,' says Aurelie. 'She needs to do my algebra.'

'You two are unbelievable!' *I can't help speaking out; the injustice has gone too far.*

Jennifer turns to me. 'It's fine,' she says.

'No, it isn't. They shouldn't be asking you to do any of their homework, let alone two identical lots!' *I jab my finger into my sister's arm.* 'Why can't you just copy what Jennifer's done for Sarah?'

Aurelie pulls away, gives me a look. 'I've told you before: keep out of things that don't concern you.'

'It *does* concern me.'

But she's gone back to pretending I don't exist, and it's Sarah who responds. 'It doesn't, Jaws,' she says. 'It's strictly a business arrangement between us and Spend-a-Penny. She does our homework for us, and we make sure everyone's nice to her.'

'But they're not nice to her.'

'They're a lot nicer than they otherwise would be. To you too. You do realise you'd get your teeth kicked in if it wasn't for your sister?'

I look at Aurelie, but she's looking at the table.

'And if your girlfriend wasn't so good at homework,' Sarah goes on.

'Why don't you shut up?'

'Oooh, that touched a nerve, didn't it?' Sarah laughs. 'Jaws and Spend-a-Penny in a tree. K-I-S-S-I-N-G.'

'I said: Shut up!'

'Quiet!' The librarian rises from her chair and comes toward us. Sarah snatches her exercise book from Jennifer, who picks up another in its place. Aurelie opens GCSE Physics *to a page on the laws of motion and I read it upside-down, from across the table.*

For every action in nature there is an equal and opposite reaction.

So perhaps that's why I care so much for Jennifer. To counteract the hatred I feel for Sarah.

Sarah is waiting for me at the top of the stairwell on the fifth floor. As I come closer, clutching my sketch pad and pencils in my arms, she taps her foot.

'It's cold out here,' she says. She opens the door into the fifth-floor corridor but doesn't hold it, so it swings back as she goes through. She walks off, not bothering to check if I am following. Clearly too used to being followed. I watch the pale nape of her neck, moving away, and wonder whether a person could be strangled with their own hair.

There are so many ways to die. Bullets, drowning, strangulation. Stabbing, electrocution, poison. When it comes to murder, the options reduce: people are killed by pythons, for example, and yet pythons are largely unviable as murder weapons. But a plethora of choice remains. The thing which really narrows down options is not so much wanting to kill someone as wanting to get away with it.

'Stephanie! Are you coming?' Sarah has finally looked round.

I want to say no. I should say no.

'Stephanie?'

I have lived in a different country from my family for five years. During that time, I have considered myself independent, free from their bindings.

And yet my feet are now travelling down the corridor toward my sister's room, as if the bindings have been in place all along, and I just couldn't see them.

Aurelie's room is similar to my mother's: large and luxurious, decorated in neutral tones. There is a vast bed at its centre on which my sister sits, cross-legged in a white bathrobe, like a wart on the bed linen's skin. She doesn't acknowledge me. Our mother is in an armchair next to the window. 'Stephanie,' she says. She struggles to her feet.

'Don't get up,' I say, but it's too late. She walks toward me, gives me a kiss on the cheek. She is wearing a kimono-style top which ties at the front, and which brushes, cold and silky, against my hand. I grip my sketch pad more tightly.

Sarah removes her slippers and climbs on to the bed beside my sister.

'What's going on?' I can feel a pencil pressing into my arm.

'Aurelie's received a letter.'

'What do you mean, she's received a letter? What kind of letter?'

'It's more of a note, really.' Our mother watches me carefully.

'A note?'

'Yes. An anonymous note.'

'Right. And is that . . . a bad thing?'

'Of course it's a bad thing!' My sister glares at me. 'People don't feel the need to write anonymously when they're being nice, do they?'

'Why, what does it say?'

My sister tucks her hair behind her ears. Her cheeks are flushed a deep red which borders on purple. 'You tell me.'

'Aurelie!' Our mother turns toward the bed. 'I know it's a stressful situation, sweetheart, but flinging accusations around won't help anybody.'

'Oh, come on, Mum! Who the hell else would write it?'

My abdomen tightens at the realisation of what's being said. Tiny knots pulling beneath the surface. 'You think I wrote it?'

'Of course not,' our mother says, but Aurelie talks over her. 'The evidence certainly points that way.'

'What evidence? I've been outside for the past couple of hours.'

'Girls, please!'

'The note was left earlier than that,' says Sarah. She is sitting cross-legged now too, next to my sister. Together, two sets of blonde hair cascading across two white bathrobes, they resemble a double-headed monster with a penchant for bleach. The Home Counties' answer to the Hydra.

Our mother sighs and leans against the wardrobe. 'Your sister found it just now,' she says. 'Next to her washbag in the bathroom. But she's been here all morning, so it must have been put there yesterday. Apparently she didn't brush her teeth last night, so she might not have seen—'

'It's not like I don't brush my teeth, Mum,' Aurelie says. 'It's just that I'd brushed them before the dinner—'

'I'm not criticising you, love.'

'I know.' Her tone suggests otherwise. 'I just don't want anyone to think that I don't value hygiene, or—'

'Oh, for fuck's sake,' I break in. 'What does the note say?'

My mother passes me a piece of plain paper, folded into quarters. I open it to reveal nine words, handwritten in black ballpoint pen.

Don't marry a man with blood on his hands.

'What the hell?' I say.

'It's obviously nonsense,' says my mother.

'What's Alistair supposed to have done?' I ask.

'You tell me,' my sister says.

My mind returns to the night of the storm: to the flapping tent and Aurelie's empty sleeping bag. And then further back, to the morning before the storm, in the restaurant at the North Ness Hotel. To the napkin Alistair left under Aurelie's plate, a message scrawled across one corner. *Meet me tonight, by the boathouse.*

I meet her gaze evenly. 'How would I know what he's done? I've barely met him.'

'That's right,' she says in a taut voice. 'You've barely met him. And yet you somehow think it's all right to cast aspersions on his character—'

'I didn't write the bloody note!'

'— simply because you can't cope with the idea of me being happy.'

'That's where you're wrong.' I look down at the bed, and try to unpick what's happening here. Did our mother write the note, as part of an extended plan she's neglected to tell me about? Or could it have something to do with Peter's disappearance?

'I don't have a view one way or the other about your happiness,' I go on, trying to remember the precise expression on Alistair's face at last night's dinner, 'because *I don't care*. I don't give a shit whether you're ecstatic or miserable, rich or poor, in sickness or in health. In fact, as far as I'm concerned, your entire existence is irrelevant.'

The room falls silent. Our mother reaches a hand to my arm. 'Stephanie, remember that it's your sister's wedding day—'

'Like I have any chance of forgetting—'

'And she's had a stressful experience with this note—'

'Which she's blaming on me!'

'Nobody's blaming anyone. I'm sure it's just a prank.' Our mother coughs into a tissue. 'A misguided prank, but a prank nonetheless. Perhaps the sort of thing Alistair's friends find funny.'

'I don't think Ally's friends would find this funny,' says Sarah. 'Or, at least, I don't think Mike would.'

'No, Mike wouldn't,' our mother agrees.

'Ally's friends wouldn't do this,' Aurelie says. 'They have nothing against me.'

I press the pencil more deeply into my arm. 'And you think I do?'

'Of course you do!' My sister's eyes are blazing. 'You've hated me for years. Ignoring me or making horrible comments, finding reasons not to meet up with me. Ignoring all my emails and phone calls, all my attempts to make things better between us. How can you possibly say you have nothing against me?'

For once, she is right. I can't.

'Girls,' our mother says again. 'This isn't going to help anyone.'

But something has shifted and I can't unhook myself from my sister's gaze. 'So why do you think I'd want to start writing to you this weekend?' I say. 'Why break a wonderful habit of ignoring you completely?'

'Girls, please!'

'I don't know!' Aurelie is screaming now. 'I don't know why you hate me so much, why you fling any kindness I try to show you back in my face, why you lie and go out of your way to make my life a misery! I can only assume you're jealous.'

'Jealous?' It's almost laughable. 'Jealous! Why would I be jealous of you?'

'Because I've got a good job! Because I've got friends! Because I'm getting married!'

I walk to the edge of the bed and drop the note beside her. 'You're completely deluded,' I say, my voice cold. 'I can't think of anything worse than spending every day in an office, like a rat in a cage, doing the dirty work of the rich. Except perhaps for spending time with your *friends* . . .' I wave a hand at Sarah. 'Or getting married to some greasy-haired charlatan who inspires anonymous notes. Which I didn't write, by the way!' I pause for breath; try to suck oxygen down to my abdomen, where the knots are pulling tighter. 'You are fake and cruel and don't care who you hurt. You're the very last person whose life I want.'

She continues to stare at me, tears pooling in her eyes, and then she turns away, and Sarah turns too, putting an arm around Aurelie's shoulders. Forming a barrier of bathrobe.

I look at our mother, who shakes her head. 'You've gone too far, Stephanie. I think it might be best if you leave for a bit. Give your sister some space.'

So I go, resisting the urge to tell our mother that this is exactly what I've been trying to do all these years, that space is precisely what I've been seeking.

That I'm here only because she asked me to come, because she begged me.

And if I go too far, she only has herself to blame.

SATURDAY, 12.50 P.M.

In films, crises usually get resolved before a marriage takes place. The timings are often ridiculously tight – the groom realising he loves someone else while standing at the altar, or the bride running in, veil askew, just in time for the ceremony – yet everything ends well.

But real life is not like that. In real life, the bride's sister can know something is wrong but not be able to fix it. She can be too angry with her family to think who might have left a note in the bride's bathroom. Too angry to remember – until it's too late – the red-haired woman from the night before. Too angry to recall the click that marked her appearance on the fifth floor, as if a nearby door had just been closed, or the way she fled down the corridor when confronted.

In real life, the bride's sister can sit alone for nearly three hours, staring at an old newspaper article and placing pen to paper, when she could have been doing something constructive. Stroke upon stroke: looping layers of ink on a hotel notepad.

In real life, as the deadline approaches, the case can remain unsolved. The bride's sister can pull on a tunic, with no revelations beyond the fact green doesn't suit her. Can arrive at the Darwin Hall late and out-of-breath, aware she is unfit but thinking, *Screw you, Darwin, I'll survive anyway.*

In real life, there doesn't need to be a happy ending. A bride can be told her fiancé has blood on his hands.

And then vow to stay with him until death does them part.

◆ ◆ ◆

The Darwin Hall is the grandest room in the hotel, some thirty metres long, with a high, intricately carved ceiling and a gleaming black and white parquet floor. The walls on either side have dark wood panelling on their lower halves and enormous paintings above, of overfed men in lace ruffs and stern women in voluminous dresses. The wall at the far end of the hall has no paintings but instead consists solely of wood, with ornate arches reaching up to panels with finicky, scalloped edges. A couple of hundred chairs festooned with giant gauze bows have been set out in rows down the length of the hall, and nearly all of them are full. The people in them are dressed in bright clothing and ridiculous headwear. They are talking to one another excitedly, their collective noise surging over me as I enter the room. And their smell hits me too: spice, musk, rose. Or perhaps that's just the flowers: two bouquets flank the doorway, wide and imposing, like bouncers.

A young man in a kilt and jacket approaches. 'Bride or groom?' he asks.

'Bride.'

He looks at the rows of chairs. 'There aren't many left for the bride. You could sit at the back here – or, if you'd prefer, you could sneak across to the groom's side.'

'I'm fine at the back.'

'Okay then. Here you are.' He hands me an Order of Service, which is made of stiff cream card. Aurelie and Alistair's names are embossed on the front, next to a heart of dried rose petals.

'Aurelie's sister!'

I look up to see Lewis coming toward me. Also in a kilt and jacket, with a sprig of heather hanging from his lapel.

'Hello.'

He runs a hand across his chin, which has been shaved since last night. 'I remember you from my North Ness days,' he says. 'Although you've changed a lot.'

'You too.'

'Grown more handsome, right?' He tilts his head to one side and grins. There is a piece of food stuck in his teeth. Something green, spinach perhaps.

'You've got something . . .' I point to the matching location in my own mouth.

He roars with laughter. 'Your mum asked me to look out for you.'

'She did?'

'Aye. I'm glad she's feeling better after last night.'

'Me too.' I think back to Lewis lowering her to the floor, clearing the area around us. 'Thank you for your help.'

'Don't be daft.' He waves a hand at me. 'Anyhow, there's a space saved for you up at the front.'

'I'm fine at the back.'

'No. Aurelie wants you at the front.'

'Well, if Aurelie wants it . . .' The sarcasm in my voice must be lost on him, for he takes my arm and starts walking up the aisle. Faces turn to look at us, most of them smiling, and I wonder if it's a reflex thing – if society has conditioned people to smile at a man and woman walking up an aisle together. Because if they bothered to look more closely, they would see he is holding my arm but I'm not holding his; that I am trying to pull clear, to get away from the insistent bulge of his bicep.

We pass Aunt Jane, who's wearing what looks like a pink-ribboned frisbee on her head; she nudges Grant and whispers something I can't hear. I notice other relatives too, some of whom I haven't seen for years, including Great-Uncle Charles, who must be pushing ninety. My mother is up at the very front, wearing a blue and white floral dress. Aurelie is right about the poor fit: it hangs slackly from her arms and gapes at the neck, drawing attention to the severe ridge of her collarbone. Her fingers worry at her wig, which has been threaded with flowers.

'Here you are,' Lewis says, depositing me on the chair beside her. 'One daughter safely delivered!'

'Oh! Thank you.'

'All part of the service!' He speaks more loudly than is necessary. 'Just let me know if you need anything else. Anything at all!'

'I will. Thank you.'

'Enjoy the nuptials!' He strides away.

My mother turns to me. 'He's not so bad, is he? As men go.' She's trying to sound cheery, but there's tension in her voice. 'And I like the fact they're all wearing Scottish outfits.' She gestures across the aisle to Alistair and Mike, who are standing side by side, facing forward. Like Lewis and the ushers, they are bedecked in tartan, with grey jackets and waistcoats, and knee-high grey socks. Or hose, as Kirsty would say. She has talked me through Scottish wedding attire: the Prince Charlie jackets, with three prominent buttons on each sleeve; the three-buttoned waistcoat; the full dress sporran, which hangs down across the front of the kilt like a large pocket. And of course the sgian dubh: a small, single-edged knife which is kept inside the hose, with just its hilt visible. Kirsty says these days they are only used for chopping fruit and the like, but originally they were a means of defence. To be kept hidden away, even when other weapons had been offered up.

In case of a surprise attack.

'And you look very pretty,' my mother says.

'You look nice too,' I lie.

'Oh, this old thing!' She pulls at the fabric and attempts to laugh.

Then there is silence. The argument in Aurelie's bedroom earlier sits between us like an uninvited guest. 'So,' I manage.

'So?'

'Is Aurelie okay? After . . . what happened?'

My mother sighs. 'She's a bit shaken, but she'll be fine.'

'I promise I didn't write the note.'

'I know, love.'

'Do you know who did?'

'Of course not!' She says this so sharply that I think I believe her. I open my mouth to tell her about the red-haired woman in the corridor last night, outside Aurelie's room, but change my mind as I start to speak.

'You don't think' – I lower my voice to a whisper – 'there's any truth in it? That Alistair might have done something bad?' The three notes are starting to merge in my head: Alistair's scrawl on a napkin twelve years ago, inviting Aurelie to meet him by the boathouse. The anonymous note my sister found this morning, warning her not to marry him. The letter from my mother, six months ago, saying the past was coming back to haunt us.

An unholy trinity.

'No!' My mother says this too loudly and a few heads turn our way. She drops her voice and I have to lean closer to hear her. 'I mean . . . he's a man . . . so we should manage our expectations about his levels of virtue and general competence, but . . . blood on his hands? No.'

I want to share her confidence, but the truth is: none of us knows the deeds of which others are capable. The lies they'll tell, the crimes they'll commit. The unseen monsters which lurk in their depths.

93

The heads turn back. When my mother speaks again, her voice is soft and wistful. 'I just wish things were better between you and your sister.'

I say nothing to this. Let my eyes follow the path of one of the wood carvings instead: long and sinuous, winding its way toward an arch.

'You used to be so close.' She smooths her dress across her knees. 'Back when you were little. When your father left me for the first time.'

I keep my eyes on the wooden path.

'I remember, one of those nights just after he'd gone, you couldn't sleep. You kept coming downstairs, with all these questions – you had so many questions! – and I kept taking you back up, tucking you in, only for you to come down again five minutes later. And then, finally, you stayed upstairs, and when I went to check on you, I found you'd got into bed with Aurelie. She had her arms wrapped around you.'

The path turns back on itself, splits into three.

'And if you fell over, she would bandage your knee. She loved playing Doctors and Nurses with you: cleaning up your cuts and sticking on a plaster, and wrapping toilet roll around it, like a bandage. We got through a ridiculous quantity of toilet roll, and the house used to stink of TCP, but it made you both happy. And God knows' – her voice cracks a little – 'with everything that was going on, that was what I wanted most of all. To make you happy.'

She sniffs, and coughs. Dabs at her nose with a tissue. 'It's what I still want. For my children to be happy. To be reunited. To be *properly* reunited. I don't want you to end up like me and your Aunt Jane, just pretending to like each other.'

I touch one hand to her arm, try not to recoil at how little flesh is left. 'We'll be okay, Mum.'

'I know you'll be okay, my angel. But I want you to be okay *together*.'

There is no good response to this. I could say I'll try to make up with Aurelie, but she'll know I don't mean it. So what's the point? Today I'm trying to uncover the truth, not push it further away.

Although, perhaps it makes little difference. Because, right now, with strange notes turning up, mysterious women fleeing down corridors, and Aurelie refusing to speak to me, I feel about as far from the truth as I've ever been.

◆ ◆ ◆

When a cello begins to play, the crowd falls silent and everyone stands. Most people turn to the back of the room: excited, expectant. I watch the cellist. She is in a tiny room behind one of the arches along with three other members of a string quartet, but she is the only one playing, her right arm extended to allow her bow smooth passage. Eight simple notes, on repeat. Her body sways slightly, and the instrument sways with her, held by her knees, her thighs.

The other musicians join in. The first violinist gets the melody, her fingers skipping across the strings.

My mother nudges me. 'Look,' she says. 'Look!'

Aurelie is gliding up the aisle in a white strapless silk dress and a long white veil embroidered with tiny stars. She appears limbless, her legs and feet hidden beneath her dress and her arms masked by flowers. The only thing mooring her to the ground is (oh irony of ironies) our father, who walks at a slow, deliberate pace. He is wearing a morning suit and a lopsided grin, nodding at several of the guests as he passes. As if he is integral to proceedings; as if he always has been. When the truth is, he did next to nothing to help bring us up. The only thing he successfully brought up – or, strictly speaking, out – was the worst in our mother.

Who, in turn, brought out the worst in us.

◆ ◆ ◆

December 2004

I take another mouthful of spaghetti as my sister runs to the window for the fifth time. She hasn't eaten anything, despite it being a rare family dinner – one where all of us, plus Jennifer, are present. Instead, she flits between table and window, clutching a hand to her sequinned stomach.

'Do sit down,' our mother says. 'Would you like some garlic bread?'

'No, no!' Aurelie turns from the window to face us. 'Can you imagine how embarrassing that would be? If I stank of garlic?'

'It would scare off any vampires.' Our father grins.

Aurelie turns back to the window.

'I don't see why anyone would want to go to a school disco in the first place,' I say.

'That's because you don't have any friends.'

'So who's this person sitting beside me?' I gesture to Jennifer. 'A phantom?'

Aurelie doesn't bother to reply.

'Girls! Don't start,' says our mother.

'This is delicious,' says Jennifer.

Aurelie makes a vomiting motion at the window, behind Jennifer's back.

'Glad you like it,' our father says.

'I don't recall you cooking it,' says our mother.

'I never said I did.'

I tear off another slice of garlic bread. The crust comes away as I pull, dangling from the greasy dough like a hangnail. On the opposite side of the table, our mother drains her wine and pours herself another glass.

When the doorbell sounds, Aurelie runs from the room before it's even finished ringing. There's a creak as the front door opens.

Seconds later, Jennifer's mother, Lan, appears. Aurelie follows behind, shoulders slumped, returning to her sentry post by the window while our mother half rises from her chair. 'Hello, Lan. We weren't expecting you for another half hour.'

'Sorry, I didn't mean to interrupt—'

'You're not interrupting anything; we just—'

'I don't think we've met.' Our father jumps up and holds out his hand. 'I'm Dom.'

'Lan.' Everything about Jennifer's mother is pretty: her fringe, her slim frame, her uncreased blouse with its lacy collar, even the way she takes our father's hand as if it were a rare bird's egg.

He gestures to the table. 'Can I get you something?'

'No. Thank you.'

'Are you sure?' Our father is in many ways Lan's opposite: large and loud, with receding, flyaway hair. The sort of person who fills a room even when the room's quite happy to be left empty. 'There's too much bolognese, so you'd be doing us a favour. And Jennifer can vouch for its tastiness!'

'Perhaps we could get the recipe,' said Lan. 'But I've already eaten, at . . .' She stops abruptly, and I look at Jennifer. But she's looking at the table, while running her front teeth across her lower lip. Her telltale sign of unease.

'I could put some in a pot for you,' our father says.

'Just leave it, Dominic.' Our mother stands up and begins to stack the plates with an uncharacteristic carelessness, each plate at a different angle from the one underneath, the cutlery sliding around on top. 'She said no. And we might want some ourselves tomorrow.'

'But there's not enough for all of us.'

'There's plenty.'

A fork falls to the floor, landing with a clang upon the tiles. Lan reaches down but our mother beats her to it, scooping up the fork while holding the stack of plates against her body.

'Thank you, but I have food at home,' says Lan.

'Of course, of course,' our father says. He runs one hand across his forehead and sits back down.

'Thank you for looking after Jennifer too.'

'You're most welcome.'

Our mother slams the dishes into the sink. There's an orange stain on her top from where she held the plates.

The doorbell rings again, and Aurelie rushes to the hall.

Our mother switches on the tap, squeezes in too much washing-up liquid. I watch as the sink fills with water and bubbles. Watch the straight line of our mother's back, unbending as the water threatens to breach its surrounds.

I run to turn the tap off. An act unacknowledged by our mother, who simply hands me the brush. 'You wash and I'll dry.'

Scrub scrub scrub. I'm halfway through cleaning a colander – trying to remove the starchy residue from around its holes – when our mother throws down her tea towel and leaves the room.

'You're not going to the disco with him.' Her voice is clear. 'You told me a girlfriend was driving you.'

'But Mum!' Aurelie sounds aggrieved. 'What does it matter? He's only giving me a lift.'

'No he isn't. You know the rules.'

'The rules are ridiculous!'

For once, I agree with my sister: the rules are ridiculous. No spending time alone with a non-familial member of the opposite sex: not in a cinema, not in a car, not even in a classroom. Not until we've left school. Whenever we ask why, our mother says it could lead to pregnancy, that it could ruin our young lives. Which is illogical. I might not be familiar with the precise mechanics of procreation, but I know it involves a great deal more than talking to a man, or driving in a car with one.

Fortunately, however, I've no desire to do either of these things anyway.

The front door shuts and our mother comes back into the room, picks up the tea towel and resumes drying.

Then Aurelie appears in the doorway, her face streaked with tears. 'What's wrong with you? It's a school disco, not an orgy!'

Our mother doesn't turn, just keeps drying.

'Aurelie!' says our father. 'We have guests.'

'But it's so stupid! How am I supposed to get there without a lift?'

'I can drive you.' Our father leans forward across the table. 'And Lan, I can give you and Jennifer a lift home too. If you'd like.'

◆ ◆ ◆

Now, walking up the aisle, Aurelie's face is far from tear-streaked; instead she is smiling, albeit in a calibrated way, with her lips turned up just-so at the edges. No beaming or crying; nothing which betrays any underlying emotion. And Alistair is equally composed: he stands at the front of the room with his eyes fixed upon her and his hands locked behind his back, pushing his chest forward. When my father passes Aurelie to him and retreats, there is a symmetry to it. A woman being given away while giving nothing away, by a man who should have been in her life, but wasn't, to a man who shouldn't, but is.

Or perhaps it's just the wedding procession which makes me think of symmetry. Sarah is in a purple dress, holding magnolias, while the two flower girls wear white dresses and carry lilacs. I reappraise Alistair and Mike's kilts and, sure enough, they are striped with white and purple too. Mike sees me looking and his eyes sear across me, before returning to the bride.

Women shouldn't be given away at all, of course.

'Welcome.' A registrar in a sensible brown suit – a poor match for the lilac (Aurelie must be twitching) – comes to the front of the gathering. 'Please be seated.'

There is a loud rustling as everyone sits. I help my mother into her chair and notice the wetness of her eyes. Not quite crying, but close enough to tug at something inside me.

'Good afternoon, ladies and gentlemen,' the registrar continues. 'May I begin by welcoming you all here today to the delightful setting of the Goreton Manor Hotel for the marriage of Alistair and Aurelie. Today marks a new beginning in their lives together and it means a lot to both of them that you, their family and friends, are here to witness their wedding vows and celebrate their marriage.'

She talks for a while about the sanctity of marriage as an institution, before inviting a woman called Felicity to give a reading. Tall and jewellery-adorned, with something of a nasal tone, I assume she is one of Aurelie's lawyer friends. She recites a poem by Elizabeth Barrett Browning about accepting love for love's sake, which strikes me as a circular argument, but then I am not a poet. Perhaps, to them, a note about blood on a man's hands could be viewed simply as a metaphor for passion, whereas I see it as a puzzle to be solved. A puzzle which *must* be solved, in case it relates in any way to what happened twelve years ago.

Did Alistair do, or see, something the night that Peter disappeared? And, if so, does the red-haired woman know? Does *Sarah* know? Is it even possible Sarah was the one who left the note in the first place?

But that doesn't make sense. None of it makes sense. I survey the watching faces, and wonder if the author of the note is among them. If I'll be able to tell from some giveaway clue in their expression: a mocking grin if it's really nothing more than a prank, or a nervousness in their eyes if their warning was well-intentioned; if they think there's a genuine reason why my sister shouldn't marry Alistair.

'It is one of my duties to inform you that this room in which we are now met has been duly sanctioned according to law for the celebration of marriages,' says the registrar. 'You are here to witness the joining in marriage of Alistair John Brown and Aurelie Rose Trent.'

Even their names have symmetry. So much symmetry. I keep looking at the faces and it occurs to me that if I can somehow determine the author of the note – if I can decipher a message about bloodied hands from an expression, a glance, a pinched lip – then perhaps the reverse is also true: perhaps someone can breach my thoughts and see the question marks in my mind.

My eyes travel across my sister, my father, my mother. One smiling, one nodding, one crying. (Blood may be thicker than water, but that just means it makes more of a mess.)

The registrar clears her throat, looks around the hall. 'If any person present knows of any lawful impediment why these two people may not be joined in marriage, he or she should declare it now.'

There is a hushed still and I search for the right words to break it. But what could I say?

Speak. Somebody speak.

'No.' It's said so quietly that I think I must have imagined it – hoped it into being – except everyone is turning, so I turn too, see a flustered woman saying, 'I'm really sorry, it was Jemima,' and pointing to one of the flower girls, who is trying to retrieve a book from a small boy beside her, and then there is laughter; great, gulping, relieved laughter, which spreads through the hall and builds in volume, and I want to put my hands over my ears because it's like the tale of 'The Emperor's New Clothes', where only the child is wise and the adults are loud and ignorant, but I keep my hands wrapped around the Order of Service, let my mother lean against me, and say nothing.

Five minutes later, Aurelie and Alistair are married.

SATURDAY, 1.35 P.M.

March 2005

There's an empty chair between me and my mother. A chair where my father is supposed to be. A chair which my mother looks at every couple of minutes, with an audible grunt each time. Grunts which are asynchronous with the pieces being performed on stage, and yet almost succeed in elevating them.

The pupils of Waldenborough High are not a musically talented bunch. There's a brass ensemble which sounds like a herd of maimed elephants, and a choir singing 'Love Me Do' so tunelessly that surely no one ever could. There's a recorder quintet, a mewling electric guitar, and a misguided attempt by a clarinettist to play the opening to 'Rhapsody in Blue'. Plus Aurelie and Sarah's flute duet, which sounds like a dose of television static.

But then there's Jennifer. The sound she creates belies her size and, even more miraculously, defies the dirge of the orchestra behind her. While the other pupils scrape and squeak, her notes soar and swell, dance and fly, until the whole room is permeated by them, alive with them.

My mother stops looking at the empty chair. Her eyes gather tears and, instead of grunting, she begins to sob. I contemplate doing something, but can't decide what. So I focus on Jennifer: on the way her fingers caress the strings, and the way she cradles the violin between chin and shoulder, in the spot where a resting head would fit. I've known for some time that she plays the violin: I've seen her go off for lessons, and been told by Lan she can't come out because she has to practise. But I never knew she could play like this, as if funnelling her very essence into the music. A near-perfect symbiosis of person and instrument.

I glance away, and immediately wish I hadn't. For there, in the woodwind section of the orchestra, are my sister and Sarah, the former stony-faced and the latter impersonating Jennifer's movements: bobbing her head and swaying from side to side. When the last note sounds, and a brief, charged hush gives way to frenzied applause, the two of them are the only people in the hall not to leap to their feet. My sister watches the floor as the ovation burns itself out around her, so she doesn't see the tears which shine on our mother's cheeks, nor the sheepish smile of our father, who has arrived just in time to leave again.

Afterwards, in the car, he remarks on how wonderfully Jennifer played.

'I don't see how you'd know.' Our mother changes gears with a vengeance. 'Given you only heard the closing bars.'

'I heard a bit more than that! Besides, you can tell, can't you? When someone is brilliant.'

'I thought her piece went on too long,' says Aurelie, crossing and uncrossing her legs next to me. 'And I don't understand why she had to fling herself about.'

'I think she was just absorbed in the music.'

'But don't you think she looked ridiculous? All that quivering and everything?'

I point out that it's called vibrato.

'I just think they should give other people more of a chance to perform.' My sister taps her fingernails on her flute case. 'Rather than making it The Jennifer Show.'

'It was hardly The Jennifer Show—'

'Says the man who wasn't there.' Our mother accelerates hard.

'Look, I'm sorry I was late. But I had to work—'

'But don't you think it's unfair?' Aurelie's voice is whiny. 'That one person gets all the attention just because she's been hothoused from birth?'

I look out of the window, past a queue of traffic to the water beyond. 'She's not been hothoused, she's naturally talented.'

'Oh come on, her mum makes her practise all the time.'

'How would you know?'

'Everyone knows. She's one of those pushy parents; she doesn't want her daughter to end up jobless like her, so she pushes her crazily hard at everything, all the time.'

'That seems a little unfair.' Our father swivels round in the front passenger seat to face us. 'Lan's qualified as a doctor.'

'But she doesn't work as a doctor.'

'That's not her fault.'

'Whose fault is it, then?'

'The UK government's. Its immigration policy. Mind you, it's the UK's loss too.'

'Let's not get carried away, Dominic.' Our mother's hands tighten upon the steering wheel. 'This isn't an issue of national importance.'

'I don't know about that – the NHS is crying out for more doctors.'

'Maybe, but that's a separate issue from whether Lan puts too much pressure on Jennifer.'

'Jennifer seems well-adjusted enough to me.' Our father turns back to face the front. 'And I don't think Lan is particularly unusual in her approach. She looked happy and proud tonight, just like any parent in her position would be.'

'So you were watching her?'

There was a pause. 'Not watching. But I did see her, yes.'

Our mother keeps her eyes on the road ahead.

'Just like I saw lots of other parents,' he goes on.

'Right.'

I feel the creep of sweat across my body. It's too hot in the car, and everything itches: my nylon shirt against my back, the sticky seat against my thighs. I run my fingers across my scalp and down my neck.

'What's that supposed to mean?' our father asks.

Our mother doesn't reply. I open the window, but the air is still and heavy, drenched with petrol.

Scratch.

Scratch.

'Eve?'

If you scratch skin hard enough, you'll draw blood.

'Oh, for goodness' sake! Can you stop with all the questions? I'm trying to get us home in one piece.'

I wind the window up again and shut my eyes.

'Stephanie? Stephanie! They're done.' My mother points to the reappearance of the wedding party, their signing of the register complete. Two arches along, the violinists from the string quartet finish their duet and fall into silence.

The registrar holds out her hands. 'Thank you for coming together today to celebrate this most special of events. Alistair and Aurelie, may I wish you both a wonderful day, a very long and happy marriage, and all the very best for your future lives together!'

The string quartet starts up again – loud triumphal music this time – and the newlyweds make their way back down the aisle, followed by Sarah and Mike. When it's our turn, my mother and I walk slowly, her hand wrapped around my arm. Lewis appears as we're leaving the hall. He gives a ridiculous little bow to my mother. 'I am here to accompany you to the next stage of proceedings.'

'She's fine with me,' I say, noting the spinach is still in his teeth.

'No, no, I'll go with Lewis.' She gestures to a waiter standing in the corridor with a tray of champagne flutes. 'Try to have some fun, Stephanie. I think we should all try to have some fun this afternoon. Not worry about . . . later. Live for the moment!'

I don't understand how my mother's moods can change so quickly. One moment she is sombre, or angry, and then all of a sudden she morphs into a wannabe party animal. Perhaps this is what terminal cancer does to a person.

Perhaps she's had terminal cancer all her life.

Lewis remains blithely unaware. 'That's the spirit, Ms Harman!'

'Call me Eve.'

'That's the spirit, Eve!' Lewis offers his arm, and she takes hold of it. 'And talking of spirits, would you care for a drink? There's champagne, of course, but I also happen to have inside information on the location of the cocktail bar.'

'A cocktail sounds good.'

So she's intending to fall off the wagon. 'Mum—'

'Splendid!' He leads her away and takes two champagne glasses in his free hand. 'Just in case we want these too,' he says loudly, and she laughs. 'Now, cocktail-wards!'

I start to go after them but am halted by an usher, who hands me a small cardboard box. 'Confetti,' he says. 'Please make your way to the Gladstone Steps to scatter it.'

'No. Thank you.' I try to hand it back, but he is giving out more boxes. The flow of people is rapid; my mother already lost among them.

'This way.' There are ushers everywhere. This one is pointing down the corridor. 'Left at the end, and then left again,' he says. 'For the Gladstone Steps.'

I take a glass of champagne and let myself be carried along with the rest of the crowd. Through a set of open doors to some wide stone steps, where a photographer is directing everyone into position. The sky is cloudless now and the sun fierce, unrelenting. Heat hits my bare shoulders and seeps through the soles of the uncomfortable, impractical shoes Kirsty insisted I wear (ones with pointed toes and small, narrow heels). I swallow some champagne, which already tastes too warm, and listen to the conversations nearby. Beauty and perfection are mentioned in relation to both the bride and the weather, with one voice asserting you couldn't ask for a better day. As if there is something innately good about hot weather, when statistics actually show the opposite is true. That an increase in temperature is associated with an increase in serious crimes. Sexual assault. Domestic violence.

Murder.

The photographer (a different one from yesterday) steers me to one of the lower steps and positions me side-on, next to a woman with short grey hair and glasses. He asks us to throw our confetti a second or two after the guests on the higher steps, to make sure there is a continuous arc of celebration.

'Have you ever heard such nonsense?' the grey-haired woman says as the photographer climbs the steps again. '"A continuous arc of celebration"!'

I like her instantly, and turn for a closer inspection. She's wearing a knee-length navy dress and flat shoes, and looks fairly old, in her sixties, perhaps.

'Perhaps he thinks it makes him sound clever,' I say.

'When in fact it does exactly the opposite.'

'Yes.'

'I'm Enid.' She doesn't attempt to shake my hand.

'Stephanie.'

'So how do you know the bride and groom?'

'I'm Aurelie's sister.'

'Ah.' She takes a mouthful of champagne.

'And you?'

'I'm Alistair's PA.'

Now it is my turn to drink. The swallowing sound I make is too loud, almost a gulp. 'So,' I say, trying to keep my voice light. 'What's he like? To work for?'

Enid gazes out across the gardens. 'He's wonderful.'

I study her expression; there is no tension in her face, just the hint of a smile. Either her assessment is genuine, or else she's an excellent liar.

'Do you mean he's wonderful at his job?' I ask. 'I've heard he's a very good lawyer.'

'Yes, he's very good at his job. But also more generally. He's a wonderful man.'

'Not too much of a taskmaster?' My attempt at a chuckle is unconvincing.

'He expects a lot of his staff. But he's also very generous to us.'

'In terms of Christmas gifts and things?'

'Yes, but not just that. He's supportive. My husband died last year—'

'I'm sorry—'

'Thank you. He died last year and Alistair was so good about it. Told me to take as much time off work as I needed. Sent me flowers. He even came to the funeral.'

'Right.'

'Not many bosses would do that.'

'No.'

'And he's very generous to others, too; gives a lot of money to charity. Particularly those charities which are closest to his heart, like the anti-bullying one, and Great Ormond Street Hospital.'

I look up sharply. 'Why is that close to his heart?' I think of the day, aged thirteen, when I discovered my pencil case had been vandalised. Aurelie's face as I confronted her, case in hand; the slight curl of a smile as she claimed she had nothing to do with it. That she didn't know why my pencil sharpener was full of chewing gum.

But I'd already thrown the pencil sharpener away.

'Well, he hates the idea of children getting sick and dying,' says Enid.

'What?' I blink a couple of times into the sunlight. 'No, I mean the other one. The anti-bullying one?'

'He feels very strongly that everyone deserves to be treated with respect.'

'Right.' A couple of hours after I'd confronted Aurelie with my graffiti-daubed case and snapped pencils, I heard her giggling on the phone to Sarah. And the next day an older boy at school approached me to say he'd heard my rubber had split. The whole corridor laughed at that one.

'And he says he wishes he'd done more to stop bullying, when he was younger.'

If that's true, he should never have married my sister. I wonder if it's possible she bullies him too; if Sarah ever goads her into acts of cruelty against him, just like she did with me and Jennifer. If it's possible that's what the anonymous note is all about.

Except, I remind myself: she was the recipient of the note, not its subject.

'Your sister is a lucky woman.'

I'm saved from having to respond by a shout from one of the ushers. 'They're coming! Get your confetti ready!'

There is excited chatter and rustling and the occasional clink of glasses changing hands or being deposited as everyone rushes to open their boxes. I succeed in opening mine one-handed, levering the flap against my hip. The confetti inside is purple and white and, according to a label on the underside of the lid, made from real flower petals. One hundred per cent biodegradable.

It makes me think of the flowers at Loch Ness – the ones marking the spot where Peter was last seen alive. They're deposited almost every day along the water's edge: a constant and inescapable reminder of the tragedy which took place there. Some come from family members, but most are left by tourists, conspiracy theorists and Nessie hunters (or some combination thereof) in ostentatious, quick-to-wither heaps. Worse even than the botanical wastage is the chronicling of it: recent postings on the 'Peter's Page' website have included a photo of a big, burly man with a bunch of limp carnations (captioned 'RIP Pete mate'), a photo of a family of five with a sunflower ('You left this world before you're time'), and a photo of a twenty-something woman whose pink roses match her hair ('sexyt1tt1es [website link]'). I find it macabre and distasteful – a family's loss being used for online hits – but Kirsty says she likes the fact he's being remembered. That these are 'Peter's people', whatever the hell that means.

I think back to the photos in Kirsty's living room. Peter as a baby, fat-cheeked and swaddled in a blanket. Peter as a chubby-armed toddler, ice cream dribbling down his chin. Peter on the beach with his parents, eyes squinting against the sun. Peter climbing a mountain with his aunt, cameras around their necks and hoods around their faces to keep out the rain. Peter at all ages, in all weathers, and somehow more alive to me than the people standing just metres away at this very moment.

'Ladies and gentlemen!' Lewis is at the top of the steps, holding a cocktail and a box. My mother (and the spinach in his teeth) no longer with him. 'I am delighted to present to you . . . Mr and Mrs Brown!'

There is a huge cheer as he moves to the side and Aurelie and Alistair appear, hand in hand. They pause for a second, framed by the arch of the doorway, until Lewis throws a fistful of confetti over their heads and Aurelie squeals, at which point the confetti starts coming thick and fast and Alistair laughs, leading my sister down the steps. The petals fall on their ears, their eyelashes, their shoulders, land on Aurelie's chest and the insides of Alistair's elbows, touch down briefly on their legs before swirling to the ground. There is more cheering and clapping and some guffaws from a man a couple of steps up from me, who scores a direct hit on Alastair's head, leaving a trail of petals in his oil-slick hair. As the newlyweds pass us, Enid scatters her confetti across the lower section of Aurelie's dress, while I upend my box on the steps. The heel of Aurelie's shoe leaves an indentation upon one of the petals and I try to track it, see how long I can hold it within sight, just like I once did with a released helium balloon at Weston-super-Mare. The balloon was shiny and orange, ostensibly obvious, yet within seconds it was tiny, and seconds later just a speck, and soon it became indiscernible from other spots of light in the sky.

The petal is easier to track: it lies dormant before fluttering like a maimed butterfly to the step below.

I can hear Aurelie and Alistair laughing, commenting on the process of cleaning each other up. 'We're basically chimps picking off fleas,' Alistair says.

'Speak for yourself.'

'You need to get the confetti off his backside, Aurelie!' a female voice shouts.

I look up to see my sister running one hand down Alistair's back and then quickly over his buttocks. Applause breaks out and she giggles.

'Again!' A male voice this time. 'If you don't remove all the confetti from his arse, everyone will think he's a party pooper!'

This brings a couple of laughs, and a ripple of further laughter as others catch on to the joke.

Enid taps my arm. 'Do you have a copy of the wedding schedule? I've lost mine.'

I unzip my crossbody bag and pull out the schedule, folded into quarters. I shake it open and pass it across.

She places her empty box and glass onto a low wall and takes the schedule in both hands; holds it out at arm's length to read. 'Over two hours until food,' she says. 'Let's just hope they provide some nibbles to keep us going.'

'Talking of food . . .' I try to keep my tone casual. 'Do you happen to know the woman who mentioned Loch Ness last night?'

'I only arrived this morning.'

'Oh. In that case, perhaps you can tell me: does anyone in your office have red hair?'

'Of course.' She doesn't look up. 'It's a big office. Red hair isn't uncommon. Oh strewth, they're having group photos. They always take an age, don't they? Trying to get everyone into shot and smiling at the camera. A losing battle.'

I try again. 'Is there anyone with red hair in your office who's Scottish, and about fifty or so?'

She shrugs. 'Possibly. Nobody springs to mind, but as I say the company is large; I don't know everyone. Oh, thank goodness, they're having a band rather than a ceilidh. I can't stand enforced dancing. All those Gay Gordons and whatnot. Why do you ask, by the way? About the woman?'

'I'm just wondering . . . is there anyone at your work who holds a grudge against Alistair?'

Her eyes harden. 'What do you mean?'

'Does anyone have anything against him?'

'Well, he's senior.' She holds my gaze. 'And still young. Some people probably resent him for that.'

'I'm not talking about people being envious, or not liking him because he's their boss.'

'So what are you talking about?' The earlier friendliness in her voice has gone.

'I don't know. Something from his past, perhaps. Something for which he hasn't been forgiven.'

'This seems like a very strange line of questioning.' She pushes her glasses back up her nose. 'Particularly on his wedding day.'

'Yes. I'm sorry. It's just . . . I'm trying . . . So you're not aware of anything, or anyone, out of the ordinary?'

'No, I'm not.' Enid hands back my schedule and picks up her glass. It is done swiftly, decisively, and yet doesn't disguise a slight tremor in her arm. 'I'd suggest you stop with these sorts of questions, on today of all days. Weddings are meant to be about love and happiness, not grudges and threats.'

She walks off, leaving her box on the wall. I look at the ground with its covering of discarded petals and think back through our conversation. Perhaps it was inappropriate of me to question her in that way. To mention Alistair's past and long-harboured grudges.

But I never said anything about threats.

SATURDAY, 2.20 P.M.

There's a common belief that, at the edge of death, life flashes before your eyes. That, in a matter of seconds, you remember past moments, people, events; things of significance. And there's evidence to back this up: scientists have shown the brain undergoes a surge in electrical activity when dying, with a marked increase in brain waves for up to half a minute after the heart stops beating.

But this activity has only ever been observed from the outside, not the inside, of the dying brain. What nobody knows is what the organ perceives during its own demise. We can use the testimony of near-death survivors to posit that a dying person sees bright lights, enters a higher state of consciousness, remembers loved ones, but these are necessarily self-selecting; the experiences of those who survived. We don't know anything of the final perceptions of those who are killed; those who, by definition, fail to make it back.

Which leads me to wonder: does a murdered person also receive a flash of happier times, even as darkness engulfs them?

The wait staff at the hotel are nothing if not attentive; I turn down five offers of a champagne top-up in a ten-minute period. Today, more than ever, I must stick to my limit, must guard against possible indiscretions or lapses in judgement. As I sift through bad memories, and walk among those who generated them, it's critical I stay emotionally level. And so I finish my first drink and place my hand over my glass.

The other guests don't share my caution; all around me, they are drinking, laughing, offering up their glasses to the waiters. Their conversations are loud, their gestures exaggerated: hands pumped, cheeks kissed, hair flicked. We are here to have fun, they seem to be saying; we must have fun. There is something almost primal about their collective rush to hedonism – the way they hunt down pleasure without thought. I remember my mother's rallying cry to 'live for the moment', and can only hope her 'moment' doesn't involve sinking a jeroboam's worth of champagne. I haven't seen her since she left with Lewis, which might mean she's having a sit down somewhere, but could equally mean she's already inebriated, staggering through corridors and swearing.

My father, on the other hand, is right in front of me: at the centre of a cluster of women, talking and waving his glass around. He appears to be regaling them with a long story; every few seconds, one of the women gives a hissing laugh, like a saucepan overboiling, and each time she laughs, he becomes yet more animated, leaning forward and whirling his arms. I'm sure Lucille wouldn't approve. Not because she'd be jealous, but because he looks ridiculous. As far as I can tell, she's always valued elegance over enjoyment.

I hear her name mentioned and draw closer. My father is acting more seriously now, his voice lower and his arms by his side, as if the mere sound of those two syllables is enough to bring him into line. *Lu-cille*. It's an objectively annoying name – impossible to say without stretching the mouth into a gritted smile, and also smug, convinced of its own importance.

'Lucille thinks olfactory therapy is going to be huge,' my father says. 'It's not really caught on yet, but she thinks it will, because it allows people to revisit the past in a non-threatening way.'

'Fascinating,' says one of the women. 'A bit like Proust's madeleines.'

He nods. 'Yes. The power of smell has often been appreciated from a cultural perspective, but not from a wider one; certainly not in the arena of healing. But Lucille thinks everyone *intuitively* understands the power of smell without necessarily realising that they do. We've all had that moment where we've smelled something from our past and been transported.'

'The smell of suntan lotion reminds me of a fling I had in Spain back in the 1970s,' says one woman, sighing and looking to the sky. 'With a guitarist called Juan, who had dreamy eyes and an even dreamier body.'

'The smell of rubbish makes me think of my ex-husband,' says another woman. 'Probably because he never took the bins out.'

'So is your wife trained as an olfactory therapist?' the Proust woman asks.

'Not yet,' my father says. 'But she's in the process of training. And then she plans to train others, and to provide retreats where people can come to heal or to refresh their skills.'

He has some gall to talk about healing, when he's spent his life inflicting wounds. But it's a good business model, I suppose. Hurt them and they'll pay to be mended.

'How wonderful. So that's why you're setting up the centre?'

'That's right. Although we still need to decide on a location. I personally think we should go for the New Forest, as it will enable us to attract the London pound, but Lucille's keen on the north of Scotland. She likes the idea of the centre being somewhere secluded. Free from the odours of human cities and roads.'

'The north of Scotland is certainly secluded.'

'Yes, but it's also a long distance away . . . from anywhere. Plus . . .' He trails off.

'Plus?'

'Oh, nothing.' He jigs his shoulders and smiles. 'Let's just say that my ex-partner and I used to go there a lot. Bad memories!'

Bad memories indeed. As he goes on to explain about the costs of such an undertaking – how they're looking for investors but also putting in a significant portion of their own money – I start to understand why he wants to change his will. Why he wants to talk to me about it.

He's giving his money to Lucille, not me or my sister. He's choosing to invest in her, not us, even if that means putting what wealth he has into an 'olfactory centre': a concept that literally stinks.

There's a bad smell in the air right now, one which is all too recognisable. One which overrides the scent of champagne, wilting flowers and sunbaked earth.

The smell of being shafted.

I never heard from Jennifer after she was taken. For months, I kept hoping for a letter; for news; for confirmation she thought of me as much as I did of her. But no envelope with her neat, even script ever came, nor any phone call from abroad. Which means I just don't know. Whether she settled happily (or not so happily) elsewhere, or was left, like me, with an unfinished story.

Of course I've tried to find her. I've typed her name into every search engine I've come across, always hoping *this will be the one*. The one capable of cutting through the Jennifer Chen haystack – the consultants, the academics, the influencers, the journalists, the architects, the doctors, the lawyers, the business owners – to find my Jennifer, sharp and shiny just like the proverbial needle.

But Chen is one of the most common surnames in China and, thus, the world. Which is too big a haystack, even for me.

◆　◆　◆

'Stephanie!'

I look up to see Aunt Jane barrelling in my direction in a blur of pink: pink dress, pink eyeshadow, pink necklace. Pink ribbons on her pink, frisbee-shaped hat. Perhaps she thinks she's at a seven-year-old's birthday party. 'Isn't it marvellous?' she says.

'What?'

'This!' She flings her hands out to either side of her. 'The weather, the setting. All being here together.'

I look down at the ground, run my foot across a gap in the paving stones.

'And wasn't it a beautiful ceremony?'

'Mmm.'

'Your sister's dress is a showstopper. Must have cost your father a fair penny, I daresay. Or did Alistair foot the bill?'

I shrug.

'In fact, this whole shindig must have cost a packet.'

'Mmm,' I say again. Alistair is standing nearby, his back being hug-slapped by another man. He returns the gesture: arm hooked, palm flat. He's a tall man – over six foot – but slim, suave, not the sort of person I can picture in a fight. He looks like someone who doesn't like mess, who pays others to clean up for him. Or who pays others to pay them, removing himself as far as possible from any dirt.

And yet I remember what Enid said. *Weddings are meant to be about love and happiness, not grudges and threats.*

So the question is: is he threatening, or being threatened? Once again, my memory is drawn to that scrawled message on Aurelie's napkin. *Meet me tonight, by the boathouse.* The newspapers explained that the empty canoe – the one that was found on the loch after Peter vanished – had come from the boathouse. That it was owned by the hotel. That it would have been difficult for one man to carry on his own.

'Don't you think?' Aunt Jane nudges my arm.

'Sorry, what?'

'That your father's looking well?'

A woman in a blue hat is talking to my father now, clasping his hand while he nods.

'Sprightly!' Jane continues. 'And dapper. A morning suit suits him. Suits him – ha! Mind you, your father has always been very . . . hmm . . . what's the word?'

'Adulterous? Fickle? A turncoat?'

If she hears my suggestions, she makes no indication of it. Instead, she gazes at the sky until she finds the word she wants. 'Twinkly!' she says.

'Oh, good God.' I hold out my glass to a passing waiter and let him fill it to the brim. Aware it shouldn't be so easy for my resolve to break. But dwelling on my weakness is hardly going to help either, so I take a mouthful of champagne and shut my eyes briefly, focus on the sensation of bubbles popping as they travel down my throat. Then, when Jane isn't looking, I toss the remainder of the champagne on to the grass.

'I know your parents have had their . . . *issues*,' she says. 'But I've always had a soft spot for your father.'

'A blind spot, more like.' When it comes to my parents, Jane is undoubtedly on my father's side. She has always rushed up to him at family gatherings, squeezing his arm and laughing at his unfunny jokes. Whispered to him in corners. Advised my mother to pay him more attention, to make him feel loved. Even after he cheated on her. Even when she sat on one of Jane's hard-backed dining room chairs, crying into a glass of wine and saying she didn't know how to go on.

Jane looks at me, head tipped to one side so her hat sits straight. 'Your father's a better man than you think.'

'Given what I think, that's hardly an endorsement.'

She tuts at me. 'I've been talking to him recently. He wants to help you.'

'It's a bit late for that.'

'It's never too late.' She presses one hand to her neck, and it strikes me how wrong she is. How sometimes the worst can happen, and nothing can be done to fix it. 'Besides, your mother's not perfect either, you know.'

A guttural sound escapes from deep within me: part laugh, part growl. As if I might think my mother's perfect. As if I might think, just because my father is a shit, my mother must be a saint. As if parents must hold a constant quantity of goodness between them. When, in fact, they can both be heinous.

And their children can be too.

I look across to Aurelie, who is clutching her train as she walks from guest to guest, smiling and laughing. Blushing just a little when they say how beautiful she is, letting hands stroke the silk of her dress, turning to give her best angle for photographs, fake eyelashes fluttering. I don't understand how she can do it. Has she concluded the note in her room was a joke, or is she pretending? Trying to convince herself it doesn't matter – or, worse, that it never happened?

But perhaps I shouldn't be surprised. My sister is good at rewriting history. Just like she did after Jennifer was taken away. Insisting – even when I shouted, raved, threatened – that she and Sarah hadn't contacted the authorities, or mentioned Lan's job to anyone. Tears in her eyes, hands in her lap; a picture of wronged innocence.

But tonight I'll find out the truth. I'll find out which one of them betrayed Jennifer. Or whether they did it together.

I look back at Jane, who is still watching me. 'Your mother wasn't always honest with your father, you know,' she says.

'Maybe,' I say. 'But he *always* wasn't honest with her.'

'But she kept something important from him. Something big.'

'What?' My voice sounds a little higher than usual as I think of the tent that night, flapping in the wind. 'What did she keep from him? Does it relate to Loch Ness?'

She frowns. 'Pardon?'

'Does the thing she didn't tell him relate to Loch Ness? To our camping holidays there?'

Jane takes a swig of champagne. 'Loosely, I suppose, although it goes back a lot further than that. But I can't say anything more; it's not for me to tell you.'

This is classic Aunt Jane: to tell me what she can't tell me. And not to tell me what she can. On this occasion, I wonder if she's referring to their childhood. My mother has relayed fragments of it over the years: their mother dying; their father checking out of his responsibilities. Jane adopting the role of parent, taking my mother to school and cooking her meals. Telling her she was a terrible burden. That she was stupid and nobody would ever want her. And, later, when men did want her, that she was a slut.

My mother's childhood sounds pretty horrific. But that doesn't mean she gets a pass to act with impunity now.

◆ ◆ ◆

When Jane eventually leaves, I take my phone from my bag. There are three messages: one from my network provider and two from

Kirsty, asking me to ring. She's probably still worrying because of the lake. I walk away from the Gladstone Steps, into a walled garden whose borders are rife with yellow dahlias. It is secluded here, and relatively quiet, the noise of the other guests little more than a hum.

'Hello?' Kirsty answers almost immediately.

'Hi. You asked me to ring.'

'Aye, thanks for getting back to me. I just wanted to check how things are going.'

'They're . . . going.' I sit down on a bench that is shaded by a couple of trees.

'That good, huh? Tell me what's been happening.'

I talk her through the events of the day, being careful not to mention the anonymous note, or the lake. To steer clear of the fact I have an ulterior motive for being here, and that others might too. Instead, I focus on safer subjects: the string quartet, the Scottish outfits, the weather. She asks a couple of questions about the ceremony, and I do my best to reply. And then she asks something odd.

'Did your sister seem at all nervous? About getting married?'

I lean back against the bench, my dress sticking to my thighs. Even in the shade it is too hot. 'She was nervous last night,' I say. 'According to her maid of honour, anyway.'

'Really? Do you know why?'

'Just pre-wedding jitters, I think. Or perhaps anxiety about our mother. But who knows? It's not as if she confides in me.'

'No.' There is a pause. 'And today?'

I suppress the memory of Aurelie sitting cross-legged on the hotel bed, her eyes filled with tears. 'She's in her element today. The perfect bride, the centre of everyone's attention. She's always wanted to get married. As a child she used to put a towel over her head and pretend it was a veil.'

Kirsty doesn't reply, so I keep talking. 'She made me be the groom.' I have a sudden desire to free my tongue, which feels cooped up inside my mouth. 'There was this old tie of my father's that my mother kept in her bedside drawer, which I had to wear. Although neither Aurelie nor I knew how to knot it, so I just wore it slung around my neck. Until my mother found me with it and said never to wear it again.'

Except she didn't say it; she yelled it. Smashed a mug against the bedroom wall to emphasise her point.

'Kirsty?' I say. 'Kirsty, can you hear me?'

Silence. I wonder if she's fallen asleep; she sometimes does in the afternoon, particularly when it's hot. It's because she doesn't sleep at night – even in the earliest hours of the morning, long before the birds begin their symphony of chirps and trills, there is always a square of light at her cottage window. I asked her about it once and she looked away from me, held a hand to her forehead as if shielding herself from a blow. She was quiet for so long I thought she'd forgotten the question. But then she replied, telling me she couldn't shut her eyes without seeing Peter's face. The scared, unspeaking face of her lost son. His skin wrinkled from the water and his mouth open in a silent scream.

'Kirsty?'

Still nothing. I want to tell her that I see him too, and not just in my sleep. Sometimes when I'm awake and looking at something innocuous – a tiled floor, say, or a scattering of autumn leaves – it arranges itself into his features. His slanted eyebrows, his rounded cheeks. And perhaps I shouldn't worry about this, as I've read that humans are evolutionarily primed to see faces in random patterns, but it's always *his* face that I see. Which doesn't seem random at all.

'Kirsty? Can you hear me? Are you sleeping? I'm going to hang up and try ringing you back.'

'I'm here.'

'Oh.'

'Sorry.' Her voice is thicker than usual.

'That's okay.'

'I'm really sorry.'

'It's not a problem. Are you feeling tired?'

'No. I'm sorry for . . .' She trails off.

'Kirsty?'

'I'm still here. It's just . . . I'm sorry you're on your own down there.'

Unease prickles at the back of my neck and I scan the garden. No one is watching me. Obviously no one is watching me. Kirsty is in Scotland. And she was referring to my estrangement from my family, not being alone in a literal sense.

'I'm hardly on my own,' I said. 'I wish I were! There are far too many people here.'

'I hope you know how highly I think of you.'

Guilt whips across my body now, hot and stinging. I can't bear for her to think of me as a good person. Not when I can still picture that night so clearly. The full moon, the flapping tent, the empty sleeping bag.

'I think highly of you too,' I say.

'Thank you,' she says. 'Although I'm not sure you should.'

'Are you all right, Kirsty?' Perhaps she has resorted to alcohol to numb the pain of it all. The past, her son's death, existence.

'You made it to the wedding ceremony,' she says. 'So there would be no shame in leaving now. No reason to feel bad.'

She's wrong about that. 'I have to stay for my mother,' I explain. 'It's what she wants and . . . well . . . she's ill, so—'

'I'm sorry.' There is a pause. 'People do the damnedest things for their families, don't they?'

My neck prickles again, but more sharply than before.

'Just promise me you'll be careful,' she says.

'I promise.'

'And don't go near the lake.'

'Okay.'

But this time I don't promise anything.

SATURDAY, 2.50 P.M.

I remain in the walled garden for some time after speaking to Kirsty. Mulling over our strange conversation and trying to welcome the heat, instead of treating it as an oppressor. Maggie, my counsellor, was always big on this sort of stuff, advising me not to view my environment or the people around me as the enemy – like the English teacher who'd first sent me to see her after I wrote in an essay that Hamlet was 'a weak, narcissistic protagonist with Mummy issues who should just stick his fucking rapier in Claudius's chest and be done with it'. She told me that mindset makes a huge difference to how we see the world around us, not just by framing our mood, but through actual physiological effects. She said if we try to see the best in people, and adopt a more positive attitude to difficulty, we can reduce the quantity of pain experienced.

But my mindset must have been wrong then, and it's certainly wrong now, because the sun feels even hotter than before.

Something has upset Kirsty. Something more than simple tiredness, or missing me. Maybe my being at my sister's wedding makes her think of what could have been, if Peter hadn't gone into the storm that night. Leads her to imagine another future in which he stayed at home – in which he grew into middle age, found a nice Scottish lass and produced a clutch of grandchildren. She thrives on caring for others, on dispensing affection and food to those around her. Even that very first evening at White Croft, I could sense her reservoirs of love: brimming and eddying, desperately seeking an outlet. Seeking an empty person like me.

Except I can never be Peter, nor she my mother. However hard we will it.

Peter didn't deserve to die. I mean, obviously no one *deserves* to die, but some people are more deserving than others. Everything I've learned about Peter suggests he was intrinsically good, that he was open-hearted and curious, and incapable of being unkind. And I appreciate no one speaks ill of the dead, but what I've heard about Peter goes beyond the normal platitudes. One local news report, for example, dispensed with the usual 'he was a bright, popular boy' shtick, and instead had a teacher recall his incredible knowledge of botany. 'He was passionate about the flora of Scotland,' she said. 'So curious, so knowledgeable, and so generous in sharing his knowledge with others. He would contribute to national surveys on local plant life, and was overjoyed when he once found a rare tufted saxifrage. His absence is a loss for all of us, not just for those of us who knew him, but for everyone who seeks to understand the world that little bit better.'

I've learned something of him first-hand too. One Sunday lunchtime, Kirsty and Rob had to run off unexpectedly when a pipe burst in their holiday cottage, leaving me alone with a table of food. I ate my fill, plus an additional Yorkshire pudding and the charred fragments of potato at the bottom of the roasting tin, then sat back on the sofa to await their return. When they still weren't back after twenty minutes, I did some clearing up, and then sat back on the sofa again. But when a further ten minutes had elapsed, I grew restless, and found myself staring at the door to Peter's old room, which his parents always kept shut. Perhaps there would be clues in there, something which could make sense of what had happened. Something which Kirsty and Rob might have missed.

128

I approached the door tentatively at first, palm flat against the wood, gently pushing, but it didn't budge, so I took the handle and tried to turn it with the tiniest tilt of my wrist, but that didn't work either, so then I stopped pussyfooting around and just opened it. The room within was, at first glance, ordinary-looking: a double bed against one wall, a desk against another, a wardrobe and bookshelf against a third. The walls painted white and the window over the desk framed with navy curtains. Everything orderly: the bed made up with chequered blue and white bed linen, and three pairs of shoes in a neat row underneath. On the walls were several botanical illustrations, showing ferns, flowers and fruit, all in matching matte black frames. Three notebooks were stacked on the desk, in front of a pot of pens and a large teddy bear wearing a knitted jumper saying 'I♥Ben Nevis'. There was also an old-style CD player, and a rack of CDs containing an eclectic mix of music: Bach's *Goldberg Variations*, Madonna's *Greatest Hits*, Happy Hardcore compilations.

But it was the bookshelf that really caught my attention. For, in addition to comics, botany and wildlife tomes, and a few 'classic' books – Dickens, Orwell and the like – there was an extensive collection of books about the Loch Ness monster. These ranged from a colourful cartoony book called *Nessie!* to an arcane-looking hardback entitled *What the Surgeon Saw: Sightings of the Loch Ness Monster from Saint Columba to the Modern Age*. There were thick books, thin books, tall arty books and short, text-heavy books, all focused upon the long-standing myth that the loch contained some sort of otherworldly beast. And it seemed both apt and impossibly sad that Peter, a boy who grew up fascinated by this myth, should have ended up as a footnote to it.

My mind is snatched back to the present by voices beyond the garden's walls. Seconds later, Alistair and Aurelie appear, accompanied by a photographer, and I shrink back against the bench to evade their notice. Fortunately, they're too preoccupied with posing in front of the dahlias to see me. The heat of the wood leaches into my flesh as I watch them holding hands and smiling, kissing. Nothing passionate, just a touching of lips. The photographer takes tens, possibly hundreds, of photos before she stops, adjusts Aurelie's train, repositions Alistair's hand upon the small of her back, and waves at them to resume.

When my sister and I stopped talking, our mother used to say it was a blip, that we'd work it all out in the end. That blood was thicker than water. But she was wrong, because the blip grew older, larger, and is now sixteen years in the making.

Old enough to create a child of its own.

I walk across the grass instead of on the gravel path, to avoid drawing their attention, but as I reach the corner the photographer stops them again.

'Lovely,' she says, glancing at her watch. 'If you could just turn to the side slightly . . .'

Aurelie turns in my direction and I hurry away without looking back, out of the walled garden, through the revellers, up the Gladstone Steps and into the hotel. Only once I'm inside do I stop to let my breath catch up. Sweat has plastered my hair to my forehead, and the cleft between my breasts is damp. My feet are slick and slippery, my toes aching from where I've clenched them to keep my stupid shoes in place.

At least it is cooler in here and not too busy: just a few guests and a couple of waiters getting rid of empty bottles. A woman passes me with orange-pink liquid in a bulbous glass, a slice of grapefruit skewered on its rim. Shortly after, a man appears with a tray of cocktails and shouts at the woman to wait up. He walks slowly, watching the glasses the entire time, their contents threatening to spill.

'Aurelie's sister!'

The voice comes from the direction of the Gladstone Steps and I turn to see Lewis bounding toward me, a glass of champagne in either hand. Just behind him is Mike with a bottle of beer.

'Hello,' I say.

'Her name's Stephanie,' Mike says to Lewis.

'I know that; I'm being witty.'

Mike raises his eyebrows. 'You call that wit?'

Lewis taps him on the shoulder with the edge of one glass. 'You wouldn't understand, Mikey-boy, what with your dark, repressed persona. All those moody Heathcliff vibes.'

'Fuck off.'

'Spoken like a true Heathcliff.' Lewis turns to me. 'The thing you have to understand about the two of us, Aurelie's sister—'

'Stephanie—'

'—is that he has the looks, and I have the charm. So, between us, we're the perfect man.'

I've no idea what I'm supposed to say to this. I glance between the two men, note the marked difference in their expressions. Lewis is smiling broadly, his eyes creased at the corners, while Mike is closed off: eyebrows lowered, mouth firm. When he sees me looking he returns my gaze with an unnerving intensity. I drop my eyes but can still feel his upon me: deeply focused, almost forcible, as if he's trying to strip something away.

'How are you finding the wedding so far?' Lewis asks.

I shrug. 'It's a wedding.'

He laughs. 'You're just like Mike – not prone to effusiveness. A person of few words!'

'I know plenty of words. I just choose not to use them.'

He laughs again, and a brief smile passes across Mike's face too. It softens the contours of his jaw, provides a momentary backlight to his eyes, and although I'm not that way inclined, I get a glimpse of why Sarah is drawn to him.

But I'm at a loss to understand what he sees in her. He seems so quiet and reserved, whereas she's wholly incapable of keeping her mouth shut. As exemplified perfectly by her earlier comments to me about his penis. The smirk on her face when she said she could verify its size from the night of Aurelie's housewarming.

And then it strikes me. The housewarming took place the night before the dress fitting. The night before my mother wrote her panicked letter.

'You seem perilously devoid of a drink,' Lewis says. 'Can Mike and I get you something?'

'No. Thank you.' I need to speak to my mother. If Mike and Sarah spent the night before the dress fitting together, then perhaps it was Mike who told her something about Peter's disappearance. I look at him again and am unnerved to find he's still looking at me, still staring with that penetrating gaze, as if he knows exactly what I'm thinking.

'Oh, go on – we could recreate the old times! Us serving you—'

'No. Really.' I have no desire to recreate the old times. No desire to re-see the dining room at the North Ness Hotel, or the boathouse and campsite just beyond it. No desire to relive that stormy night in July twelve years ago, when the tent flapped and the waters churned.

They left me. They all bloody left me.

'I can't promise pancakes, but I could rustle up a cocktail. I could even put it into a cracked teacup to properly conjure up the North Ness ambience—'

'Jesus, Lewis, nobody wants to conjure up the North Ness ambience.' Mike says this firmly, but his left hand is shaking. He moves it across to join his right hand, clasps his beer tightly between them.

'All right, Heathcliff, keep your knickers on. It wasn't *that* bad. The hotel was a shithole, admittedly, but you had such a fetching haircut. Those delightful, floppy curtains—'

'Why don't you do us all a favour and shut the fuck up?'

There is a long pause. Mike's face and body are giving out contradictory messages: he is staring at Lewis, eyes unblinking; but his hands are twitching, scraping shards of paper from the label of his bottle.

It seems to me that he's trying to hide something. And that it could be linked to what Sarah said to my sister at the dress fitting; to what panicked my mother into action. 'Have you seen my mother recently?' I ask.

'Aye.' Lewis takes a large draught of champagne. 'Or at least, fairly recently. In the Nightingale Suite.'

'Where's that?'

'The lounge area.'

I raise my eyebrows.

'Where the cocktail bar is. Back past the Darwin Hall.'

I thank him and make to leave, but he pulls a sad face. 'Going so soon?'

'I should make sure she's okay.'

'Can't I persuade you to stay a while longer? How about if I do a dance for you?' He raises a hairy knee and smiles at me. 'Everyone enjoys a Highland Fling.'

Mike grabs his arm. 'For fuck's sake, Lewis. Let her go.'

'See!' Lewis calls after me, as I walk away down the corridor. 'No charm at all!'

Returning to the Darwin Hall, there is a renewed knotting in my abdomen. Only eight hours remain until the end of the celebrations, and I feel increasingly confused – losing clarity when I should be gaining it. It's like I've been submerged and am watching the world from underwater. Watching blurred, shadowy forms moving in an ecosystem where everything is linked but predator is indistinguishable from prey.

I wish I could teleport myself back to Scotland, even if only for a few minutes. I can think more clearly up there, my mind free from unwanted memories. My days unsullied by family. My life relatively unscathed (so to speak).

But it's just one weekend, and teleportation hasn't been invented yet, so on I walk down the corridor. A newly erected sign for *Brown Wedding – Lounge Area* directs me past three doorways to another sign, with an arrow pointing to a room on the right. The Nightingale Suite. It looks cosy inside: full of plump sofas and armchairs and small coffee tables instead of the hard-backed chairs and long tables that feature in most of the function rooms. There is a makeshift bar in one corner, with bottles, glasses, and a cocktail menu written on a blackboard. A dancing pineapple drawn in yellow chalk advertises 'tropical cocktails': Piña Colada and Sex on the Beach. There are also 'traditional cocktails', 'party cocktails', and the day's special, the 'Aura Lee', which is made with vodka, vermouth, grapefruit and tangerine. Presumably sweet on first taste and bitter underneath.

And now, at last, I see my mother. But she isn't alone. She and another woman are in armchairs on the far side of the room, deep in conversation, heads bent together. A wig threaded with flowers next to a ribbon-festooned, frisbee-shaped hat. Aunt Jane. An array of drinks sits on the table between them: three glasses of champagne (empty), two cocktails (almost empty) and two glasses of water (barely touched). My questions about Mike and Sarah will have to wait.

But, as I'm about to turn away, I notice Jane is gripping the seat of her chair with both hands, and her cheeks are taut, sucked in. She and my mother are whispering urgently to one another.

I stop where I am, halfway across the room. Try to make out their words, but hear only agitated whispers, interspersed with noises from the bar behind me. The sound of chopping, knife against wood. The clink of glasses being placed on a counter.

A low hum from the fridge.

◆ ◆ ◆

November 2001

I lean in closer, my ear pressed against the wood of the kitchen door. 'She's only just started at Waldenborough High,' my mother is saying. 'It's been a big change for her. Unsettling.'

'What she did was violent,' Jane replies. 'I don't think it can be explained by being unsettled.'

'But there's been other stuff to contend with too.' My mother sounds tired. 'Dom leaving, and coming back; the arguments between the two of us. It's been difficult for the girls, Stephanie particularly. She's sensitive to that sort of thing.'

'Everyone has difficulty in their lives. It doesn't mean they turn feral.'

'Feral!' My mother's voice grows louder. 'She's a child, not a dog!'

'Grant says a dog would be put down for less.'

I become conscious of the patterns in the wood: a dark knot encased in tiny circles, surrounded by other, larger circles, which spin out yet further, in rings of ever-increasing size.

'Fuck Grant! And fuck you too, for listening to him.'

'He's my husband.'

'And Stephanie's my daughter! What right do you have to talk about her like that?'

A sigh, and the clatter of plates being stacked. 'We're just concerned. When it comes to families and children, you haven't always shown the best judgement.'

A pause. 'You always do this.' My mother's voice is trembling. 'Put me down. Question my decisions. Well, I've realised: the only truly bad decision I ever made was letting you decide for me.'

'Let's not start on that again.'

'That? That? He was a person, not a thing.'

'And you were a child! I was responsible for you, for your welfare.'

'And I was responsible for his.'

A pause. 'Well, now you're responsible for Stephanie's. And I think you need to do something. It's not normal for a child to behave like that.'

'What would you know about what's normal? You don't have any idea what it's like—'

Another sigh. 'There's no point getting worked up.'

'—trying to do your best, day in, day out, when you're worried your partner might run off again at any moment—'

'And whose fault is that?' A cold chafe of a laugh. 'Perhaps if you paid Dominic more attention, he wouldn't feel compelled to look elsewhere.'

Another silence, then a chair scraping across the floor. My cue to move. I back away from the kitchen, turn and run the length of the hall. Perch on the lowest step of the staircase, flexing my feet inside my too-tight shoes. Watch over my shoulder as the kitchen door opens and my mother appears, her mouth set in a crooked line.

'Stephanie,' she says. 'Get your sister. We're going.'

◆　◆　◆

I walk closer, to hear what they're saying. 'He's agreed?' my mother says.

'In theory,' Jane replies. 'But he wants to speak to Stephanie first. Before he agrees for definite.'

'Who wants to speak to me first?'

Jane springs away from my mother and claps her hands together. 'You startled me, Stephanie!' And then, 'We need some more cocktails!' Her eyes are too bright, her cheerfulness more forced than a constipated shit. When I say thank you but no, she explains she was asking, not offering. I turn to my mother and she nods.

'Yes, Stephanie,' she says. 'I think we could all use a cocktail.'

'Who wants to speak to me first?' I say again.

'Oh.' Jane waves a hand in the air. 'That groomsman.' She doesn't look at me as she says it.

'Which groomsman?'

She exchanges a glance with my mother. 'The one who does the toasts and things.'

'Lewis?'

'Yes, him.' She takes an almost-empty cocktail glass from the table and consumes its dregs, before launching into a garbled monologue about how Lewis might ask me to dance later. How we'd make a handsome couple, alongside Mike and Sarah, and my sister and Alistair. My mother stares at the table throughout.

'Are you seriously discussing this?'

'You're right it's silly let's get cocktails,' my mother says in a single breath. She takes my arm when I open my mouth to object. 'I'll pay.'

'It's not the money—' I begin, but Jane cuts across me.

'They're free,' she says. 'The whole bar is, apparently, courtesy of Alistair. Which is a good sign. So many women don't let men pay for anything these days. Which is perverse, don't you think?'

'It depends what they're paying for.'

She lets out a shriek of laughter. 'Oh, you are funny, Stephanie. But anyway, good on your sister, I say. And I'd like a Screwdriver.'

My mother nods. 'Three Screwdrivers, please.'

'It will be fun.' Jane gives a pink-lipsticked smile. 'Us girls drinking together.'

Encouraging my mother to fall (further) off the wagon seems like a warped idea of fun, and I'm about to imply as much when my mother squeezes her hand around my arm. 'Please, love.'

I pause.

'Or I suppose I can get them myself.' She makes a motion as if to rise.

'No, no, I'll do it.' I set off for the bar and decide to ask for orange juice without any vodka. That way we can stay alcohol-free but Jane will think we're drinking, so I won't have to listen to her complaints about my lack of *joie de vivre*. I've heard them enough over the years, normally when she's throwing half a bottle of gin down her gullet. Just before she starts singing Barbra Streisand songs and Grant retreats to a different room.

After a few steps, I turn. See that my mother's head is by Jane's again, their whispering resumed. Surely they're not actually discussing dance partners? Or, worse, partners more generally? Remembering last night's conversation with my mother, a sour taste develops at the back of my mouth. I shouldn't have told her about Jennifer. Shouldn't have opened myself up, when I'm meant to be closing things down.

I arrive at the bar to find three drinks on the counter. 'I overheard what you wanted,' the barman says. 'So I took the liberty of getting it ready. Five-star service!'

'Right.' I want to point out that five-star service is not about taking liberties – that taking liberties can never be seen as a positive – but I'm hardly in a position to occupy the moral high ground right now. So instead I lean toward him and run my hand through my hair like I've seen Sarah do. 'I'm so sorry,' I say, dropping my voice to a near-whisper. 'But do you think it might be possible just to have three orange juices? My mother and aunt are a bit worse for wear. And . . . I'd be grateful . . . can you make them look like cocktails?'

He laughs. 'Of course. Your secret is safe with me.'

Three cocktail glasses are duly fetched and filled with ice and orange juice. The barman then adds a slice of orange to the rim of each, along with a sprig of mint. He winks at me. 'To make them look the part.'

'Thanks,' I say, doing my best to ignore the wink. I carry the glasses over to the table and Jane coos with delight, before diving straight in.

'Delicious,' she pronounces. 'Thank you so much, Stephanie. It's exactly what the doctor ordered.'

But I'm barely listening. Instead I'm watching the barman wipe down the counter, and thinking how wrong he is.

Because the truth is: my secrets are no longer safe with anyone.

SATURDAY, 4.15 P.M.

By the time we finally sit down to eat, everyone is ravenous. Nobody says so – we go through the usual rigmarole of greetings and hand-shakes and comments on the decor – but as soon as Aurelie and Alistair have made their grand entrance, a roomful of mouths make contact with the poppy seed rolls. Quentin Parlee-Smythe, the long-chinned man on my left whose name only just fits on his place card, eats his in two bites, before dabbing at the remaining poppy seeds on his plate with a moistened finger. On my right, my great-uncle Charles seems too hungry to spread his butter properly; just squashes a couple of pats on to the top of his roll and eats it that way, his mouth partly open as he chews.

We're back in the Darwin Hall, where the gauze-bow chairs have been reconfigured to accommodate a series of round tables. At the centre of the room is the Gold Table, where the newlyweds are seated, along with my mother and Lewis, Mike and Sarah, and Alistair's parents. From there, the tables spread out in concentric circles, with the least important guests seated the greatest distance away. The ring closest to Aurelie contains just three tables, and it seems I've been deemed worthy of a place at one of them. As has my father, although at least Aurelie's had the sense not to put us together. I'm on the Iridium Table while he's on the far side of Copper. Out of earshot if not sight; he eats his roll by splitting it open, cutting it into pieces and using his knife to raise the pieces to his mouth.

I hope he cuts his tongue.

Besides Quentin, Charles and me, the Iridium Table also hosts two of the ushers and their partners and a woman called Lisa. She has a small mouth which she uses to nibble her roll, hamster-like, scattering crumbs toward the vase at the centre of the table. The vase is enormous and silvery-white, which I presume is a nod to iridium, given the one on my father's table is painted copper, and the one on the table to my left (Palladium) is white-grey. All precious metals.

The vase on my sister's table is, obviously, gold. The most coveted metal, the metal of winning, the metal that matches her name. I had briefly wondered if she might theme the tables by famous Victorians, as per the rest of the hotel, but should have guessed the theme would actually revolve around her. When we were children, she told me repeatedly that Aurelie means 'golden' in French, while Stephanie is merely Greek for 'crown'. And when I argued that made me royal, and therefore better, she said crowns are worthless unless smothered in gold.

Quentin pours me a glass of white wine before I can stop him. 'It's prawns for the first course,' he says, as if that explains it. I nod, don't tell him I'm done with drinking for the day.

'You're Aurelie's sister?' he asks me.

'Yes.'

'I can see the family resemblance. And are you a lawyer too?'

'Definitely not.'

He laughs, his chin wobbling, and holds his hands up. 'Confession time!' he says. 'I *am* a lawyer.'

'Right.'

'Thought it best to get that out in the open straight away! If you don't like lawyers!'

'Mmm.' His pattern of speech – the repeated exclamations – reminds me of Sarah. Perhaps I should introduce them in the hope they might like each other! Get married! Have children! Except the idea of Sarah reproducing is horrifying. I had wondered, before this weekend, if it were possible she might have improved with age. If the years might have made her reflective, ashamed of the way she treated us at school. Remorseful about what happened to Jennifer.

But she's barely changed at all. She is currently leaning toward Mike, one elbow on the table in such a way that she's pressing her breasts together. She looks a little nervous, but also excited; her eyes sparkling as she uses her non-breast arm to brush her hair away from her shoulder.

'Although I actually studied sociology at university,' Quentin goes on. 'Not law!'

Sociology: the science of human relations. A topic which eludes my understanding both in a general sense and when it comes to my mother in particular. Because I've asked her about Mike and Sarah three times in the last hour, and she's shut me down abruptly on each occasion. First, in the bar (while Jane was in the toilet), when she shushed me like a naughty child, saying it wasn't the time or the place for such a conversation. Second, by the Gladstone Steps, when she left me to join a conversation about Brentwood Town FC (despite the fact she never watches football). And third, after I cornered her by the goat's cheese and honey crostinis, when she resorted to coughing until second cousin Ann came to her aid with a glass of water. So I'm pretty certain something (besides semen) passed between Mike and Sarah on the night of the housewarming six months ago. Something which prompted Sarah's whispers to my sister the following day, at the dress fitting, which in turn prompted my mother's panicked letter to me.

But I don't know what, nor why my mother is being so evasive about it.

'What did you learn in your sociology degree?' I ask Quentin.

'All sorts!' He gives a big, self-satisfied smile and reaches for his wine. 'The usual stuff: theory and research methods. But I also did some modules on cyberculture and cybercrime. And on the sociology of intoxication!'

'Intoxication?'

'Yes.' He tells me how intoxication is not just a physiological phenomenon but has a significant social dimension. How there are many cultural norms tied up with drinking and taking drugs. How these norms have a key role in building interpersonal bonds.

But can also break them.

◆ ◆ ◆

May 2005

My mother turns to wine as soon as she hears the ding of the text message, before she's even looked at her phone. 'I know what it's going to say,' she says, taking hold of a corkscrew and jamming it into the nearest bottle. 'He's doing it again. He's bloody well doing it again!'

I say nothing. Just wait until my mother is absorbed in extracting the cork to walk to the sideboard and peer down at her phone. See the message from my father: Working late – sorry.

'It just says he's working late.'

'Working late.' My mother lets go of the bottle to make air quotes. 'Working late! He's worked late five times already this month.'

'Maybe he's just got a lot on.'

'Oh, don't be so naive, Stephanie. Men never have a lot on.' She pours the wine into a Bristol Cathedral mug and begins to drink.

'Do you want a wine glass?'

'No!' She surfaces from her mug and refills it. 'That will just make me think of him, sitting with some fancy woman in some fancy restaurant . . .' She begins to drink again.

'You've got no evidence he's—'

'Of course I have. He's done it before, with Lucille. He becomes all distant, barely talks to me, says he has to work all the time . . . he has a pattern.'

'A sample size of one is hardly a pattern.'

'Oh, don't get all statistical on me. I know your father. I know the look he gets in his eyes when he sees a woman he likes, and I know how he looks at me after it's happened.'

'But—'

'He looks at me like a piece of furniture. Like I'm no better than our battered old sofa . . .' Spit flies from her mouth as she speaks. 'Which, by the way, we might be able to replace if he didn't spend all our money on his whores.' She takes another draught, spit included. 'He looks at me as if I'm cheap, just like Jane used to.'

She continues to drink and rant, rant and drink, and I know better than to try to stop her. Instead, I gather rubber gloves, a bowl and flannel, ready for the inevitable aftermath. I spring into action as soon as it begins: tying back my mother's hair, wiping her mouth between retches, periodically rinsing the gloves. And then, when the contents of her stomach are spent, I remove her vomit-splattered clothes, haul her into bed. I turn to go but she grabs my still-gloved hand. 'Don't leave me, my angel,' she says, her voice slurred. 'Everyone always leaves me, and I couldn't bear it if you did too.'

And so I stay on the edge of the bed, staring at the plastic bowl I've placed on the floor in case she's sick again. Staring at its wide base and shallow sides, at its lip which curls toward the carpet.

I stay in that exact position for over an hour, until my mother's breath finally becomes even. At which point I peel off my gloves and head to the window in the front room. I watch as a motorbike roars past and a couple amble hand in hand beneath the diffuse orange glow of a street lamp. As a cat slinks between parked cars like a comma between clauses. Movement, movement everywhere while I. Stand. Still.

It reminds me of that trick where a cloth is pulled from a table without disturbing the plate on top. Which is all very well when the plate is pristine, but pointless when it's already cracked.

I open the kitchen cupboard and take out boxes of cereal, bags of pasta, tins of soup, to reach the stash of wine at the back. All bottles of red with foreign names. I choose one with a picture of an eagle on its label.

Then I pick up the phone and dial Jennifer's number.

Ten minutes later, the two of us are in the communal gardens, hidden from the street by the metal railings and overgrown shrubs. We drink the warm, vinegary wine straight from the bottle, talking between gulps. Talking with more feeling and less sense as it takes effect. I've read all about the impact of alcohol: how it impedes the communication channels within the brain; makes the neurons sluggish. But I hadn't expected it to feel so good. Hadn't realised I wouldn't be anxious about the neural impact once it was underway.

When the bottle is empty, we lie down on the grass and look at the sky. The clouds are grey and frayed, their edges lit white by the moon.

Jennifer sighs happily. 'I could lie here forever.'

'Me too,' I say. 'I've been in this garden loads of times, but it's so much better with you.'

'And with wine.'

'Because it blocks out the weeds and dog shit?'

She laughs.

'How long have you got?' I ask. 'Before your mum gets back?'

She wafts her hand through the air. 'She'll be out most of the night. Yours?'

'She's at home, but she won't notice I'm out. She's drunk herself into oblivion again.'

There's a pause. 'I'm sorry.'

'Yeah, well.' I place my fingers in a sideways V around the moon, as if to snip it from the sky. 'She's got it into her head that Dad's cheating on her.'

'I'm sorry.' And then: 'Is he?'

'I don't know.' Now it's my turn to sigh. 'I really don't know. He has before but . . . well . . . it might just be paranoia this time. She's all over the place. Massive mood swings.' I trail a hand through the grass, hoping there's no dog shit nearby. 'I don't know what to do.'

'How about Aurelie?'

'What about her?'

'Can't she help?'

'No.'

I think of my mother the morning after the last time, her voice a murmur in the half-light. I'm so sorry, my angel. You shouldn't have to see me like that. Shouldn't have to deal with my . . . mess. *And then her little laugh, and the words that cut the deepest.* But maybe it's not so terrible that you did. Because you and I are similar, and perhaps it's best you understand. What it's like when you're capable of love, but not of keeping people close. Which is why we must always stick together.

Jennifer looks confused. 'No?'

'No.' I try to refocus. 'She's gone to a party tonight. And also . . . I don't know . . . it's different with her.'

'How so?'

I shrug, unable to explain what I mean. But my mother's relationship with Aurelie is different: the two of them argue all the time and yet don't seem troubled by this, seem almost energised, in fact. Whereas I spend most of my time trying to act as a shock absorber for my mother's volatile moods, and the result is a sense not of energy, but of being worn slowly down into oblivion.

'It must be strange, having a sibling.' Jennifer props herself up on one elbow. 'When I was younger, I always wanted an older sister. Somebody who could lend me her clothes and braid my hair.'

'I wouldn't want Aurelie's clothes. Or for her to braid my hair.'

'No. But the two of you have never got on, have you?'

Flashes of memory: of me and Aurelie sitting in a swing together, laughing. Spreading a dressing gown on the floor and seating our teddies around it; pouring 'tea' into small plastic cups. Climbing trees, wading through a river, upending rocks to look for woodlice. Of my sister's hand taking mine, leading me into the bathroom. Telling me not to be afraid.

And then other memories: Aurelie at Waldenborough High, watching as my lunch tray was knocked to the ground, saying nothing as the hall erupted into cheers. Of her smiling as Sarah hummed the theme tune from Jaws. *Looking away when a boy stuck his foot out in the corridor, sending me sprawling across the floor.*

Our mother's words again. You're capable of love, but not of keeping people close.

I shut them from my mind. 'No,' I say to Jennifer. 'No, we haven't.'

'It's strange how some forms of dependency are socially sanctioned,' Quentin is saying, between swigs of wine. 'While others are frowned upon by society. And it's even stranger how the distinction between the two can change fairly rapidly over time.'

'Mmm,' I say. 'Like with cannabis.'

'Exactly.' He sounds pleased. 'Cannabis is particularly interesting, because the British population is overwhelmingly in favour of it being legalised for medical purposes, but more divided on whether it should be legalised for recreational purposes! And yet where do you draw the line between the two? If somebody with chronic back pain takes cannabis in a social setting, is that medical or recreational?'

'I suppose it depends whether the product is regulated.'

'Indeed! The medicinal products contain tiny quantities of tetrahydrocannabinol, whereas the street products tend to contain far more.' He looks at me. 'Tetrahydrocannabinol is the active substance in cannabis—'

'I know.'

'—the bit that gives you the high, but can also make you feel sick.'

'Yes.'

'It can speed your heart up too, cause arrhythmia! That's when you get an irregular—'

'Heartbeat; yes, I know.'

He leans forward in his chair. 'Are you a medic?'

'No.' I straighten the cutlery at my place setting. 'But I'm familiar with some of the possible effects of too much cannabis. Nausea, arrhythmia, paranoia. Made more likely when the cannabis is taken in edible form, as it's harder to monitor the quantity of THC being ingested.'

He chuckles, shakes his head a little. 'I'd never have guessed you were the type of person to get high.'

'Really?' I say, angling my spoon away from him. 'That's funny.'

Because I'd definitely have guessed he was the type of person to jump to the wrong conclusion.

◆　◆　◆

May 2005

Jennifer and I are still in the garden when we hear footsteps, followed closely by Aurelie's voice, high-pitched and panicked. 'Help, help! I'm dying!'

My body rises of its own accord and runs into the street, where I see my sister stumbling toward our house, bent over and gasping. Sarah is behind her, reaching out with one arm as if to provide comfort, but touching only air.

'I'm dying!' Aurelie shrieks again. She presses a hand to her chest. 'My heart's gone crazy; I think it's going to explode!'

My head is suddenly, miraculously, clear. 'You need to take deep breaths,' I say, wrapping an arm around her shoulders. 'In from your abdomen, and then out. Slowly, slowly.'

'I can't! I can't breathe!'

'You can. You're breathing now. You wouldn't be able to speak if you couldn't breathe.'

'You're lying!' Aurelie turns to Sarah. 'She's lying!'

'She's not lying.' Sarah's face is pale, her eyes wide.

'She is lying, and so are you! I know I'm dying. Or maybe I'm already dead.'

'Stop that!' Sarah's voice is shaking. 'Of course you're not dead!'

'What's happened?' I ask.

'She's killed me, that's what's happened!' Aurelie slumps down on to the front steps and curls into a ball.

Sarah looks close to tears. 'It was only a hash brownie. Doug made them for a laugh. It was just a brownie.'

'It was a poisoned brownie!' Aurelie begins to rock back and forth. 'I'm dead, I'm dead, I'm dead.'

'You're not dead.' I sit down beside her and take her hand in mine. 'You're very much alive. Here, can you feel my fingers?' I run the pad of my thumb around Aurelie's palm.

'Yes.'

'Good. Then just concentrate on that sensation. On my fingers against yours.'

Sarah taps my arm. 'You should take her inside.'

'No.' The idea of being left alone with my mother and sister – one comatose with alcohol and the other in the grip of a drug-related panic – is unthinkable. Aurelie is moaning now, moaning and rocking.

'We can't just leave her on the street!'

'I'm not suggesting we do.'

'Then what are you suggesting?'

'I'm not sure yet.' I continue to stroke my sister's hand while I consider the options. Our mother can't help. Aunt Jane believes anyone who takes drugs should be locked up. And our father . . . no. Not him. 'I guess we should take her to hospital.'

'That's a bit over the top, isn't it?'

I look at my sister's coiled, rocking body, and then at Sarah, whose face is full of fear. And I wonder if she's scared for my sister, or worried she'll be held responsible for the state my sister is in. 'Is it?' I say.

'She just needs some sleep,' Sarah insists.

'Then take her to your house.'

'But we're right by yours!'

I stand up, put one hand upon our front door. 'I'm going to call an ambulance.'

'You can't call an ambulance because someone's had a bit of cannabis!' Sarah runs up the steps, positions herself between me and the door.

'Move out of the bloody way!' I tug at Sarah's shoulders, but weakly, ineffectually, because Aurelie is still on the steps below us.

'No!'

'I need to help my sister!'

'She's fine!'

'I'm dying!'

'Stop it!' Jennifer's voice cuts cleanly through the night air. 'I know who can help us.'

I release my hands from Sarah, my breath still rough in my throat, and turn to Jennifer. 'Who?'

'My mum.' But she is biting her lip as she says it, like she's already regretting her suggestion.

◆ ◆ ◆

The starter is too small – only three prawns per plate – but Great-Uncle Charles seems to enjoy it. He spears the prawns with his fork and holds them up to the light; surveys their pink, veined bellies before bringing them to his mouth and chewing. 'I haven't eaten prawns for years,' he says. 'Not since the eighties.'

This kickstarts a conversation about 1980s food, which everyone round the table has a view on, even though most of us weren't alive during the decade itself. I look across to the Gold Table, where Lewis is refilling my mother's wine glass and she is flexing her elbows, making him laugh. They drink and my mother brings her glass down on to her plate, dissolves into giggles as wine slops over her prawns and the tablecloth. Laughs even harder as she tries to gather the spilled wine with a spoon, before holding out her glass for a refill.

I don't understand what she's doing. I mean, I understand she's nervous, but she must know drinking is a terrible idea.

Great-Uncle Charles grabs my arm. 'To new beginnings!' he says. 'That was the toast my father always gave.' He lifts his glass and I feel obliged to lift mine too, to touch it to his.

'To new beginnings,' I say. But it doesn't feel right.

We should be toasting an ending. Or, at least: the beginnings of one.

◆ ◆ ◆

Another opportunity to talk to my mother finally presents itself after the main course, when she gets up from her seat. I watch as she crosses the room, using the backs of the chairs to steady herself. She chats to some of the people she passes, wipes her forehead with a lilac napkin. Her progress is slow, but when I am satisfied she is making her way to the exit, and not simply catching up with old acquaintances, I run to join her.

'Hi Mum.'

'Stephanie.' She tries to walk faster, but stumbles, and I reach out to catch her. She flings my arm away. 'I'm fine! Just going to the toilet.' Her words are slurred.

'Right.'

'You should go and have fun. I don't need an escort.'

'I know you don't, but I'm escorting you anyway.'

She looks at me and shakes her head, before hobbling forward again. This time, when I reach out to take her arm, she doesn't resist. I can feel her bones beneath her skin: the hard length of her humerus, the protrusion of her ulna. She stops to cough, and her shoulders rock with the force of it. I look down at her bowed head, at the flowers leaning sideways in her wig. Each cough dislodging them further. 'You've been avoiding me,' I say.

'No.' She coughs again.

'Yes, you have.'

We walk in silence past the board with the table plan and out through the double doors into the corridor. She touches her fingers to the wall. 'I don't remember this wallpaper,' she says. 'So many stripes! Was it like this earlier?'

'Yes. Funnily enough, they haven't changed the wallpaper while we've been eating dinner.'

'No, I don't suppose they have. But was it always this *bright*?'

Jesus, she must be more drunk than I thought. 'Did you know that Sarah slept with Mike?' I stop and turn to face her.

She turns too, gives an exaggerated raise of her eyebrows. 'Of course I knew. How could I not, when I was next door; when I had to listen to her caterwauling—'

'No, not at Aurelie's twenty-fifth; on the night of her and Alistair's housewarming. The night before the dress fitting.'

'What?' She looks back at the wall. 'Possibly. But I'm not interested in Sarah's sex life.'

'Of course not. But did Sarah mention it at the dress fitting?'

She moves away from me, runs a finger along the wallpaper.

'Mum?'

'What?'

'Did Sarah mention it at the dress fitting? That she'd slept with Mike?'

She keeps her back to me, gives a little shrug. 'Yes, I think she might have done. You know what she's like, always boasting and gossiping.'

I am seized by a desire to grip my mother's bony shoulders. To shake, shake, shake until the truth finally drops out. Although, in her current state, vomit is more likely.

'And?'

'And what?'

'Does it have anything to do with Peter's disappearance? With Sarah saying she knows something about it?'

She sighs. 'Why would Sarah's sex life have anything to do with that poor boy's disappearance?'

'Because Mike might have told her something.' I walk round in front of her so she can't avoid me.

'I'm sorry, Stephanie, but I don't know what you want me to say.' She pushes past me and continues along the corridor with unsteady steps.

'I want you to tell me the truth!'

'I have.'

'Not all of it.' I run to catch up with her. 'Look, you said in your letter that you overheard Sarah at the dress fitting, telling Aurelie she knew something about Peter's disappearance.'

'Yes.'

'Well, if that's true, don't you think Mike might have something to do with it? Given the timing, given the two of them slept together the night before?'

'But I thought you thought Sarah was making the whole thing up?' She turns her head to the side as she says this, refusing to meet my gaze.

'I did – I do – but I also think it might have something to do with Mike.'

'Both of those things can't be true.'

'I'm not so sure.' I run in front of her again, try to catch her line of sight. 'What if Mike said something about Peter – that he saw him the night he disappeared, or saw . . . something else – and Sarah turned it into a big deal, into a point of intrigue, to make herself feel important?'

'You're just speculating—'

'Or what if Alistair said something to Mike, who said something to Sarah, who then twisted it—'

'Well, now you're definitely speculating—'

'But it's possible, right?' I think again of the note in my sister's room. *Don't marry a man with blood on his hands.* 'We shouldn't rule it out. If we want to make sure our family is protected?'

My mother shrugs, her eyes upon the carpet. 'I don't see the point in all this. We'll talk to Sarah tonight.'

'Or we could try to find out before tonight?'

'What?' My mother looks up from the carpet in a jerky, awkward motion. 'What do you mean?'

'I could talk to Alistair, or Mike—'

'No!' She presses one hand to the wall. 'That's a terrible idea!'

'Why?'

'Because it's ridiculous. We mustn't make a scene or do anything dramatic—'

'Says the woman who's planning to lure the maid of honour to the lake—'

'Shh!' My mother says this theatrically, one finger pressed to her mouth.

'So, what? Now you want my silence too?'

'No.' She glances up and down the corridor. 'Look – you're a practical person, Stephanie, and you know as well as I do we weren't entirely truthful with the police about our comings and goings that night. So the only way to keep our family *protected*, as you put it, is to ensure the case doesn't get reopened. So we need to keep Sarah quiet, regardless of what got her talking about it in the first place.'

'Or who,' I say.

'Or who,' my mother agrees. 'So, can I rely on you to be discreet?'

I look at her glazed eyes, which can't quite seem to focus, and frustration pulses through me. 'If you're so concerned about discretion, why are you drinking?' I ask.

'If I were a better person, I wouldn't. But I'm not a better person. I'm not even a good person.'

'Mum—'

'I'm not, Stephanie; I'm really not.'

We've reached the door to the toilets. I open it and help her through. The room inside smells of orange blossom – citrus and sweet.

She extricates herself from my grip and leans against the sinks. 'My mascara's smudged.' She takes a tiny towel from a stack on the side and dabs it ineffectually at her eyes. I notice some china cups nearby and fill one with water, but when I offer it to her, she knocks it away, sloshing water down my front. 'I'm not drinking from that.'

'Suit yourself.' I empty the cup and return it to its former position. Dry my tunic with another of the tiny towels. 'I just thought it might help. Sober you up a little.'

'It won't help anything if I contract cholera.'

'I don't think you can contract cholera from—'

'You think you know everything, Stephanie, but you don't.'

I look in the mirror at her reflected face, at the black flecks of mascara under her eyes, and the seams of lipstick in the skin above her upper lip. 'Then tell me,' I say. 'What don't I know?'

'You don't know how spineless I am. How bad I've been at sticking up for myself.' She leans closer to the mirror. 'And the repercussions that can have.'

'What are you talking about?' I hate that drinking makes her like this: all morose and spiky. Full of self-pity and loathing in equal measure.

She presses one palm to the glass. 'It was my fault he left.'

'But he had an affair!'

'No.' She swings round toward me. 'The only reason we're going through all this is because I let him go.'

I shake my head. 'I disagree.'

'I don't care if you agree or not. The fact is, it's my fault we were by the loch that night, when that poor boy disappeared. And it's my fault that I went out, that I didn't stay in the tent.'

I have to admit there's some truth in this. Our mother abandoned Aurelie and me at the campsite to find a pub and drink away her sorrows. And once she had gone, there was nothing to stop

Aurelie from going too; from unzipping the tent and running out to meet Alistair at the boathouse.

But the events of that night weren't entirely of our mother's making. If our father hadn't left earlier that day, claiming a work emergency, she might have stayed calm, instead of screaming and throwing his clothes into the loch. She might have stayed inside the tent, instead of finishing off a box of wine and tramping off down the track to search for more.

If our father hadn't left, everything could have been so different.

SATURDAY, 5.25 P.M.

October 1999

I am sitting, cross-legged, on the landing floor when my mother hurries up the stairs, already buttoning her coat. 'What are you doing here?' she says. 'You're supposed to be brushing your teeth!'

'I don't like the bathroom.'

'I don't care if you don't like the bathroom. Go and brush your teeth!'

'But it's scary.' If I do as my mother says, I won't be able to avoid the mirror above the sink.

'Things will be a lot scarier if you don't brush them.'

I'm not sure if this is a reference to my teeth rotting, or being told off. I don't know which is worse. But I do know either is better than having to see myself in the mirror, teeth bared and mouth frothing.

'Stephanie! Now!'

'I can't!'

'Of course you can!' My mother tugs at her bag strap. 'If I can keep everything going single-handed – if I can deal with all the laundry and shopping and cooking and cleaning and looking after you and your sister while your father swans around with that harlot of his – I think you can manage to put some toothpaste on a brush. You're nine years old, for crying out loud! Not a baby. Go! Now!'

'I can't!'

She starts to shout, then: words of anger which stumble in her haste to expel them. I lean toward the carpet, place my head between my legs. There's a sound of cracking, of hard surfaces colliding, but I don't look up. There are other noises too: more screaming and the thud of feet.

And then a light touch at the back of my neck. A whisper by my ear. 'Stephanie. It's okay.'

I look up a little, see my sister's shoes beside me. Black with silver threads in their laces.

'It's okay,' she says again. 'Mummy's gone downstairs, and I'll help you. Here.' She holds out her hand and I let its softness encase mine. Let it lead me into the bathroom. I keep my head down, see a broken eyeshadow palette on the floor, blue powder scattered across the pedestal of the sink.

'What are you scared of?' my sister asks.

'The mirror.'

'Why?'

I can only shrug.

'You don't need to be scared of the mirror. The mirror just reflects you. Go on, look up.'

I shake my head.

'I've got an idea. If you make a silly face at the mirror, then all you'll see is something silly, and you won't be scared anymore.'

'I can't.'

'You can. I'll do it too. Look at me.'

I turn to see Aurelie hooking her index fingers between her upper and lower lips, to stretch her mouth sideways. Then she sticks out her tongue and widens her eyes, nostrils flaring.

I must smile because she lets her face loosen and smiles too. 'Now it's your turn. Make the silliest face you can.'

I pull my ears and scrunch my mouth toward my nose.

'Great! Now keep doing that while you look in the mirror. On the count of three: one, two . . .'

I jerk my head up, forcing myself to confront my contorted face, and my sister's beside it. Aurelie dances and waves her arms around, before pretending to comb her hair with a tube of toothpaste.

And, despite everything, I start to laugh.

◆ ◆ ◆

I'm looking in a bathroom mirror again now, as my mother returns from the toilet. I watch her reflection as she runs the hot water, extracts soap from the dispenser and rubs her hands together, but her coordination is off; she has to jab the dispenser a couple of times before any soap is released. After drying her hands, she misses the bin with her hand towel. Then she drops her keycard on the floor while trying to locate her mascara. I reach down, pick up both card and towel, and discard the latter in the bin (which is not actually a bin, but a large wicker basket under the sink).

'Thank you.' She stabs at her eyes with the mascara wand, before depositing it back in her bag. There is a click as she closes the clasp. 'Now,' she says. 'We should get back to the Darwin Hall quickly if we don't want to miss the speeches.'

I would very much like to miss the speeches, but decide it's best not to admit this. I hold the door open instead, watch as she shuffles into the corridor, support her weight as we walk back toward the hall, her feet dragging across the carpet. They are grossly swollen, bulging from her shoes like sausage meat escaping its skin.

She grips my arm. 'Let's not go this way.'

'What? But it's just—'

'Quickly!' she hisses. 'Turn around.'

I am about to protest again when I notice Sarah coming toward us in lilac stilettos, eyes fixed on her phone.

'Come on!'

'There's no point,' I say. 'She's much faster than us. Even in those shoes.'

My mother tries to squirm away from me. 'I don't want to talk to her. I *can't* talk to her.'

'You've managed it up to now.'

'Well, I'm drunk now. And I can't be around her anymore. All through dinner, I've had to watch her fawning over Mike like some salivating teenager, or making plans with Aurelie for the two of them to go to Ibiza. After what she did, it's like rubbing salt in a wound.'

I don't care if Sarah's fawning over Mike or making plans with Aurelie, but I understand how my mother feels about her in a more general sense. Just watching her now – the way she's waltzing along the corridor, not looking where she's going, expecting everyone else to move for her – brings bile to my throat.

'I met a woman in the chemo surgery whose daughter went to Ibiza.' My mother is in full drunken flow, her eyes darting about as she speaks. 'The place is riddled with drugs, by all accounts; everyone takes them. And I don't want your sister having another incident.'

It's all very well, her saying that, but the truth is, when my sister had her 'incident', as she puts it, she wasn't the one who had to deal with it. She was lying comatose, in bed, and it fell to me and Jennifer to pick up the pieces.

◆ ◆ ◆

May 2005

The car pulls up outside our house, and there's a bad atmosphere from the off. Jennifer called her mother from our landline, and there's a stiffness to her now as Lan emerges from the driver's seat. 'Aurelie's just over there,' Jennifer says, unnecessarily, pointing at the coiled form of my sister upon the front steps.

Lan walks over to Aurelie, crouches in front of her. 'How are you feeling?' she asks.

My sister just whimpers.

'I'm going to check a few things, Aurelie, all right?' She speaks slowly and simply, as if talking to a four-year-old.

'I'm dead,' my sister moans.

Lan feels her pulse, while glancing round at the rest of us. Jennifer looks down at the pavement. 'What's she taken?'

'Only a small hash brownie.' Sarah's voice is shaky.

'Anything else?'

'I don't think so. Well, a few drinks—'

'Alcoholic?'

'Yes, just some beers, and maybe some cider. But I don't understand!' Sarah sounds petulant now. 'She didn't even have that much brownie; I had more than her and I feel fine!'

Lan ignores this, looks up at me instead. 'Is your mother around?'

I think of the body inside, slumped on a bed with a sick bowl beside it, and shake my head. 'Is she going to be okay?' I ask.

'She'll be fine,' Lan says. 'But we should get her to a hospital. Just to be on the safe side.'

I can feel my arms starting to tremble, even though the night air is warm. 'Should I call an ambulance?' I ask.

And that's when Jennifer and her mother start to talk in Mandarin: rapid, breathless streams of words I can't decipher. Lan seems angry – she raises and lowers one hand repeatedly in a chopping motion – while Jennifer appears plaintive, hands squeezed together as she talks. 'Should I call an ambulance?' I ask again.

The two of them look at me. Before looking at each other, and back to me again. 'No,' Lan says eventually. 'No, you don't need to call an ambulance. You can come in my taxi.'

Her car has an unpleasant smell: sweet and chemical, like artificial cherries. Jennifer helps me bundle my sister into the back seat, where she sits between the two of us, hunched over with her head between her knees. I somehow manage to fasten a seat belt across her. Sarah sits in the front, next to Lan, glancing around with a pale, pinched face as we drive away.

'Is this hell?' Aurelie asks.

'No,' I say. 'It's a car.'

'I don't want to be in hell.'

'You're not in hell; you're not even dead.' I squeeze my sister's hand. 'You're going to be absolutely fine.'

'You promise?'

'It was just a brownie, for God's sake!' says Sarah.

We're silent for a while after that, gliding through the night-time city. I notice that the car is immaculately clean, with smooth, wipe-down seats and tinted windows. And then I notice the air freshener, dangling from the rear-view mirror, and the phone attached to the dashboard. 'Is this actually a taxi?' I ask.

'Yes, it is.' Lan's voice is tight.

'Oh.' I'm about to ask more questions when I feel a hand gently touch mine. Jennifer's. I look across at her but she gives a tiny, almost imperceptible shake of her head.

'Oh gosh, hi!' Sarah is so busy looking at her phone that she almost trips over us. 'Eve! Stephanie!' She sounds delighted, like she's stumbled across long-lost friends, the earlier argument in my sister's room clearly forgotten.

'Hello,' I say. My mother just nods in Sarah's direction.

'What an incredible night! Don't you think?'

It occurs to me to ask whether her night with Mike six months ago was incredible too, whether he told her any incredible things. But my mother's hand is clamped tightly round my arm. 'Yes,' I manage.

'Such lovely food, and wine. And company!'

'Yes,' I say again. 'I enjoyed . . . the chicken.'

'Oh gosh, yes – the chicken was amazing! So tender. And the vegetables were delicious. Even if all those heritage potatoes mean I'll have to spend longer at the gym tomorrow.'

'Tomorrow?' I say. 'A lot can happen before tomorrow.'

My mother squeezes my arm. *Stop talking.*

But any tension between the two of us goes unnoticed by Sarah, who tells us how excited she is about the rest of the evening. About the speeches, the cake cutting and the first dance. About the cheese and whisky that will be served later. 'It's a nice touch, don't you think? Providing refreshments for the evening guests. So they don't feel they've missed out. I know Aurelie feels a bit bad about having evening guests at all – doesn't want them to feel like second-class citizens or anything! – but she and Alistair have so many friends that it just wouldn't have been practical to have had everybody in one room for the ceremony and dinner and everything.'

'Mmm.'

'I expect you must be excited too,' she says to me. 'About seeing your younger siblings again.'

I stare at her. 'Half-siblings,' I say.

'Oh. Yes. That's what I meant.'

'Right.' I refuse to give her a reaction. 'And no, I'm not excited.'

Sarah raises her eyebrows as we leave, but I don't give a damn. I don't want to think about Lucille and the twins right now. Not in the company of my sick mother, with her wig and emaciated body. With her distended feet and difficulty walking. With her way of still seeing me, when everyone else has forgotten I exist.

After she dies, I wonder if anyone will ever see me again. Or if, to all intents and purposes, I will simply disappear.

Just like Jennifer did, all those years ago.

◆　◆　◆

May 2005

Lan drops us off outside the hospital, says she can't park or come in. So Jennifer and I take my sister between us and half walk, half drag her to the entrance.

The light inside is painfully, glaringly white, and there are several disoriented-looking people stumbling around or draped, zombie-like, on hard plastic chairs. An official examines Aurelie and asks a few questions, before telling us to find some seats.

Sarah disappears off to the toilets and I buy a couple of cans from the vending machine, handing one to my sister, who clutches it without drinking. I give the other to Jennifer, who thanks me and opens it immediately. 'What was all that about?' I ask.

'They were triaging us—'

'No, not that. All that stuff with your mother. Was she angry with you?'

Silence, and then a nod. 'Yes.'

'Why?'

She takes a large gulp from her can, swallows slowly. 'Because I wanted her to drive your sister to hospital, and she didn't.'

'Because she was working?'

'Yes, but not just that.'

I wait for a couple of seconds, but Jennifer is staring at the drink in her hands. 'What, then?' I ask gently.

'Look – she works as a taxi driver, okay?' Jennifer turns to me with something like panic in her eyes.

'That's nothing to be ashamed of,' I say. 'We need taxi drivers.'

'I'm not ashamed.' A faint flush comes into her cheeks. 'The problem is she's not supposed to be working at all. She's working illegally as a taxi driver.'

'Oh.'

'Yes, oh. My mum said I shouldn't have rung her. She said Aurelie is an ignorant, privileged girl, and I've put our livelihood at risk by helping her.'

'I'm sorry.' I try to take her hand but she shakes me away. 'You don't need to worry, though,' I say, my voice pleading. 'We won't tell anyone.' I look at my sister, who is still hunched on her seat, unopened can in hand. I don't think she's registered our conversation at all.

But then I notice Sarah just behind her, returning from the toilets. And she's smiling like she's heard every word.

We approach the Darwin Hall without speaking, listening to Sarah's footfall on the carpet behind us. Then there's the creak of the toilet door as she goes inside. My mother begins to cough, and we stop as she takes a lilac napkin from her handbag and brings it to her mouth. After a few splutters her chest settles, but she keeps the napkin balled in one fist, held up against her throat. The gesture reminds me of Jane, talking to me at the foot of the Gladstone Steps earlier. *Your mother wasn't always honest with your father, you know.*

'Mum,' I begin.

She sighs, but it's more wheeze than exhalation. 'Please don't tell me you're having any more doubts about the plan. Just trust me that it's the right thing to do, to keep our family safe. That—'

'It's not about the plan,' I say. 'It's about Aunt Jane.'

'What? Why in God's name do you want to talk about her?'

'Because . . . it's just . . . she said something strange.'

'Everything Jane says is strange.' My mother puts the balled-up napkin back into her bag. 'It would be more newsworthy if she said something ordinary.'

'But it involved you and Dad.' I know I'm treading on dangerous ground here, so I speak gently, cautiously. 'She said you've kept a secret from him for many years. Something big.'

Her mouth constricts and puckers, as if a drawstring has been pulled through her lips. 'What?'

'I asked her what she was talking about but—'

'But?'

'—she said it was up to you to tell me. That it goes back a long way.'

My mother shakes her head a little, turns to the side. 'She always has to interfere, doesn't she? Stick her oar in where it's not wanted.' She walks off.

'Mum?'

She keeps walking, her gait stiff and uneven.

'Mum!'

Now she's pushing ineffectually at the double doors to the hall.

'Mum!' I run up beside her. 'Tell me.'

'Oh, Stephanie.' She pushes at the doors again, and I notice there are tears in her eyes. 'I was planning to, but in my own time. It's difficult.'

I study her face: the creasing of her forehead, her damp eyes and sunken cheeks. But she won't look at me, just keeps on pushing at the door. Finally she succeeds in opening it, and we're hit by the noise of talking and laughter on the other side.

'Please,' I say, more loudly. 'Please tell me.'

She takes a couple more steps, apparently unmoved by my request. But then she stops. 'It's about that night in Scotland again.' She mutters this at the parquet floor and I have to lean closer to hear her. 'The one when he disappeared; that poor boy—'

'Peter—'

'Yes, the night he disappeared. I . . .' She trails off.

My heart begins to hammer. 'What?'

'I . . .' She hesitates. 'I wasn't alone. I was with someone. At the pub.'

'What? Who?'

She pauses, looks at me and then away again. 'A man.'

I stare at her. I'm not sure what I was expecting, but it certainly wasn't this. Not after the vitriol she spewed at my father, her repeated condemnation of his affairs and the damage they caused. The way she hounded Aurelie, in her teens, for displaying any sort of interest in the opposite sex.

'You . . .' I begin. 'But . . . who was it?' I don't recall her ever bringing a man back to our house, or even talking about any adult male other than my father. And in the years since I left home, there's never been so much as a passing mention of a date, let alone a long-term partner.

She shakes her head more vigorously.

I've branded her many things over the years. Controlling. Out-of-control. Caring. Suffocating. But not unfaithful. Never unfaithful.

'It's not like you think,' she says, looking toward a raised platform at one side of the hall, where Lewis is adjusting a microphone.

'Then what is it like?'

But I never get to hear what it's like – or even what it isn't – because, at that precise moment, Lewis cuts across us. 'Ladies and gentlemen,' he says, in a voice that has little need for amplification. 'Please be seated. The speeches are about to begin.'

SATURDAY, 5.45 P.M.

My father is up first; Lewis introduces him to a burst of applause and he makes his way to the platform slowly, shoulders back, smiling and waving as if he's at a political rally.

'Good evening,' he says into the microphone. 'And what an evening it is!'

There is some clapping and a bit of cheering. But it's like it's happening somewhere else, muted by a mental image of my mother's body under the weight of a man. An anonymous man, his face indistinct but his torso heavy and sprawling.

'I'm Dominic,' my father says. 'Dad to Aurelie. Who I'm sure you'll all agree is the most beautiful, brilliant bride imaginable!'

There is more clapping and cheering, and he smiles, nodding. I look at my mother, who is sitting with her hands in her lap, watching him through narrowed eyes. To think how I've despised him for his lying and cheating, for picking away at the scab of her sanity, when, all along, she may have been lying and cheating too.

'It's my job to welcome you here today, on this most happy and memorable occasion. Thanks to everyone for coming, for giving up your time to celebrate the marriage of Alistair and Aurelie. And a particular shout-out to those of you who have travelled a long distance, especially Jasmine, who has come all the way from Fiji!'

There are loud whoops from a group of young women on the Rhodium Table.

'I would also like to give a special mention to Aurelie's Great-Uncle Charles – who, at ninety-two, is the oldest person here.'

On my table, everyone claps in Charles's direction. He dismisses us with a wave of his napkin.

My father clears his throat. 'I am absolutely delighted to be welcoming Alistair to the family today, along with his parents, Judy and Martin.' He extends a hand toward the older couple on the Gold Table. 'And all of their relatives too. I believe it to be a cause for great joy when two families are brought together as one. So long as you don't beat me on the golf course, Martin!'

There is laughter, and Martin says something I can't quite hear, about a driver. The sheer banality of it all is gut-wrenching.

'But my main job today is to say a few words about my amazing daughter, Aurelie. Not only is she, as I'm sure you'll agree, absolutely beautiful' – he pauses for the inevitable cheers – 'but she's also resourceful and ambitious and brilliant. She didn't always have the easiest childhood, but, instead of letting it get her down, it only made her more determined to succeed.'

He says this as if our childhood was only difficult because of some abstract external factors. As if he had nothing to do with it. When, actually, he had nothing to do with *us*, which is far from the same thing, and possibly its opposite.

'Aurelie was accepted into Durham University, where she got a First in Law, and was taken on by one of the top law firms in the country. A long-hours, high-pressure environment, where she has not only thrived but excelled, leading her to be named one of OBW's Top Young Lawyers in 2015. I'm so proud of what she has achieved. She approaches everything with commitment and passion, which are laudable qualities, except perhaps when applied to her singing.'

This gets a big laugh, and Aurelie smiles.

'But perhaps I'm being unfair,' our father goes on. 'As a young girl, Aurelie's singing was actually quite good . . . compared to her recorder-playing.'

More laughter. Aurelie places her head in her hands and Alistair puts an arm around her. Pulls her close.

Of course, my mother's revelation isn't merely nausea-inducing. If she was with a man on the night of Peter's disappearance, that brings another person into the mix. Another person who might have borne witness to the night's events.

'Love is both precious and unusual,' my father says. 'Normally, when something is precious, we guard it closely, share it sparingly. But with love there are no limits. Instead it is like a flame: the more we love, the brighter it burns.'

And, he might have added: the more complicated everything becomes.

◆ ◆ ◆

November 1996

I spin around on my father's chair, faster and faster, until the papers on his desk are a blur. I use the green of the pot plant on the bookshelf as a marker to count my revolutions: eight, nine, ten. After slowing to a standstill, I set off in the other direction, pulling on the edge of the desk to help build up speed. Dizzying myself once again, enjoying the way my surroundings fold in upon themselves: ceiling to desk, desk to floor. Flashes of green.

He's told me to stay here, that he won't be long. We were at home when he said he needed to swing by the office, and promised me a McDonald's if I came with him. But I would have come anyway. I like the spinning chairs, the jar of boiled sweets at reception, the silver balls on his desk which swing from side to side when the first ball is knocked into the others. I also like the lift, which is lined with mirrors so you can see the reflection of your reflection, and the reflection of that: endless versions of yourself in ever-smaller boxes.

It's a Sunday, which means the office is quiet. Deserted, in fact. A series of empty rooms and desks, like a mouth without teeth. No secretaries, but the sweets are still here; I helped myself to a couple on the way in. I ran up and down the beige carpet too, triggering the automatic strip lighting, until my father put me in his office. 'Don't go anywhere,' he said, throwing a book down in front of me. A compilation of stories: Tales for Nine-Year-Olds.

'It's too old for me, Daddy. I'm only six.'

'But you're a good reader.' He smoothed out his shirt; he's wearing his smart one today, the one with the blue checked pattern. 'Tell you what, if you stay here and read fifty pages, I'll buy you a milkshake as well as a burger. I won't be long.'

I picked up the book after he left and trawled through the words on the first page. I understood there was a woman with a house full of cats, but not much else. One of the cats was described as a tortoiseshell and I wondered if that meant it was half cat, half tortoise, or whether it was a cat with hard skin. I flicked ahead but there were no pictures to help, just row upon row of text. So I put the book down and played with the silver balls. And then, when I tired of their gentle clacking, I turned to chair-spinning. But now even that is beginning to lose its appeal. My head is tired and my tummy is making gurgling noises.

After a few more spins, I've had enough. Bored of waiting, and ready for my cheeseburger, I decide to leave the room. 'Daddy?' I say as I pass the secretaries' empty desks. 'Daddy?'

There's no sign of him out here, nor of anybody else. No sound either, beyond the low-level hum of the ceiling lights and the occasional growl of a car outside. As I creep forward, I enter a new and menacing realm: the bulbs in the desk lamps look like giant eyes, watching my

every step, and the photocopier a beast, waiting to pounce. 'Daddy?' I'm
whispering now, my voice barely carrying above my breath. 'Daddy?'

When it becomes clear he isn't coming, I start to run. Out to the
lobby where I stretch up to reach the lift button: jab, jab, jab. If I don't
move quickly enough, the monsters will get me.

But I've run the wrong way. The lift doors open to reveal my father
crushing somebody against the wall inside. He has his mouth against
her neck and his hand under her skirt and she is moaning, her skin
deathly pale. I turn, only to be confronted in the mirror with a reflec-
tion of his back: his hair dark against her pale white neck. And a
reflection of the reflection, and a reflection of that, on and on.

Infinite glimpses of a world in which I want no part.

The dark hair is no longer there, replaced by a sheen of sweat across
his bald scalp – but, in other respects, my father hasn't changed. He
is still assured of his righteousness, still in thrall to his own voice.
He waves his arms almost ecstatically as he relays how Aurelie once
had a tantrum over the colour of her bicycle. 'A word of advice,
Alistair: if you want to stay married, for God's sake leave her in
charge of interior design!'

When the audience stops laughing, he adopts a serene expression. 'But, if I could offer you one piece of serious advice, based on
my own experience, it would be this: stay true to yourselves and
one another.' I can't help but let out an involuntary snort, and have
to cover it with a cough. 'I've learned the hard way that, whatever
life flings at you, honesty is the most important thing.' He smiles
at Aurelie and she smiles back, dewy-eyed. My mother takes a pre-
mature gulp of champagne.

'So I'd like to raise a toast.' My father raises his glass and everybody stands. 'To love, and honesty.'

'To love and honesty,' the crowd choruses back, before drinking and breaking into applause.

◆ ◆ ◆

November 1996

'Stephanie, I was thinking: it might be best if we kept this quiet. Made it our little secret.'

'The milkshake?' He's bought me one even though I didn't read fifty pages, or stay where I was put.

'No. Well, yes, the whole of today. Our outing. It might be best to say we stayed at home.'

I extract the pickle from my cheeseburger and lie it flat upon the waxy wrapper. 'Why?'

He shifts in his chair. 'I wouldn't want to make anybody feel bad.'

'Why would they feel bad?'

He sticks his straw into the opening of his cup and wiggles it around so I can hear the ice cubes rattle. 'They might feel a bit jealous. That we had a day out without them.'

'Aurelie likes McDonald's.'

'Exactly. We don't want to make Aurelie feel bad, do we?'

'But she likes chicken nuggets, not cheeseburgers.'

'She might still be sad.'

I nod. 'And Mummy doesn't think it's healthy.'

'No.' He takes a large bite of his burger, looks off into the distance as he chews. 'Mummy also doesn't think it's healthy to go into the office too much.'

'Why? Is it because of the sweets?'

'The sweets?'

'In the jar.'

'What? No. She just thinks I shouldn't . . .' He looks down at his cup, wiggles his straw again.

'What, Daddy?'

'She thinks I shouldn't work too hard. The thing is . . . it's difficult being a grown-up. You have lots of responsibilities, which are important, but sometimes you have to do things for yourself too. Things that make you happy.'

'Can I have some of your Coke?'

'Okay. But only a sip.' He pushes the cup toward me, watches as I put the straw in my mouth and slurp. 'So, do you think you can keep today a secret? Our lunch here, our trip to the office, and everything? It would stop Mummy, and Aurelie, from being sad.'

The Coke is very sweet and very cold. So cold it feels as if my gums are receding.

'Stephanie?'

I swallow. 'I had a mouthful. Mummy says I shouldn't speak when I have a mouthful.'

'Yes, quite right. But what do you think? Can you keep it a secret?'

'Yes, Daddy.'

'Good girl.' He places a hand on mine, and I try not to think about earlier: the way his hand was inside the woman's skirt, as if she were a glove puppet.

'Who was that woman?'

'Which woman?'

'The one in the lift.'

'Oh, just somebody I work with.' He removes his hand, scrunches up his empty burger wrapper and places it to one side of the plastic table. 'Her name is Lucille.'

◆ ◆ ◆

Alistair's speech begins with the obligatory 'My wife and I' reference, which sends everyone into a frenzy of excitement. Hooray for another woman being shackled! He continues by thanking half the room – my parents, his parents, the groomsmen and ushers, Sarah and the flower girls – although there's no thanks for the rest of us who have to sit through his benedictions. A couple of enormous bouquets of lilac and white roses are produced for the two mothers: mine perches hers on her lap until she realises it obstructs her champagne, at which point she dumps it on the floor against the leg of her chair.

Then we are on to Aurelie. 'Now, as many of you know, I didn't meet my wife' – more inane cheers – 'in the most conventional of circumstances. I actually met her while working as a waiter in a hotel restaurant. A holiday job during sixth form and university, which bored me out of my mind. I spent hour after hour on my feet, serving hot drinks and teacakes to pensioners. Wiping down tables and making small talk about the weather. Counting down the hours until I could leave. But then, one day, all of that changed, when the most gorgeous girl I'd ever seen walked into the dining room. I couldn't believe it; couldn't take my eyes off her, partly because she was wearing hideous orange walking trousers' – this gets a big laugh – 'but also because she was unfeasibly beautiful. And although I would never describe myself as shy when it comes to the opposite sex—'

'Or when it comes to any sex!' shouts one of the ushers, leading to some rowdy applause.

'Thank you, Aidan,' says Alistair. 'Remind me never to invite you anywhere again.' Laughter. 'So, where was I?'

'Sex!' shouts Aidan.

Alistair sweeps a strand of shiny hair away from his face. 'Although I would never describe myself as *shy*,' he says pointedly, 'even I was rendered dumbstruck by the arrival of this gorgeous girl into my restaurant. Into my *life*.' There are several *aww* noises as he gestures toward Aurelie. 'I took her order, served her pancakes, brought her parents the bill' – another laugh – 'but I couldn't pluck up the courage to do anything more: to ask her about herself, to take her phone number. And so she left, and I was absolutely livid at myself for being so cowardly. Full of regret for what might have been.'

He pauses. Many of the guests are wearing wistful smiles, perhaps thinking about their own might-have-beens. I, however, am more preoccupied with what *might be*. With who in this room knows what, and where that could lead.

'But, ladies and gentlemen, I'm pleased to say the story has a happy ending. Because she came back the next summer, and the following summer, and the summer after that! And gradually I got over my shyness, found out more about her, struck up a friendship. I wrote long, rambling letters to her in the gaps between summers: long, rambling, embarrassing letters which I very much hope she hasn't kept and which, miracle of miracles, she replied to. And it was through those replies that I realised she wasn't just stunning, she was also super smart and funny, with all sorts of interesting things to say.' This gets some whoops from the women on the Rhodium Table (who apparently don't see the irony in a man praising a woman's ability to say interesting things while she herself says nothing). 'It was a very old-fashioned courtship, I suppose – played out through letters over a period of many years. Until, at long last, we were both living in London, and were able to take our relationship to the next level. And then the level after that!' He holds his left hand aloft, displaying his wedding ring to great cheers. 'But we will remain forever bonded by those letters; by the long-distance, slow-burning start we had to our relationship.'

It might be a sweet story, if it were true. But it isn't. They did exchange a few letters, but the focus on these has always been for my mother's benefit. In reality, their bond came not from long missives but from a scrawled message on a napkin. Not slowly, over a period of years, but quickly, one stormy night, from a rendezvous in a boathouse.

'So what have I learned from this?' Alistair asks. 'Well, I've learned love at first sight is real but that it doesn't need to be rushed; that, actually, taking things slowly can lead to a more wonderful, rewarding outcome than I ever thought possible.'

He smiles at Aurelie and she smiles back, her eyes full of tears.

'Shout-out for the tantric, mate!' says Aidan.

'And the other thing I've realised,' says Alistair, ignoring Aidan, 'is that, if there's any truth in the expression "start as you mean to go on", I'm screwed. Because I'll have to wait on Aurelie for the rest of my life.'

While most of the guests dissolve into laughter, I look at my mother, whose gaze is fixed on Mike and Sarah at the opposite side of the table.

She isn't laughing.

Mike is last to speak. He takes his time walking up to the plat-form and even longer to say anything. There are a few giggles as he adjusts the microphone: down, and up again, as if he can't decide on his height. Despite his muscular stature, he cuts an oddly forlorn figure without Lewis by his side. He brushes one sleeve across his forehead, straightens the heather in his buttonhole.

'Good evening,' he says, his voice a little shaky. 'I'm Mike, Alistair's best man. I've spent a lot of time worrying about this moment . . .'

There is a long pause.

'. . . although probably less than Alistair has.' This gets a few weak laughs. 'When he asked me to be his best man, I was delighted but also terrified. I didn't know where to start.'

He pauses again, swallows. 'So I decided to trawl the internet, and after a couple of hours I'd found some really, really good stuff. But then I remembered I was supposed to be writing a speech.'

This gets more laughter, and Mike seems to relax a little as he moves on to complimenting the bridal party. My mother, whom he's foolishly entrusted with his phone, attempts to take some photographs, but her finger is over the lens for most of them. Sarah, meanwhile, reddens when he says how wonderful the maid of honour and flower girls look, and I can't tell whether she is pleased with his praise, or annoyed at being mentioned alongside six-year-olds. Her words replay inside my head: *Mike has a big cock too. As I can verify from the night of your sister's housewarming.* And then my mother's, when I asked her about him and Sarah. *Why would Sarah's sex life have anything to do with that poor boy's disappearance?* She said it convincingly enough, but the way she turned from me while speaking, unwilling to meet my gaze, only magnified the question marks in my mind.

'And now . . . drum roll please, Lewis' – Lewis obliges by hammering his hands upon the table, causing the cutlery to rattle – 'the moment you've been waiting for. The truth about the groom!'

There are roars of approval from the crowd as Mike launches into stories about Alistair. Stories of japery at the posh sixth-form college where they met and became friends. Stories of drunkenness and sexual shenanigans. Stories of him embarrassing himself in Brighton and Leeds.

And yet no stories about the Scottish Highlands. No stories about where they grew up, or their summers spent working together at the North Ness Hotel.

No mention of Loch Ness at all.

◆ ◆ ◆

'I was once told that the best man's speech should last for as long as it takes the groom to make love. But I decided to ignore that advice, for obvious reasons: you can't say much in thirty seconds.' Mike waits for the laughter to ease. 'However, I don't want to go too far the other way, not when it's so hot and you're waiting to get on with the important business of getting totally steaming . . . I mean, celebrating a wonderful union. So I'm going to wrap up. However, before I do, I'd like to engage you all in a wee quiz.'

He looks out at the audience. 'Raise your hand if you can name at least one person who's been to the moon.'

There is an instant tide of hands – a roomful of fingers surging to the ceiling as if pulled by the moon itself.

'Now,' Mike goes on, 'keep your hand in the air if you can name at least two people who've been to the moon.'

The majority of hands stay raised.

Mike smiles. 'As I suspected. But here's the real test: keep your hand in the air if you can name at least *three* people who've been to the moon.'

Almost all the arms drop back. There are a few exceptions, including Great-Uncle Charles and one of the women on the Rhodium Table.

'So here's the thing,' says Mike. 'Twenty-four people have been to the moon, on nine separate missions, but the only well-known mission is that of Apollo 11 in 1969. Almost everyone has heard of Neil Armstrong, the first man on the moon, and almost as many have heard of Buzz Aldrin, the second. But there was a third astronaut on Apollo 11 who barely gets any attention at all. Michael Collins.'

'Can I put my hand down now?' the woman on the Rhodium Table calls, to laughter from those around her.

'Aye, sorry. Please do. Now the point of all this is that I feel an affinity with Michael Collins today, and not just because he and I share a name. I feel an affinity because he's the third wheel to a well-established pair. Just like me.' He looks across to Alistair and Aurelie. 'And I say this not to be churlish or attention-seeking, but to make the point that some couples just go together. Like Lennon and McCartney. Mario and Luigi. Bonnie and Clyde. Some couples just . . . fit.'

There is a chorus of *aww* noises, despite the fact Lennon was shot, Mario and Luigi are computer game characters, and Bonnie and Clyde committed thirteen murders. Sarah sits up straighter, her body turned fully toward Mike, and I feel a renewed wave of hatred flooding through me.

Perhaps Bonnie and Clyde had the right idea.

'I've never seen Alistair happier than when he's with Aurelie,' Mike says. 'And I've been told the reverse is also true. They are perfect together.'

More *aww* noises. 'It's kind of a miracle, really,' he goes on. 'That a meeting between two teenagers in a hotel restaurant should have ended up not just as a fling, not even as a long-term relationship, but here today in a full-blown marriage. And it gives me faith that sometimes remarkable things can happen. That love can find a way through, even in the most improbable of circumstances. That anyone can find happiness, even a lanky, cocky Scotsman who spends far too much time styling his hair.'

The room fills with laughter and Mike waits for the noise to subside. 'And yet,' he says, 'even for them, there are bound to be obstacles along the way. For partnerships – for families – to work, one must seek not just to understand the obvious, but to understand the less obvious too. And one must strive to forgive mistakes, even when they are apparently unforgivable.'

He looks toward the Gold Table, and I follow his gaze. Alistair wraps his arm around Aurelie, while his father takes his mother's hand. Sarah is in a trance, her eyes locked on to Mike, and I stiffen my resolve to extract the truth about them – about everything – before the night is out. Lewis, meanwhile, passes a handkerchief to my mother, who uses it to wipe the tears from her face.

'So, let me propose a toast!'

Even after wiping, there are still tears. The last time I saw my mother cry like this was when the pistachios ran out, after our father left (for the second time).

'To perfect partnerships, love and forgiveness,' says Mike.

'Perfect partnerships, love and forgiveness!' chants the crowd.

I take a swig of my champagne, and say nothing.

SATURDAY, 7 P.M.

After dessert, we gather round a flower-strewn table at one end of the hall to watch the newlyweds cut their cake. The cake has four tiers, iced in varying shades of purple, from lilac at the top to indigo at the bottom. The photographers spend five minutes moving us around before Aurelie and Alistair are brought across, and even then the cake isn't cut. Instead, there is much repositioning: of Aurelie's veil and hair, her body in relation to Alistair's, the configuration of their hands.

All this waiting is unbearable. Time has become like my mother's feet: swollen and slow and unpleasant to contemplate. I previously welcomed its buffer between the present and the future, but now that buffer is stretching ever thinner, I'd rather it didn't exist at all. It's like standing and waiting for the sky to fall in; waiting for that moment when the troposphere cracks and the heat of the sun pours through, boiling the oceans. No, worse than that: it's like standing and waiting for the sky to fall in while everyone else talks about fondant icing.

The knife is golden and around thirty centimetres long, with Aurelie and Alistair's names engraved across one side. The edge of the blade looks seriously sharp, capable of cutting far more than icing and sponge. I recently learned that knives are sharpened by being cut themselves, by the removal of a very thin layer of metal from the blade. And the process I had thought of as sharpening – the running of a knife across a steel – is actually honing. For it turns out that the edge of a knife is covered with scores of microscopic teeth which, over time, get bent out of shape. And honing is what realigns them, so they're ready to bite again.

◆ ◆ ◆

October 2001

Unable to find Aurelie, and rebuffed by the girls in my class, I lie by myself on the school field. Counting the blades of grass which fall within the span of my hand and estimating how many spans the field contains. How many blades of grass in total. Since starting Waldenborough High a month ago, I've learned about large numbers and exponential growth; how, if a grain of rice is placed on the first square of a chessboard, and the grains on each subsequent square are doubled, the sixty-fourth square will yield a pile of rice larger than Mount Everest.

A shadow, and a greeting. 'Hi.'

I look up to see Sarah, a pretty and popular girl from Year 9. Usually she is surrounded by others – by boys showing off and girls showing allegiance – but right now she's alone. A social butterfly without her wings. No hangers-on, not even Aurelie.

She twirls her ponytail round her middle finger. 'I've got something to show you. Come with me.'

I look around, wondering if she's speaking to someone else. But there's no one nearby.

'You don't have to, or anything. I just thought you might be bored. Lying by yourself out here.'

I nearly mention exponential growth and the chessboard but stop myself. Check myself! Aurelie has said the best way to get through school as a girl is to know a lot but pretend to know very little. While the opposite is true for boys. I stand up and press a hand to my stomach. 'Where are we going?'

'This way.' She strides off across the field, arms swinging, and I follow. She stops when we reach the railings at the front of the cricket pavilion. 'Go round there.' She points to the shadowy area between the back of the pavilion and the beech trees that mark the edge of the field.

I lean forward to get a better view, but can't see beyond the corner of the pavilion. 'Is it safe?'

'Oh gosh, yes.' Sarah taps a hand upon the railings. 'Go on.'

'Aren't you coming?'

'No. I've already seen it.'

There's something in her tone that seems off, like a wrong note in an otherwise harmonious chord. But perhaps that's just how popular people speak.

'Go on.' She nudges me forward.

I creep into the relative darkness of the trees' shade, and then further, turning the corner of the pavilion into grass strewn with rubbish: drinks cans and crisp packets and chewing gum wrappers. I try not to tread on any of it; worry about getting gum on the soles of my shoes. So sticky and almost impossible to scrub off. When I look up I see the broad back of a boy, bent over someone smaller, pinning her against the wooden slats of the building. The girl's face is hidden but she's wearing a skirt, and his hand is underneath it. Her legs are slightly bent and her shoes scuffed. Silver threads in her laces.

I know those threads. The sight of them is like a shutter falling. When it lifts, my teeth are in the boy's arm and he is screaming. I pull away.

'She bit me!' the boy screams, clutching his arm. 'She bloody bit me!'

Aurelie – no longer trapped – stares at me with wide, pale eyes. 'What the hell, Stephanie?' Her voice is quiet, almost a whisper.

'He shouldn't be doing that. He shouldn't be doing that to you.'

She shakes her head. 'No, you shouldn't be doing that to him.' She looks at the wound on the boy's arm, at the beads of blood gathering on his skin.

The boy looks too. 'Fuck!' he shouts. 'Aurelie, your sister is a fucking crazy bitch!'

She dabs at his arm with the sleeve of her shirt. 'I'm sorry,' she says. 'I'm so sorry. Stephanie shouldn't have done that.'

'That's the understatement of the fucking year. She should be locked up!'

By now a small crowd has begun to gather, peering round the edge of the pavilion and nudging one another. Some giggle at the boy's raging while others point and whisper. I withdraw into myself, imagine I'm a single grain of sand on a wide, desolate beach. That the metallic taste in my mouth is silica. That all around me are fragments of rock and long-dead living matter.

I'm pulled back to the field by the arrival of a teacher, who disperses the crowd before turning his attention in our direction.

'You three,' he says. 'Up to school with me. Now.'

Later, at home, I approach my sister on the sofa. 'I'm sorry,' I say. 'I was just trying to help.' A silence, long and unbridgeable. Aurelie's knees are hunched to her chest.

'I . . .' I try again.

'You want to help me?' There are spots of colour in her cheeks. Movement too: her jaw engaged in a series of tiny, rapid oscillations. 'You really want to help?'

But this is one of those times when a question is not actually a question, for she speaks again before I can respond.

'If you really want to help, don't tell anyone why you bit Chris. Not the teachers, not Dad, not Mum. Especially not Mum.'

'I haven't told anyone anything.' It's true: in the headmaster's office earlier, I simply stared at the floor. Not because I thought I shouldn't tell, but because I didn't know how to articulate what had happened. *'What he did was bad.'*

'It wasn't bad! It . . .' Aurelie stops and shakes her head. *'Sarah was right when she said you're ignorant.'*

'It was Sarah who showed me.'

'Who showed you what?'

'You. With . . . him.'

'She showed you?' Confusion flits across her features, but is soon replaced with a scowl. *'Well, so what if she did? You didn't have to bite him.'*

I run my tongue around my mouth, feeling where gum and teeth meet. Where flesh gives way to bone.

'I mean, what is wrong with you!'

There's no answer to that. Or, alternatively, there are too many to list.

Aurelie pulls her knees closer to her body. *'I want you to leave me alone.'*

'Okay. I'll go out in the garden.'

'I don't mean now; I mean at school. I don't want you coming up to me anymore. Or talking to my friends.'

Silence.

'You should hang out with people your own age.'

I pick at the edge of the sofa with my thumbnail. *'They don't want to hang out with me.'*

'I'm sure they would if you would just . . . chill a bit.'

The fabric is coming away from the frame. *'Okay. I'll try not to talk to you as much. We can swap crisps without speaking.'*

'No, Stephanie! You're not getting it! I don't want you to approach me at school at all. Not to talk about what you've learned, or to swap crisps, or anything!'

'But we've always swapped crisps.' Unable to decide whether we prefer Cheese and Onion or Ready Salted, we've developed a habit of taking a bag of each, and splitting them.

'That doesn't mean we always have to.'

I use my thumb to lever the fabric further away from the frame. 'So you'd rather split the crisps before we go to school?'

'I don't care about the bloody crisps!'

It feels as if someone has punched me in the stomach. Or perhaps as if some crisps are stuck there: large and sharp, slicing into my stomach's lining.

'Look, it's very simple,' she says. 'At Waldenborough, we're no longer related.'

'But being related means sharing genes—'

'Oh Jesus, Stephanie, do you have to take everything quite so literally! Yes, fine, we can't stop sharing genes, but we can stop sharing any sort of physical space, or spoken contact.'

'Is that what you want?'

'Yes.'

'To stay away from each other completely?'

'Completely.'

'Oh.'

'Is that clear now? Do. You. Understand?'

I nod, because I want the conversation to stop. I want to escape to the gardens, to lie in the long grass and breathe in the smell of the dirt. 'Yes, I understand.'

But it isn't true. I don't understand at all.

An outbreak of clapping alerts me to the fact the cake has finally been cut. I look up to see Aurelie smiling for the cameras, and shift my weight. The balls of my feet are aching from my ridiculous shoes.

Aurelie steps back, leaving Alistair holding the knife. It sticks out from the cake at a forty-five-degree angle, its handle a perfect match for the new gold band on his finger.

'Ladies and gentlemen!' Lewis says. 'The First Dance will take place in the Dickens Room at 7.45. The Darwin Hall will be closing to guests in a few minutes, but you are welcome to wend your way to the Dickens Room now, where coffee and champagne will be served, or to procure a cocktail in the Nightingale Suite. I look forward to seeing you all on the dance floor imminently!'

The guests start to disperse, drifting through the door in two and threes, chatting and laughing, many still clutching glasses of champagne. One man falls to the floor, his legs sliding in opposite directions and his glass breaking somewhere nearby. 'Don't worry!' he shouts, as a few people peer down in concern. 'I'm fine!' He stands up again, eyes bloodshot. 'Just lost my balance. Need to find . . .' He stumbles off without finishing his sentence, and a waitress appears to clean up the mess.

When I glance round again, I notice Sarah standing nearby, looking at her phone while fanning herself with a discarded menu. She is alone, which is unusual; at Waldenborough High she was always surrounded by a band of acolytes, jostling for her favour. Copying her hairstyle and laughing at her barbed remarks. Watching her now, I contemplate what I'd do if we were to find ourselves back there. Slam her head inside a locker? Tip a plate of baked beans into her hair, and laugh as they dripped orange glop down her neck? Make her write out five thousand lines saying *I should never have betrayed Jennifer*?

But we're here, not there, and I can't think about retribution just yet.

But perhaps this is a good opportunity to find out if she really knows anything about the events at Loch Ness. She's been drinking all day, so is more likely to talk freely than she was last night. I walk over to her, attempt a casual greeting. 'How's your evening going?'

She looks up, eyes off-kilter. 'Oh, hi!'

'How's your evening going?' I ask again.

'Wonderful.' Her voice is slurred. 'It's a wonderful wedding, isn't it?'

But I'm already done with the niceties. 'Can I ask you something personal?'

'Of course. I love personal.'

'You and Mike?'

'Yes?' She comes closer, the sour tang of alcohol on her breath.

'Did you . . . say something happened between the two of you? At Aurelie and Alistair's housewarming?'

She smiles and toys with a loose strand of her hair. 'Yes. Why? Has he mentioned it?'

I am about to say no when I realise that a careful untruth is more likely to yield answers. 'He alluded to it,' I say.

'Really?' She leans in. 'What did he say?'

'I can't remember, exactly—'

'Oh—'

'But it was something along the lines of how good you look tonight—'

'Oh gosh!'

'—and then he said you always look good, and he kind of *implied* . . .' I trail off, hoping she'll pick up the thread.

'He's messaged me, you know.' She smiles. 'Tonight, I mean. He wants to meet me.'

Wrong thread. 'Right,' I say.

'I mean, he wants to *meet* me.' She leans even closer.

'Right.'

'But I'm not sure if I should.'

'Why?'

She draws back, lips pressed together, and I decide to take a calculated risk. Leaning forward, I whisper, 'Is it because of Peter?'

Her eyes widen. 'What?'

'The boy . . . man who drowned in Scotland. Is it because Mike knows something about . . . what happened?'

She stares at me for a couple of seconds, her hand tightening around the menu. 'What . . .' she begins. 'I mean . . . what . . . how?'

'I know what happened,' I say.

'But he said he'd never told anyone!' She looks at the floor, and then back at me. 'He only told me because he felt he had to . . . because after we . . . you know . . .'

'Had sex?'

'Yes, after that – he fell asleep, and starting thrashing about, having a nightmare. It really freaked me out to be honest. So I woke him up, and he was in a terrible state, said he was feeling guilty.'

Why was Mike feeling guilty? I try to nod sagely. 'He wanted to unburden himself,' I say.

'Yes!' She reaches forward and clasps my hand. 'Yes, that's exactly it! But the thing is, I'm torn. Part of me thinks I should go to the police. That I should tell them what he told me, that it might be important. But another part of me thinks it might get him in trouble. He says he didn't do anything—'

'And you believe him?'

'Yes.' She nods. 'Yes, I do. But still, it doesn't look good for him, does it? That he carried the canoe to the loch?'

The base of my spine begins to tingle. 'The canoe,' I say. 'The canoe from the boathouse. No, I guess that doesn't look good for Mike.'

'But he says he never saw the boy that died that night, that he didn't have anything to do with his death! And I'm sure he was telling the truth.'

'Then why did he get the canoe out?'

She is quiet for a couple of seconds. 'I don't know. I tried asking but he just sort of . . . clammed up. And ever since then, he's acted kind of weird around me.'

I think back to the newspaper article, its report that no body had been found. Only a battered canoe. And I think about Mike's nervousness earlier when Lewis mentioned their North Ness days, the way he peeled the label from his beer with shaking hands. If that's what this has all been about – the whispers at the dress fitting, my mother's letter – then we definitely don't need to worry about Sarah. Although we do need to talk to Mike.

'Until tonight,' she goes on.

'So tonight he's acting more normally?'

'Sort of. Well, more like other people act. But not more normally for him.'

'What do you mean?'

'Oh gosh, I don't know. It's just that he seemed so peculiar about the whole canoe and drowning thing that tonight . . . well . . . it makes his message to me seem a little odd.'

'Because he wants to meet you?'

'Not *because* he wants to meet me, exactly.'

'Then what?'

'It's just . . . it's *where* he wants to meet me.'

'Why, where does he want to meet you?' But even as I ask the question, I already know the answer.

'The lake,' she says, patting her hair into position. 'He wants to meet me by the lake.'

SATURDAY, 7.30 P.M.

I find Mike sitting on the Gladstone Steps, smoking a cigarette. He is on his own, looking out at the gardens which are soaking up the evening light. The sky reminds me of a Constable painting: the sun filtering through clouds tinged with indigo, as if Aurelie persuaded the very troposphere to adhere to her colour scheme. I wouldn't put it past her.

'Hi,' I say, sitting down next to him. The step is still warm from the day's heat.

He looks across at me, raises his eyebrows. 'Evening.'

We sit in silence for a while. Then he holds his cigarette packet out to me. 'Want one?'

'No thank you.'

'Sensible.'

There is a long pause.

'I've been looking for you,' I say.

'Oh.' He sounds annoyed by this, or at least I think he does; I've always found it hard to read men's emotions. Particularly young men, who sometimes act irritated even when they're not. *Playing it cool*, Kirsty calls it.

I call it being an arse.

There is a longer pause and I scrabble for something to say. 'Your speech was . . . interesting.'

He shrugs his shoulders. 'Lewis is more of a public speaker than me.'

After that, we are silent again. I consider how to work up to the subject of sex, nightmares and drowning, but small talk has never been my forte. 'I was wondering . . .' I say eventually, 'how well you knew Peter?'

'Peter who?'

'Ferguson. From Ullapool.'

He takes a long drag on his cigarette, breathes out before replying. 'Why do you ask?'

'I know his parents. They often visit Loch Ness. And of course you all worked there: you, Alistair and Lewis, at the North Ness Hotel.'

'Aye.' He keeps looking out at the horizon. 'We didn't always overlap with Peter's shifts, though.'

'Mmm.' There is a tickling at the back of my throat. 'The thing is, I remember seeing Alistair, because Aurelie got all flustered when he was around. And I remember seeing you and Lewis, because the two of you and Alistair used to have competitions to see how much you could carry . . .'

He nods, and I take the opportunity to cough. 'But I don't remember Peter being there.' I can picture Peter's face so clearly, round and freckled with his snub nose and chipped front tooth, smiling out from my newspaper article and the frames in Kirsty and Rob's living room. And from the police photograph too, the one they showed us at the campsite the morning after he disappeared. His slanted eyebrows and mop of strawberry-blond hair. But, try as I might, I can't picture him at the North Ness Hotel.

Mike shrugs. 'Maybe you weren't there at the same time as him. Also, he tended to be back-of-house.'

'Oh?'

'Washing up, changing barrels, that sort of thing.'

'How well did you know him?'

'Not very.' Mike stubs his cigarette out on the balustrade, flicks the butt on to the gravel. 'We were out among the customers most of the time, whereas the managers preferred to keep him behind the scenes.'

'Why?'

He looks at me again, a scrutinising gaze much like my mother's when, as a teenager, I wore a skirt above the knee. 'Are you sure you know Peter's family?'

'Yes.'

'It's just you don't seem to know much about him.'

'What do you mean?'

'It's just . . . Peter was . . . I'm not sure what the right term is. When somebody is unworldly. Socially awkward.' He looks across to me for help.

I look back.

He takes another cigarette from his packet, and a lighter. Rolls the spark wheel to generate a small flame which graduates from blue to yellow. 'Anyway, I didn't see that much of him. We were all there just to earn some cash in the holidays, whereas he was there year-round. There was a bit of a divide between the holiday workers and the permanent staff.'

'You didn't like each other?'

'I wouldn't go that far. The two groups didn't mix much, that's all. We thought they were a bit stuck in their ways.'

'What did they think of you?'

He shrugs. 'Probably that we were arrogant fuckers.'

'So what do you know about the night Peter disappeared?'

He jerks back, as if I've shoved him in the chest. 'Christ, you don't believe in mincing your words, do you?'

When I don't reply, he swallows a couple of times. 'How do you know Peter's parents, anyway?'

'They're my neighbours. So what do you know about Peter's disappearance?'

'They're your *neighbours*?!' His skin blanches. 'Are you sure?'

'Yes, I'm sure I know who my neighbours are.'

'But . . .'

'But what?'

He shakes his head. 'Nothing.'

'No, go on.'

He sits back, flicks ash on to the step below. 'No, honestly. I'm all good.'

'But you seemed shocked? When I mentioned Peter's parents are my neighbours.'

'They've got to live near someone, I guess. I knew you lived in Scotland but . . .' He clamps his lips tightly around his cigarette.

'So what do you know about Peter's disappearance?'

He spins toward me suddenly. 'Look, I've been through all this before, several times, and I don't want to go through it again.' His voice has become hard. 'It's sad, what happened to Peter, and I feel guilty that we weren't nicer to him at work, but it was an accident, that's all. Sometimes shit happens.'

'What did you do to him at work?'

'What?'

'You said you could have been nicer to him at work. What did you do?'

'Nothing.' He looks off into the distance. 'Just a bit of teasing.'

Memories force themselves to the fore, much like bullies themselves. The snapped pencils. The upended tray of food. The graffiti inside my locker, of a shark and a penny kissing. The word *Lezzer* underneath.

'What kind of teasing?'

'Just stupid stuff. Replacing a glass he'd cleaned with a dirty one, to confuse him, that kind of thing. It was Lewis, mostly; he's always been keen on pranks. A bit of banter in the workplace to liven things up.'

Pranks. Banter. People believe they can trivialise an act by giving it a light-hearted name, but it's bullying, pure and simple. I think of the photo of Peter climbing a mountain with his aunt. How happy he looked; how excited, despite the rain. And then I remember what Enid said about Alistair. *He wishes he'd done more to stop bullying, when he was younger.*

'So where were you on the night he disappeared?'

Mike stands up, his body a hulking mass above me. 'Look, I didn't come here for a rehash of the past.' He drops the remainder of his cigarette on to the steps and grinds it out with his heel. 'Talk to the police if you want more information. Or his parents, seeing as you're neighbours and all.'

As he walks away, I think of Rob and Kirsty. Of our Sunday lunches, the three of us sitting together at their kitchen table eating roast lamb. Of Peter's room, with its books on botany and the Loch Ness monster, and its always-shut door. Of Kirsty's warning that even the shallowest of lakes can be dangerous.

And I think of what Sarah told me.

'Did you often use the hotel's canoe?'

He takes a couple more steps and stops in front of the doorway. Slowly turns. 'What did you say?' His voice has become soft. Threatening.

'I said, did you often use the—'

'I heard what you said.' He walks back toward me.

'Then why—' I begin, but I stop as he comes closer, and closer still. His body seems even more imposing from this perspective: his shoulders wider, his arms inflated with muscle. He leans down until his face nearly touches mine.

'Let me give you a piece of advice,' he hisses. 'Keep your nose out of other people's business.'

It's almost comical – for him to say this when his nose is close enough for me to count the hairs inside his nostrils – but I don't laugh. Nor do I point out his aggression suggests he has something to hide. Instead, I wait until he pulls back and say nothing. Aware, as all women must be, that sometimes strength trumps logic.

I stay silent as he walks to the hotel doorway and disappears inside.

What was Mike doing that night? I ponder this question from my position on the steps, wishing I'd taken a cigarette after all. (I've never smoked but have read that it focuses the mind, and right now my thoughts are bouncing around like wasps in a jar.) Mike knew Peter, admits he was mean to Peter, became aggressive when I spoke about Peter. And Sarah says he had nightmares about carrying the canoe to the loch. All of which fits with what the newspaper article said: that it would have been difficult – albeit not impossible – for someone of Peter's stature to carry the canoe from the boathouse on his own.

If Mike did just carry the canoe, we have nothing to worry about. If that's genuinely all that happened, then even if Sarah decides to go to the police, the chance of my family's testimony being re-examined seems slight. Because we didn't carry the canoe, and our links to Mike are tenuous.

But if he did or saw something else – something which places one of us near to the scene of the drowning when we claimed to be in our tent – then that's a different matter. And the problem is, what he said to Sarah doesn't ring true. Why would someone carry a canoe to the loch, only to walk away from it?

I think again of the note in my sister's room. *Don't marry a man with blood on his hands.* What the hell is going on here?

I know my mother said not to ask questions of Mike and Alistair, but I can't just stand around, doing nothing; can't just wait until we talk to Sarah later. Not when it's clear other people at this wedding know far more than she does. Mike might have refused to tell me anything, but that doesn't mean everyone will. Maybe Alistair will be more forthcoming.

Deciding on a course of action helps me feel better, a little more in control. I stand up and smooth out my dress.

I'm going to speak to Alistair.

The Dickens Room is smaller than the Darwin Hall, but just as ornate. It's square in shape, with a vast fireplace and large windows bordered by heavy crimson curtains and carved wood panels. Above the fireplace is a shield made of stone, embellished with chevrons and horse heads, and above that is the ceiling: a grid of gold squares decorated in leaves and roses, with a chandelier hanging at its centre. The walls, meanwhile, are covered in paintings of uniformed men.

And then, in a jarring juxtaposition, there is a flashing dance floor, strobed by coloured lights, and eighties pop plays at a volume which is almost certainly guidance (if not law) breaching.

Drinks stations have been set up around the perimeter of the room, and clusters of people are gathered by them. The band members are setting up in one corner amid wires, speakers and instrument cases, and a drunk man is spinning on his own in the middle of the dance floor. I can't see Alistair, but I spot Lewis standing in a group nearby.

'Hello? Lewis?'

He turns and raises his arms, spilling some champagne in the process. 'Aurelie's sister! How are you?'

'Have you seen Alistair?'

'What?'

'Have you seen Alistair?'

'What?' He leans closer and I repeat my question for a third time, in a much louder voice.

'Yes.' Lewis's voice carries above the music without any effort. 'He and Aurelie are in the antechamber, getting ready.'

'Where's the antechamber?'

'What?'

'I said, where's the antechamber?'

He smiles and raises his plastic cup. 'Yes! Cheers!'

I give up, scan around for signs of another room. The only doors are the one I entered through and a glass door leading outside, which has been propped open. There is a tall, thin painting next to one of the windows which theoretically could conceal a doorway, so I examine it more closely. It has a gilt frame and depicts a severely straight-backed man with a whiff of Uncle Grant about him. I run my fingers along the surrounding wall but can't feel any hidden furrows or hinges, so I press gently on the frame. Nothing yields.

There is a tap on my shoulder and I turn, preparing to be chastised. But it isn't a member of staff; it's a slim woman wearing a pale blue dress. The sort of dress you'd find in a catalogue for middle-age, middle-class, middle-income women who think they are anything but middling. Her hair is cropped and she wears a silver necklace which complements the silver band on her left ring finger. A band which was placed there eleven years ago in the absence of anyone bar a registrar and two witnesses sourced from the corridor of the register office. In a ceremony subsequently described by her husband, my father, as 'quiet and dignified'.

Lucille.

'Stephanie.' She kisses me on both cheeks.

200

'Hello.'

Her gaze travels down and up my dress, settles back on my face. She has a remarkable ability to look disdainful without actually changing her expression. 'How are you?'

'Sorry?'

She leans closer. 'How are you?' I can see the fine lines at the corners of her eyes, soft crinkles in the skin. She has aged better than my father (or perhaps just less defiantly).

'I can't hear; it's so noisy!' I throw my hands up to convey frustration. Resignation. 'I'm sorry. Perhaps we could talk later? Somewhere quieter.'

She nods. 'Of course. Sebastian and Imogen would like to see you too. They're just settling into their room at the moment.'

I try to smile, but the idea of seeing the twins immobilises my face and makes my chest tight. As if I'm back inside the photograph at Grandma's house, in my too-small school blouse, with Aurelie and her rictus grin beside me.

I need to focus. To find Alistair. 'Yes,' I say. 'Sebastian and Imogen.' As I leave, the friendliest gesture I can manage is an incline of my head. A semi-nod. A sod.

I am halfway out of the room before I realise I forgot not to hear her.

◆ ◆ ◆

August 2005

The ending, when it comes, is oddly quiet. No screaming, no swearing, no breakages. Just my father, with an open suitcase. With a handful of shirts, still on their hangers, which he lays flat inside. With socks and underpants which he packs in the gaps around the edges, and ties which he places on top. The red one, the blue striped one, the one with the

Christmas puddings. Perhaps he will wear it with Lucille at Christmas, and she will wince at his jocularity.

I watch from the landing as he unzips a kit bag and inserts three pairs of shoes. Work shoes, leather boots, trainers. A small black wash-bag. He likes things to be simple. He even said as much to me just half an hour ago: 'I'm sorry, but I want things to be simple. For all of us.'

My mother has shut herself in the lounge; she's turned the volume up high on the television so she won't have to hear any more. Since our recent trip to Scotland, she's been withdrawn, prone to long silences. Her drinking is less obvious, less demonstrative, but she can't hide the blotches on her cheeks and the bottles which clink inside the recycling bin like stripped bones.

I'm better at hiding my pain than she is, touching my knife solely to secret skin. To the flesh at the tops of my thighs, pale and soft, or the area above my hip. Sometimes I imagine how it would feel to run the blade along my wrist instead, to watch the blood spurt and gush; and these dark thoughts can only be released by cutting myself elsewhere.

The kit bag is zipped up, the suitcase fastened. I ask my father if he wants some books, but he says he'll leave them for my mother. That he can buy more. So I ask if he wants any photographs. He can't buy those. He looks at the assorted frames upon the sideboard: the picture of me and Aurelie as young children, eating chips by the sea; the blurry snapshot of me as the Star in the Nativity. The one of the four of us, standing by Loch Ness, taken two years ago by a man who had stopped to compare walking routes.

'I'd better not,' he says. 'Your mother would miss them.'

I want to shout at him then, to tell him it isn't the photographs she'll miss. That he should stay, that we need him, that I need him, not just because he's my father but because someone has betrayed Jennifer, and something even worse happened at Loch Ness, and I don't know what to do.

None of it is simple, and that makes it too complicated to explain.

So I look at him, implore him to see.

He places a hand on my shoulder. 'Look at you,' he says. 'So grown up now.'

He's seen the wrong thing. He gives my shoulder a pat, but the pat doesn't feel heartfelt, or proud, or somehow weighted with wisdom.

It feels as if a baton has been passed.

◆ ◆ ◆

The newlyweds arrive at the entrance to the Dickens Room as I'm leaving, but Lewis gets to them first. There's no time to question Alistair before I'm ushered back inside. Lewis removes the lone man from the dance floor and makes a hand signal to the photographers – thumb and little finger raised, other fingers bent – which they return, like they're playing at being secret agents. A few seconds later, the music is switched off.

'Ladies and gentlemen.' A shriek of feedback from the microphone sends one of the band members scurrying to the speakers.

'Ladies and gentlemen,' Lewis tries again. 'We now come to that very special part of the evening when the bride and groom will perform their first dance as man and wife. The start of a long and happy dance together. So please show your appreciation for Mr and Mrs Brown!'

My sister and Alistair walk into the centre of the dance floor, where they stand facing each other. He puts a hand on to the small of her back, and she a hand on his shoulder. They remain in this position, perfectly still, until the clapping has died out. And then the music begins, slow and syrupy, and they shuffle around, feet placed with care. I can see Alistair counting under his breath as the band's singer starts to croon, and he awkwardly twirls Aurelie under one arm.

Looking around, I locate Mike almost immediately in a corner, watching the couple. And perhaps I'm imagining it, or my vision is distorted by the lights, but he seems tense; his hands are squeezed together, his body too rigid. As I watch, I sense someone watching me, and turn to see Sarah looking in my direction. She quickly looks away, back at Alistair and Aurelie, but then I feel another gaze. And this time it's Mike, and my turn to look elsewhere. As if we're taking part in some ridiculous Victorian parlour game, where nobody can be caught watching.

At least my mother doesn't appear to be playing; she is sitting on a chair at the far side of the room, eyes fixed on the dance, while my father sways and hums next to Lucille, glancing at her every few seconds as if to seek an endorsement of his underwhelming musicality.

'*I love you, darrrrr-ling!*' A sudden change in volume returns my attention to the newlyweds and the band. The singer has his eyes closed, is almost kissing the microphone, and Aurelie leans back on to Alistair's arm, garnering great applause. There is further clapping and excitement as a cannon shoots gold confetti into the air, which falls mainly on the dancing couple, twinkling under the spotlight.

When this song and dance eventually finishes, the band launches into an upbeat number which prompts more clapping and a rash of foot-tapping. Alistair raises his arms, encouraging the clappers and foot-tappers to join them on the dance floor, and there is a surge of movement. So much movement that soon I can barely see the married couple for all the hands and handbags and hats. I focus on Alistair, try to keep his slimy hair in sight as it peaks and troughs amid the revellers.

'Stephanie.'

My father materialises at my side and I grant him a begrudging nod.

'Do you fancy going somewhere a bit quieter?' he shouts. 'The bar, maybe?'

'I don't want a drink.' I speak at my normal volume.

'What?' He leans closer. 'I just thought we could find somewhere to sit and chat.'

'No thanks.'

'Sorry? I'd really appreciate it. Besides' – he gestures to the wriggling bodies in front of us – 'it'd give us an excuse not to join the dancing just yet!'

'I don't need an excuse.'

'What? It'd be fantastic to catch up.'

'I'd rather eat my own head.'

'What? You're not going to bed already?'

It's like one of those children's stories where rhyming words are mistaken for one another to comic effect. Except being around my father is anything but funny. 'I despise you,' I mutter. 'You lied to us, and left when we needed you.'

'I can't hear you!'

'And now you're trying to pretend everything's fine. That you're the dutiful father. When in fact you've only ever been good for money, and now you're taking even that away from us.' I make my way on to the dance floor, which is already sticky underfoot, and don't look back. Head for the centre of the throng.

But I can no longer see Alistair. I cast around for his shiny hair, cursing myself for letting my attention wander. Cursing my father for yet another instance of crappy timing. I weave through the dancers, ducking under arms and slipping into gaps, searching. Once I have done an entire circuit of the dance floor and checked the drinks stations, I leave the room. Alistair can't have gone far. I round the bend to the long corridor, check inside the Nightingale Suite – just one elderly couple on a sofa and some staff behind the bar – walk past the Darwin Hall, and back toward the Gladstone Steps.

And then I see him, standing in a recess in the corridor. Facing away, talking to someone hidden in the shadows.

As I come closer, I notice his fists are clenched. His chest thrust forward.

This isn't a friendly chat.

I creep nearer, try to get a better view of what is happening. Alistair lowers his chin, stares down at his adversary. 'Keep the fuck away from my wife.'

A rival lover? The other man's face is hidden, but from what I can make out of his body, he looks to be small. At least a foot smaller than Alistair. He takes a step back.

'Then tell me the truth.' For a couple of seconds I am too preoccupied with the words spoken to consider the voice of the speaker. But then I realise.

The accent is Scottish. The pitch too high.

The man in the shadows isn't a man at all.

It's the red-haired woman. Back again.

SATURDAY, 8 P.M.

I stop where I am, suddenly conscious of the sound of my breathing.

'I'm not going to listen to any more of this fucking insanity.' Alistair is almost shouting, his fury barely contained. He turns, body trembling with rage, but there's no time for me to hide. He recoils as he sees me.

'Stephanie!' The transformation is rapid: he steps away from the red-haired woman and toward me, smiling, his posture loosening. Although, I notice he's clasping his hands together, the ends of his fingers white. 'You gave me a surprise! How are you?'

'Is everything okay?' I direct this at the red-haired woman.

'Oh yes, sorry if we alarmed you.' She comes forward out of the shadows, also smiling. Her hair is pinned up and she's wearing a trouser suit. 'It was just a bit of role play, so I could get the best shots.'

'Shots?'

'I'm a photographer.' She pulls a small camera from a bag on her shoulder and waves it at me. 'We thought it might be nice, for Aurelie, to get a few pictures of Alistair in hyper-masculine mode.'

I stare at her, wondering exactly how stupid she thinks I am. Unless she has to say this, to keep Alistair from hurting her. Could 'hyper-masculine' be code for dangerous?

'My name's Fiona,' she says, holding out a hand.

I hesitate, thinking of cool fingers, of lavender, before shaking the thoughts away. Her hand is damp with sweat – with fear? – and I leave mine entwined with hers for longer than is comfortable, in case she wants to communicate through touch. A hidden plea for help. But there is no squeeze or pressing of fingers.

'Yes, Fiona's a photographer,' Alistair says.

I look at him, try to read his expression. But he is unreadable, any fury or guilt successfully masked. 'And this is Stephanie. Aurelie's sister.'

'Hi,' Fiona says.

'Hello.'

There is a pause. I want to ask why she mentioned Loch Ness at the dinner last night, and what she was doing up on the fifth floor; whether she was the person who left the anonymous note in my sister's room. But I can't gauge the dynamics. Who is making the threats, and who is being threatened. Or are they both complicit? But in what, exactly?

'Alistair, can I have a word with you, please?'

'Of course.' He doesn't move.

'Alone?'

'No. I'm sorry, but that's not possible right now.' He clears his throat, looks across to Fiona. 'The two of us were just about to go for a walk round the gardens, weren't we?'

She nods. 'Yes. To get some sunset photos.'

'Sunset photos,' he agrees.

'Oh.' I attempt to smile, but my heart is hammering, as if all those idiotic foot-tappers from the dance floor have hopped inside my chest. 'In that case, shall I go and get Aurelie?'

'No,' says Alistair, too quickly. He runs a hand through his hair. 'I want these photos to be a surprise.'

'I'll come and get her when we're ready,' says Fiona.

'Yes,' says Alistair. 'When we're ready. Right, best be off.'

Fiona nods again. 'We don't want to miss the last of the light. See you later.'

And with that, the two of them walk away down the corridor, toward the Gladstone Steps. He, tall and loping; she, short and pigeon-toed.

Neither saying a word.

◆ ◆ ◆

I linger in the corridor, uncertain whether to follow. What I saw – Alistair looming over Fiona, fists clenched – was definitely not role play, and I'm worried she's in danger. *Don't marry a man with blood on his hands.* But then I remember the look of terror on Alistair's face at dinner last night. The trembling of his body a few minutes ago, when she demanded the truth. His PA's cryptic reference to threats earlier, when we were stood by the Gladstone Steps. And I wonder if it's possible the danger runs the other way.

Or a third possibility: it's all an act to lure me outside. But how could they know I'd come down the corridor at that precise moment? And what would they want from me, anyway?

I walk toward the exit, but turn, walk back, turn again.

I need to get a grip. Inhale for four, hold for four, exhale. *It's just you and me, my angel.* Inhale. Hold. Exhale. My breath is too shallow, not enough oxygen.

Even a metre of water is enough for an accidental death. And it's definitely enough for a deliberate one.

Something about the argument between Alistair and Fiona is troubling me. Something I've missed, something more than the aggression and subsequent pretence. I replay the scene, frame by frame: Alistair lowering his chin, staring down. Fiona stepping back. Alistair seeing me and smiling.

'Stephanie! There you are!'

The words break my concentration. I look up to see my father striding toward me. 'I need to speak to you.'

'Not now.' I try to remember the next frame.

'Yes, now. You can't avoid me forever.'

'No.' The memory is slipping from me.

'Stop acting like a child!'

'What!' It's gone.

'Look, I get it!' He waves his hands in circles as he speaks. 'You're angry with me for leaving your mother. You're angry she's ill. You're angry I married Lucille. You're angry about Sebastian and Imogen. And I'm sorry that I hurt you, that I wasn't around more. But you're an adult now, old enough to understand that your mother didn't always act perfectly either. Her mood swings and jealousy were difficult, very difficult, and perhaps I could have dealt with them better, but you know what? I'm human, and humans are flawed, and your mother and I got to a point where we just couldn't co-exist anymore. And my question for you is: are my crimes so great that you're willing to be angry with me for the rest of your life?' He pauses, his face flushed with the effort of his outburst. 'I mean, is it really worth it?'

I watch his face watching mine. His right eyelid quivers and stills.

'You made me lie,' I say.

'What?'

'You made me lie. After I saw you and Lucille in the lift . . . together . . . all those years ago, you made me pretend to Mum that nothing happened.'

He looks at me, runs a hand across his mouth and the loose skin around it. 'The thing is, Stephanie – and I know this might be hard to understand – I couldn't face a full-on confrontation with your mother back then. She was so volatile, so up and down. She

210

drank too much and became impossible to reason with. She threw things at me, smashed things—'

'Which she still did after you left. Only then you weren't there to help.' I clear my throat. 'You were never there.'

He sighs and rubs his chin. 'That's something of an exaggeration. I didn't leave your mother for good until you were, what? Fourteen?'

'Fifteen.'

'Well, there you go.'

He looks almost pleased with himself, as if he should be given credit for staying a year longer than he'd thought. But what his comment actually reveals is that leaving us was inconsequential to him. If it mattered, he would remember. He would remember not just the year he left but the month, the day, the hour, the goddamn *minute* he gave up on us.

Because I sure as hell do.

I can feel a fury rising inside me, hot and dangerous, and I know I should get away from him. That I should get away from *here*. It's only forty-five minutes until my mother and I are due to head to the lake, and I'm not ready. Not even nearly. And yet words are leaping, unstoppable, from my mouth, forcing themselves into the open. 'You weren't there when it mattered.' As I discharge them I can once again see the fat white moon in the sky above Loch Ness, the tent flapping in the wind. And I can feel the lonely girl inside me, the one whose family had abandoned her. The one whose sole friend had been removed from the country. The one who had nobody in her life, and no life in her body, just a cold, dark numbness.

The one I was, and am, and ever will be.

'Contrary to what your mother may have told you, I actually worked very long hours during your childhood—'

'When you weren't shagging Lucille, you mean.'

'Oh, come on, Stephanie!' He straightens his waistcoat. 'There's no need to be crude. I tried very hard to make things work with your mother, but she was suspicious of everything I did—'

'Rightly so—'

'But it was her suspicion which drove me away! She'd fly into a jealous rage if I so much as looked at another woman; accuse me of sleeping around if I was a minute late for anything, even the school bloody jumble sale. So can you really blame me for finding happiness elsewhere?'

'Yes.'

He ignores my response. 'Every time I stayed in the office to get away from her, her suspicions would worsen, and her drinking, so I stayed there increasingly often, and the whole situation became a vicious, toxic cycle until eventually, I admit, I did return to Lucille, and yes, perhaps I could have been more upfront about it, but by that point I was so worn down by it all, so tired of trying to give your mother the devotion she wanted, of trying to replace the voids of her childhood, that I—'

'Created a void in my childhood instead.'

He rubs a hand across his chin again. Glances down at his shoes, which are black and supremely shiny, with a ladder of laces. Alistair's looked just the same, catching the light as he stepped toward me. Just before Fiona came out of the shadows.

'I'm sorry you feel that way,' he says. A non-apology if ever I heard one. Corporate-speak for *stop wasting my time*. 'And I know there are things I could have done better. That I would go back and do differently, given the chance. But we can't change the past, only what comes next.'

What happens next is our eyes connect. And I wish they hadn't, for I can see myself in him, or him in me, our genetic common-alities brought to the surface like poisoned fish in a pond. And I hate him, I really fucking hate him, because not only has he failed

212

to apologise for his role in the shitstorm of 2005, he's also held up a mirror to my flaws.

I need to return to the business of the evening, to the train of thought I was having before my father derailed it. Fiona was wearing a dark grey suit, with a fitted jacket and wide-legged trousers. The bag on her shoulder was dark grey too: leather, with a buckled strap. I saw her reach into it.

'We still need to talk about my will,' my father says. 'I know it's a difficult topic, but it's important, and I'd much rather speak to you about it without your mother around. So there's no . . . misunderstandings.'

Fiona waved a camera at me. A flash of black; an understated silhouette.

And then I realise.

It's her; Fiona is her.

The woman I've seen inside a photo frame in Kirsty's living room, smiling next to Peter.

The woman who climbed a mountain with him, as the rain poured down around them.

The woman with a camera slung around her neck and an elasticated hood pulled tight around her face, hiding her hair.

Peter's aunt.

SATURDAY, 8.10 P.M.

I tell my father I need to make an urgent call and run to the end of the corridor. He shouts after me as I descend the Gladstone Steps into the garden, but I ignore him and keep running, pulling my phone from my bag as I go.

Kirsty picks up after two rings. 'Hello Stephanie. How's it going?'

'Why is she here?' I ask.

'Who?' She says it too breezily.

'Peter's aunt. Fiona, if that's actually her name.'

'I don't know what you're talking about.' But this time, she's not breezy enough.

'Don't lie to me.'

'I don't know what—'

'Peter's aunt. Your sister. She's here. And don't try to claim she isn't, because I've just talked to her.'

There is a long pause. When Kirsty speaks again, her voice is small, subdued. 'Yes.'

'What do you mean, *yes*?'

'Yes, Fiona is at the wedding.'

I feel a prickling sensation at the back of my neck. 'Why?' I ask.

Another pause. 'Because we need to find out the truth.'

The prickling grows sharper. 'About what?'

'Peter.'

'But why . . .' I can't get the words out, can't bring myself to ask for details. Who she and Fiona think was involved in Peter's death, and what they think that involvement entailed. Not to mention why they think those things, or what they plan to do about it.

Kirsty mistakes my silence for a sense of betrayal. 'I'm so sorry, Stephanie,' she says. 'Since you've been living with us, you've become more like a daughter to me than a lodger. Fiona and I never wanted to cause you any pain; we hoped we could find out more without you ever having to know.'

Find out more about what, exactly? I think back to our Sunday lunches, to the way we talked about my family's camping trips to Scotland, and the forthcoming wedding. To Kirsty's apparently innocent questions about Alistair and his groomsmen, and how he and my sister had originally met. Which clearly weren't so innocent after all. 'Was it Fiona who left a note in my sister's room?' I ask.

No response.

'Kirsty.' My tone increases in pitch. 'Did she leave a note in my sister's room?'

A pause. 'Aye. She bribed a member of staff for the keycard.'

'But . . . do you . . .' I'm not sure what I'm trying to say.

'I'm so sorry, but I just want to find out what happened to Peter. What really happened.' Her voice begins to waver. 'The police said it was just a tragic accident, but I know there was more to it than that. He was going to meet someone; I know he was! He said he was, and Peter never lied.' She lets out a sob. 'He never lied!'

It was a mistake, coming to the walled garden; I feel penned in. The walls too high to jump. As Kirsty continues to sob, the memories become unavoidable, seeping to the surface of my conscience, where they spread and harden.

Settling round my brain like a tight iron band.

◆ ◆ ◆

July 2005

There is a coldness at my core, despite the many layers I've put on. Despite the sleeping bag which is wrapped around my body, its hood secured over my head so just my face is exposed. Despite the fact the storm is at last subsiding: the wind no longer howling, the tent no longer straining to be free of its poles. The rain is lighter too, the deluge replaced by a patter.

And yet I can't warm up, can't shake the numbness which has settled upon me like a shroud. When at last I hear footsteps approaching our tent – hear the grate of the zip being pulled up, see the patch of brightness from a torch – I close my eyes. Keep them closed as the brightness comes closer and passes across me, to the empty sleeping bag on the neighbouring mat. Lie deathly still as the torchlight moves up and down, side to side, taking in the scene. Searching. There is a rustling at the foot of my mat, and my mother's voice, indistinct, mumbling.

I could say something. Even if my mother is drunk and my own tongue frozen and bloodied from where I've bitten it, I could say something, could wrestle with my numbness, giving shape to the secret and unspoken, instead of pushing it deeper. Could say I know where Aurelie has gone, how alone I've been, that I nearly drowned in the darkness.

But I say nothing. And as night passes to day and Aurelie climbs back into the tent beside me, the words I might once have spoken coalesce into large, hard lumps, impossible to eject from my body. So I leave them undisturbed, saying nothing to anyone about what I know.

And our mother, too, says nothing. Nothing about what she saw that night, as she cast her torch across the tent. Nothing about what was there, and what was not. Perhaps she drank too much and doesn't remember. Or perhaps she has found it easier to forget.

The only certainty: the things we bury don't disappear. Instead, they rot, decomposing into smaller parts and providing food for detritivores. Maggots, moulds and fungi, which use these nutrients to proliferate and spread.

Until breakdown is complete.

◆ ◆ ◆

The light is fading but I can still see the dahlias with their ruffs of petals, the old stone wall behind. 'You think Alistair met Peter?' There is a tremor in my voice which I try to flatten.

'Yes,' she says. 'And I think somehow he's responsible for Peter's death. I always have. So we left the note to provoke him, to get him riled up, in the hope he might then tell the truth. And also to protect your sister, to discourage her from marrying him. Although it sounds like we failed on that front.'

She's wrong. She's got this all wrong. I stare at the dahlias as she recounts how the police investigated Peter's disappearance and concluded he went to Loch Ness on his own. That his canoe capsized in bad weather, leading him to drown.

'But I don't believe it,' she says. 'He was excited that evening, saying "we're going to look for the monster by moonlight". *We*, not I. He'd always been fascinated by the idea of the Loch Ness monster – followed all the scientific theories, learned the dates of all the sightings – but other people didn't share his interest, tended to think it was silly, until this person came along and wanted to go searching with him. I asked him who he was going with before he set out that night, but he was so excited he just kept garbling about sonar readings and wave patterns. And it's my biggest regret that I didn't ask again.' She stops to blow her nose. 'But I was just so pleased he was excited, that he had friends.'

A silence follows, which I don't attempt to fill.

'But when the police failed to do their job, Fiona and I decided we'd do it ourselves. Rob didn't think it was a good idea – he thought I was distressed enough and it would just make me more upset – but I felt it was the least I could do. To seek justice for our son! So we did a bit of asking around, and discovered there was some unpleasantness going on at the North Ness Hotel.'

'Unpleasantness?' There's too much saliva in my mouth; I attempt to swallow but it refuses to shift, stays thick and cloying upon my tongue.

'Bullying, I suppose you'd call it. Peter was an easy target. And that husband of your sister's, along with his henchmen – sorry, groomsmen – were going for the bullseye. I've heard all sorts about what they got up to: shutting him in the walk-in fridge, hiding his uniform, showing him photos of pieces of driftwood they'd thrown into the loch, claiming it was Nessie.'

Memories from my schooldays swarm at me; the wasps out of their jar. The jeering, the sniping, the laughter. So much laughter. The children laughing in the lunch hall as my tray was knocked to the ground. The girls laughing in the corridor when I found the graffiti in my locker. *Lezzer.* And then I think of Peter. Of his trusting expression and long-limbed frame, of how upset he must have been when they shut him in the fridge. I picture him half standing, half crouched in the darkness, his eyes wide with fear and confusion, his shoulders trembling. The image is so vivid that I temporarily lose my footing. 'So you know about Mike and Lewis too, then?' I say, righting myself with one hand upon the wall.

'Yes,' Kirsty says. 'Or at least I know *of* them. And we told the police what we'd discovered. But they said it didn't prove anything or suggest the case should be reopened. That it was just boys being boys. Whereas I think – no, I *know* – there was more to it.'

The taxi flashes into my mind: its wipe-clean seats and tinted windows. Sarah smiling when I told Jennifer I'd keep her mum's job a secret.

'Bullying can tip into worse things.' My voice is slow, distant-sounding. 'But that doesn't mean it did, with Peter. Maybe it *was* just a terrible accident.'

'Except a waitress from the hotel said she'd heard them – Alistair, Mike and Lewis – talking about the monster with Peter the day he disappeared. Saying sightings were much more likely during a full moon. Saying they should plan an expedition to find it. To hunt it.'

I shiver, despite the evening's warmth. Press one hand to my stomach.

'And the canoe that was found, after the storm, came from the hotel's boathouse. Only staff had access to it.'

I remember Mike peeling the label on his beer bottle. His aggression when I asked him about the canoe. 'If you're right . . .' I begin tentatively, 'that someone from the hotel was with Peter when he disappeared . . . what makes you think it was Alistair?'

'Because he was the only one who wasn't with anybody else.'

It's a reasonable theory, but an incorrect one. Kirsty never saw the message on the napkin, nor the sleeping bag lying empty on the floor of the tent. 'What makes you so sure?' I ask.

'Mike and Lewis told Fiona they were with other people, and their stories checked out. But Alistair claimed to have been alone, at home. Not only that, he acted strangely when Fiona asked him about it, became fidgety and awkward. She could tell he was lying.'

More lies. It seems the last twelve years have consisted of little else. My father lying about his affair. My mother lying about hers, while claiming to abhor infidelity. My sister lying about Lan's job, saying she and Sarah didn't report it.

All of us lying to the police.

Kirsty starts to apologise again. Saying how sorry she is I've been dragged into all this, and how she hopes one day I can forgive her.

But I don't think I can. Not just because I'm bad at forgiveness, and not even because I let my guard down a little and *liked* her, but because it's hard to forgive from a place of greater sin.

For years, I've failed to tell the truth. And now that failure is coming back to bite me.

'Fiona's with Alistair,' I say. 'Somewhere in the gardens. Is she in danger?'

'Fiona can handle herself.'

'Is *he* in danger?'

Silence.

'We just want to know what happened,' Kirsty says. 'We tried sending him notes – to his home, to his office – but those weren't yielding results. So the wedding provided a perfect opportunity for Fiona to . . . go further.'

'And do what exactly . . .'

'Stephanie, my lamb,' she says. 'You need to stay out of what's going on, not worry yourself.'

'I'm not your lamb.' My head is spinning and I lean against the wall as I try to process the facts. Fiona is here, at my sister's wedding. She and Kirsty are poking around trying to find out what happened to Peter. They've left a strange note, talked to Alistair in the hotel gardens, and are maybe 'going further', whatever that means, and my head is spinning, events are spinning, history is spinning. All this time, living next door to Kirsty, being part of her artist residency, I thought I'd been finding out about her and her family, what they knew.

When actually the opposite was true. Or at least Kirsty was better at it than me.

'I'm sorry,' she says again now. 'But even if you hate me, I hope you can one day understand why we've done this. I just need to understand what happened to my son. I need the truth.'

There is a pause, and when she speaks again her voice is resolute. 'Fiona *will* get to the truth, you know,' she says. 'Whatever it takes.'

SATURDAY, 8.15 P.M.

This time, it isn't so much bindings which return me to my sister, as elastic – like the cord in one of those bungee run games – catapulting me back up the steps, along the corridor and into the Dickens Room.

The dance floor is a mass of gyrating bodies, but Aurelie's isn't among them. There is a huge cheer as the band launches into a repeated whistling and the dance floor bisects, half the people leaving and half dancing more wildly than before. I feel a tap on my shoulder and turn to see second cousin Ann, grinning at me. 'It's "Single Ladies"!' she shouts. 'Let's dance!'

On a normal day, this would prompt me to make a caustic remark about society's fixation with the relationship status of women. But this isn't a normal day. This is a day of primordial soup in my stomach, and oxygen deficiency in my lungs. 'Have you seen Aurelie?' I ask.

'What?' She adopts the posture of a teapot: left hand on her hip and right hand thrust sideways like a spout.

'Have you seen my sister?' My throat hurts with the effort of making myself heard.

'Maybe try the cheese and whisky room?'

'Where's that?'

'I don't know.' She looks like a praying mantis now: both arms and a single leg raised in the air, elbows and knee bent. 'But when that usher guy announced it was opening, loads of people left.'

I thank her and leave the room. Then I accost the first people I see: a pregnant woman in a chiffon dress and a man who is massaging her shoulders. But they don't know where the room is either, and they start discussing the perils of unpasteurised cheese, so I hurry away.

'Did you say you're looking for the cheese room?' This comes from Aunt Jane, who breaks off from the group of people she was talking at.

'Yes. Do you know where it is?'

'It's the other side of the disco, but you have to go outside to get to it. Through the smokers' area.' She pronounces the word 'smokers' like it's a delicious delicacy. 'Here, I'll come with you.'

'Thanks, but—'

'I insist. I need something to line my stomach. Although probably not as much as your mother does.'

I don't rise to her bait. 'So back this way?' I say, as I head for the Dickens Room.

'Yes. But slow down a little, will you!'

I walk faster, pointing every now and again to check I'm going in the right direction. She puffs along and nods, and soon we're past the dance floor and out of the door on the far side, into a square courtyard with a fountain at its centre. A group of smokers chat and laugh, the ends of their cigarettes glowing in the semi-darkness. 'The fun people!' Jane announces. They ignore her.

'Where now?' My voice sounds too loud away from the music.

'Here.' She points to another open door, a few metres along from the one we've just exited. I run toward it.

'Wait a sec!'

I enter a room which smells of feet and am immediately confronted by an enormous oil painting of a woman eating cheese. No doubt my sister finds this appealing – the artwork reflecting the room's function for the evening – but I find it sinister, given the smirk on the woman's face (which reminds me of Sarah) and the fact her breasts have inexplicably spilled from her dress (which also reminds me of Sarah). All around the edge of the room tables are laden with platters of cheese, crackers and grapes, while the guests are gathered in the middle, chomping and drinking. I spot Aurelie talking to two couples by the Bath Oliver biscuits.

'Look at all this cheese!' Jane says. 'What a disaster for my waistline! Oh well, *que sera, sera*, I suppose. Whatever will brie, will brie!'

I escape as quickly as I can, tap my sister on the shoulder. She turns toward me. Doesn't smile, but manages not to grimace either.

'Can I speak to you for a moment?' I ask.

She hesitates, before launching into introductions. Explaining to the people around her that I'm her sister, and a painter – 'art, not walls!' – and relaying a series of names and professions to me which I don't have the time or inclination to remember.

'Can I speak to you for a moment?' I say again. 'Privately?'

I sense her suppressing a sigh. 'Does it need to be right now?'

'Yes. It's important.'

'Fine.' She excuses herself from the other guests with a smile and an exhortation to try the Renegade Monk, and we retreat to a corner of the room.

'So,' she says, her voice low. 'You've barely spoken to me for over a decade, so what do you want now?'

'There's something important I need to tell you.'

'Okay then, Stephanie.' She adjusts her veil. 'This had better be good.'

'It isn't.'

I remind her of Peter, of his disappearance from the shores of Loch Ness twelve years ago. As I see her becoming impatient at my retelling, I quickly set out what I've learned today. That Alistair, Mike and Lewis bullied Peter at the North Ness Hotel. When she objects to this, I explain that Peter's mother and aunt believe Alistair capable of far worse.

'Worse than bullying? Do they think he's cheating on me?'

'They think he killed Peter.'

'Ha!' Her squeal of laughter is so loud that a woman in a purple hat drops a spoonful of chutney. It lands on the carpet, brown and gelatinous, and she stoops to clean it up. My sister makes a point of smiling at her before looking at me again with an expression that could stain more than carpets. 'You're being serious?'

'Unfortunately, yes.'

'But why the hell would they think that?'

'Because they've been investigating the people who bullied . . . who were not always entirely kind to Peter, and say Alistair's the only one without an alibi. The only one who claimed to be alone that night.'

She goes very quiet and I wait. Wait for her to protest, to say what she knows.

But she doesn't say a word.

◆ ◆ ◆

July 2005

The morning after the storm, the police come to the campsite. I am reading in a fold-out chair when they arrive and feel a coldness pass through me: a brief, intense coldness, like the swallowing of an ice cube. Perhaps it's because I didn't sleep well. Or perhaps it's because the morning has a chill to it – the sun more of a pulse than a presence behind the clouds – and I can't find my fleece jacket. Or perhaps it's because thoughts of the previous day have a strange, fugue-like quality, a sense of being imagined. My father leaving, my mother throwing his clothes into the loch and striding away down the track, my sister's empty sleeping bag.

At least the police don't come straight in our direction. Instead, they begin a walkabout of the campsite, beginning with the tent closest to the car park. There are two officers: a woman and a younger man. I watch them while making sure to look at my book every few seconds, to turn the pages at regular intervals. When the police reach the third set of campers, I get to my feet, place my book face down upon the chair, and go to rouse my family.

Aurelie wakes quickly, but into a state of unease. There's a skittishness to her movements as she launches herself from sleeping bag to tent floor and grabs at items of clothing, a redness in her cheeks as she pulls them on. She speaks in a higher pitch than usual as she tells me there's nothing to worry about, that maybe the police are just checking no one has come to harm in the storm. Or warning of its aftermath: a fallen tree across the track, perhaps, or a power outage.

Our mother is more obviously distressed. 'The police!' she exclaims a few times as she sits up, only to lie down again. 'My head,' she says, by way of explanation, as she buries her face into her roll mat. 'Can you fetch me some painkillers? And a drink of water?' She turns to one side, her skin pale. 'And don't say anything to the police without me.'

By the time the officers arrive at our tent, we're gathered in the communal area at its front, busying ourselves with food preparation.

Aurelie butters bread, I cut cheese, and our mother pokes about in a bag for some salad. She thinks it will improve our standing with the police to be seen to be eating salad.

'Knock knock,' says the female police officer.

'We're in here!' says our mother.

The officer puts her head inside our tent. 'Sorry to interrupt,' she says. 'Is this breakfast or lunch?'

Aurelie says 'breakfast' as I say 'lunch'.

'Brunch!' says our mother, with an unconvincing laugh.

The officer introduces herself and requests a quick chat. 'We're asking everyone in the area a few questions.'

I slip on my damp trainers and follow my mother and sister out of the tent, to where the male officer is waiting. He shows us a photo of a young man, probably no older than twenty, with a mass of strawberry-blond hair. 'He went missing in the storm last night,' the officer explains. 'Have any of you seen him?'

'No,' says Aurelie quickly. Too quickly. Our mother leans in closer, examines the round, freckled face and chipped front tooth. Then she also says no. I just shake my head.

The female officer clears her throat. 'It would be useful if you could tell us where you were last night, and whether you saw anything unusual.'

I look at my sister, watch as she taps one finger against the back of her opposite hand.

'I was here most of the night.' Our mother says this with conviction, and I wonder if she genuinely believes it. If all the alcohol has compressed her perception of time, making her hours beyond the tent feel like minutes. 'Although I popped out briefly for a walk.'

'Where did you go?'

'Oh. Just around.' She wafts a hand in the air. 'Up to The Coach and Horses and back.'

'And did you see anything out of the ordinary?' The male officer is taking notes.

'No. I mean, I saw some fallen branches but nothing . . . unusual.'

'Did you all go to the pub?'

Aurelie shakes her head and looks at the ground, and I realise I'll have to do the talking. 'Our father has gone to Edinburgh for work,' I say. It comes out too loud. 'He left yesterday afternoon. And my sister and I were here, in the tent. All night. We didn't go anywhere. Didn't see anything.'

Our mother glances at me oddly, her eyes over-bright, as if in the throes of a fever. 'You must be hungry, Officers,' she says. 'Can we rustle you up a cheese sandwich?'

As they decline any sandwiches – or tea, or biscuits – I continue to watch my sister. Her head is bowed and her shoulders are raised, while her eyes stay fixed on the ground.

She remains in that position even after the police have departed.

◆ ◆ ◆

It's left to me to broach the unsaid. 'Do you think it's time we told the truth?' I ask my sister. 'About where we actually were that night?'

I hope for a nod, or at least a sliver of emotion, but she just looks at me, steely-eyed. 'And what do you think the truth is, Stephanie?'

So this is how she wants to play it. 'You were with him,' I say, as matter of fact as I can. 'With Alistair. He wasn't alone.'

'No, he wasn't.'

I wait, give her a chance to expand, but she keeps her eyes upon mine, her gaze hard, as if daring me to say anything more. We stand like that for several seconds, staring at each other, until she eventually speaks. 'Why now?' she says. 'Why, after all this time, do you have to bring this up on my *wedding day*?'

'Because of Peter's mother and aunt. Because they believe Alistair killed Peter. Because they might wrongly condemn him or, if they're digging into the past, they might find out we lied to the police and then . . . well . . .'

'They're not going to find out! Besides, that doesn't answer my question. Why now? Why *today*?'

'Because Peter's mother and aunt are digging into it all at this very second.' I explain how Fiona is here, right now, at the wedding. That she was the one who mentioned Loch Ness last night, and left the anonymous note.

'Fucking hell.' Aurelie fiddles with her veil, running one finger along its lacy edge. 'So these two women have got it into their heads that my husband is a killer, to the point where one of them has turned up to my *wedding* – and, worse still, has been *into my room*. How did she even get in?'

'She bribed a member of staff.'

'Fuck.' She exhales loudly. 'We should call the police.'

I consider telling her about tonight. That I'm heading to the lake in twenty minutes to try to resolve this for good. That I still need answers but, however things pan out, having the police around will categorically not be helpful.

Yet telling her this will probably not help either. So I contain my concern between my clutched hands, keep my voice steady. 'Is that wise?'

She throws her arms up in the air. 'I don't know! I don't know what's *wise*.' There are bright spots of colour in her cheeks. 'It probably wasn't wise to lie to the police in the first place, but we did, *you* did, and everything settled down, everything was fine, until you had to go and stir it all up again.'

'That's not—'

'I wouldn't call it *wise* to shack up with a couple of psycho Scottish sisters. I wouldn't call it *wise* to give them all the information they needed to infiltrate my wedding.'

'Infiltrate? We're in a hotel, not MI5 headquart—'

'This was supposed to be a happy day, supposed to be *my* day, and you've gone and tried to wreck it, like you always do. You can't bear me being the centre of attention, so you've gone and regurgitated the past, *like you always do*, despite the fact the rest of us don't want to remember.'

'But how about Peter's family?' My mind returns to the closed door, and the orderly bedroom behind it. The botanical prints and the Ben Nevis teddy bear. 'Are they supposed to just forget too?'

She runs a hand across her collarbone. 'Where is she now? Peter's aunt?'

'Alistair's with her.'

'He *what!*' Aurelie shrieks this last word and several people turn in our direction. But this time she doesn't smile or attempt to placate her guests, and I tell her about stumbling upon Alistair and Fiona in the corridor, mid-argument, and how they pretended everything was fine, that Fiona was a photographer. 'But I heard them,' I say. 'I heard Alistair saying "keep the fuck away from my wife". And then they went out into the gardens.'

'So he knows she's crazy,' Aurelie says. 'And he's protecting me from her. Good.'

'But aren't you worried about him?'

'Alistair's a black belt in karate.' She leans down to adjust her shoe. 'Now, listen: I've wasted enough time on this madness; I've got guests to talk to.'

'So that's it?' I ask. 'You're willing to just . . . go on? As if nothing's happened?'

'Yes, I'm willing to just go on, and you should be too, if you've got any sense. Which, I concede, is debatable.'

And with that she walks away. Her gait is stiff and unnaturally level, like one of those Edwardian girls practising deportment by balancing a book on her head. She doesn't look back, but the train of her dress follows her in a sprawl of silk. Dragging through crumbs and the residue of spilled chutney.

Through all the shit humans leave in their wake.

SATURDAY, 8.30 P.M.

I'm running out of time; there's only fifteen minutes before I'm due to meet my mother. I leave the cheese room and cross the courtyard to the fountain, lean forward until the spray finds my face. The water is blue-black, like a shimmering bruise, with patches of green where it's lit from beneath. I let my eyesight blur, let the colours swim, try to clear my head. But the blurred colours coalesce into body parts: spreadeagled legs, dismembered arms, patches of pubic hair. People fucking and drowning.

'Stephanie!' Aunt Jane appears beside me. 'Are you all right?'

I attempt to nod, in the hope this will get rid of her.

'It's just . . . I saw you arguing with your sister.' She tips her head to one side – nosiness masquerading as concern – and all hope is eviscerated. 'Has something happened?'

'No.'

She studies me for a few seconds. 'She's told you, hasn't she?'

'What?'

'Your mother. She said she was going to.'

I am briefly confused; my mind has been so full of Alistair, Mike and Peter that I almost forgot my mother's tryst. The reminder is like a bout of period pain: a knotted, bloody mess which always arrives at the most inconvenient moment. 'Are you talking about . . . him? The man she met in the pub in Scotland?'

She nods. 'It's so strange, seeing him here.'

'You've seen him *here*?'

'Ye-es.' She gives me a quizzical look. 'It's rather hard not to, though, isn't it? When he's making speeches and handing out rings. He's sort of integral to events.'

Making speeches. Handing out rings. And then I understand. The tears in my mother's eyes as he spoke of love and forgiveness. Her jealousy of his time with Sarah. Kirsty saying he had an alibi for the night of the storm.

My mother's secret rendezvous was with Mike.

'Stephanie?' Jane reaches her hand to my shoulder and I step sideways, elude her grasping fingers. I'm not sure how long I've been staring into the water. 'What's going on? You said you *knew*.'

Mike. My brother-in-law's best man. It feels wrong, incestuous. And the age gap feels wrong too: our mother may have had us young, but the fact remains she is nearly fifty and has raised a family, while Mike is still preoccupied with tales of handcuffs and filling a suitcase with condoms. And he must have been really young that night in Scotland, not much older than a teenager. The thought makes me queasy.

'Stephanie! What exactly did your mother tell you?'

Mike has had sex with Sarah, and my mother has had sex with Mike. They are linked through sex, and the complications that come with it. Not to mention what's coming later, although it occurs to me now that perhaps that's linked too. Perhaps it's all linked: an impossible tangle of sex and death and lies.

'For goodness' sake, Stephanie. Say something.'

'Your hat looks like a frisbee.' With that I turn to go, hear her calling after me as I make my exit, out of the courtyard and into the Dickens Room, through the people dancing and drinking and into the corridor on the other side, but I don't reply, don't speak to anyone, just remove my shoes and run to the stairwell and head up the stairs as fast I can, all the way to my room.

Where I fling the door shut behind me.

I lie on the bed and gaze at the ceiling. At the new patches of paint I noticed after arriving yesterday afternoon. It seems so long ago now. I turn my phone on to silent and stuff it under the duvet.

I attempt some deep breathing but have to stop on the third exhalation; it reminds me too much of my mother. *It's just you and me*, she always said. But of course it never was.

I shut my eyes and images flood into the void. Of my mother, stroking my hair and counting breaths. Saying everything would be okay. Of her lying in bed, saying nothing, with empty bottles and a heap of pistachio shells on the table beside her. Of Mike, clearing our table at the North Ness Hotel, piling a tower of plates on his arm. Of Jane, telling my mother why she couldn't keep men interested. Of my father with his hand under Lucille's skirt. Of my sister, dancing with the toothbrush, trying to make me laugh. Of her and Sarah staying seated while the other members of the orchestra rose to their feet, clapping and cheering. Of Jennifer, taking a bow at the front of the stage, violin in hand.

Of the men coming to school to take her away.

◆ ◆ ◆

June 2005

It's break time when the men arrive. They walk into the library, accompanied by Mrs Denby, the headmistress. Jennifer is sitting on a stool next to a stack of books, reading; there's a gap in the stack where her book was previously stored. She's oblivious as the figures walk toward her; looks up only when they're close enough to block her light.

I can't hear what's being said. But I can see the expression on Jennifer's face: a deep frown, her teeth across her lower lip. One of the men is talking, his moustache rising and falling as he speaks. He is smiling, not unkindly, but as if he knows best. As if he is acting with benevolence.

I want to rush over then, to rip his fucking moustache from his face. To cover Jennifer's ears. If you can't hear their words, they don't count. They have to read you your rights.

Mrs Denby holds out an arm, gesturing to the library's exit. The other man goes first while the one with the moustache walks next to Jennifer, talking incessantly and still bloody smiling. Mrs Denby brings up the rear. I watch their little procession, willing Jennifer to turn and see me.

But she doesn't. Her gaze stays straight ahead as she walks past the stacks of books, past the tables and chairs where Aurelie and Sarah watch and whisper, and out of the room.

Lan's job. It has to be Lan's job. In the weeks since Aurelie's overdose, Jennifer has worried about her mother's secret coming out; has said she could be deported if immigration services were to learn of it. I've tried to reassure her, but my words have counted for nothing. For less than nothing, as it turns out. We should never have involved Jennifer's mother that night.

And now it's too late. I walk to the stool and sit down in the space vacated by my friend. The last vestige of her warmth seeps through my skirt while, all around, the air grows brittle and cold.

◆ ◆ ◆

I retrieve my phone from under the duvet. Ignoring the notifications on its screen, I compose a new message.

> *Kirsty, I know something about what happened that night. Ask Fiona to meet me in the car park. I'll get there as soon as I can.*

My thumb hovers over the 'send' button. Just one small tap for me, but a potentially huge deviation from my mother's plan. A tap which could unravel everything.

I close my eyes and let my thumb make contact. Then I push the phone back under the duvet, jump from the bed and pull on my trainers. Go to leave but, just as my hand is reaching the door, turn back. Pick up my utility knife from the desk and place it in my crossbody bag.

My second deviation.

Walking down the stairs, I pass the hunting knife, the tortoise-shell combs and the raven. The raven's eyes seem less glassy than before, more judgemental. '*Nevermore, evermore*,' I whisper as I descend the last few steps.

And then I enact the third deviation. Instead of going to the Nightingale Suite to collect my mother, I return to my room, and go from there to the fifth floor. And once I'm done there I make my way straight to the gardens: to the Gargoyle Trail and on to the aviary.

At which point I break into a run, and proceed to the lake, alone.

SATURDAY, 8.50 P.M.

The sky is dark now, the moon a slim grey crescent. The path around the lake's perimeter is lit by regularly spaced bollards casting orbs of light on to the ground, but beyond these spots of brightness the lake and bushes are swathed in darkness.

I pick such a dark point, between the jetty and a dense patch of reeds, and sit down. The ground has been baked hard by the sun, although there is a slight breeze, a sense of the Earth exhaling after a hot day. Resting and readying itself for what is to come.

Why didn't I tell the truth, that morning after the storm, at Loch Ness? Why didn't I tell the police that my father *wasn't* working in Edinburgh, that my mother had gone to the pub for *hours*, not minutes, that my sister had also left the tent? Was it a misguided family loyalty that kept me quiet, a protective instinct, or did I somehow detach myself from reality?

And what should I do now? Do I even have a choice? People like to believe in free will, but their choices can only ever be a product of their neural structures. So even if I think I'm deciding something, or even if I deliberately choose something else – to make a point of not succumbing to the option that I first picked, so as to prove my autonomy and ability to effect change – my actions might actually be wholly predictable, if only I could understand the full complexity of my brain. So perhaps it's better that I don't;

perhaps my brain is perfectly pitched to make me clever enough to be curious, to seek meaning, but not clever enough to understand itself and reveal there is no meaning whatsoever.

Enough. I take my knife from my bag and extend its blade. Hold my arm out straight and clench my fist, bring my blood to the surface.

Then I touch the blade to my wrist.

I press down gently, watch as a line of blood appears, only just visible in the darkness. I wipe it away with the fingers of my right hand and wait for another line to take its place. This time I allow the line to become thicker, less tidy: the penmanship of a toddler. There is pain at the point of the incision, which increases when I submerge my hand in the lake: a sting of cold and blood. Part of me is tempted to deepen the wound, to see the blood rush, instead of lazily ooze. To slather it across my skin so I become an inside-out person, in keeping with how I feel. But I can't extract my bones, can't suck the marrow from within. Can't pull out my muscles and ligaments and sinews. So I remove my hand from the water and shake it dry. Hold it tightly with my right hand and bring it to my heart, let mother-and-baby pulse reunite.

◆ ◆ ◆

April 2003

Of course it has to happen the night before my swimming lesson. I stare at the toilet paper in my hand, at the smear of blood across it. A red dash: no letters spelling out 'Welcome to Womanhood' or 'Sorry'. Just blood.

I drop the paper into the toilet and take another piece, wipe again. The same outcome. So this is it. I wonder if I should keep wiping or accept I can't be staunched. With pants and jeans around my ankles,

I waddle to the drawer where I know the sanitary products are kept. Open it to find a confusing array of boxes and packets. Light flow, heavy flow, applicators, wings. I opt for the most basic pad I can see, peel back the paper and stick it to my pants. Throw the wrapper in the bin, flush the toilet, pull up my clothes. Wash my hands and take my jeans and pants down again, to check the blood hasn't already soaked through. But there's only a tiny patch.

I go downstairs. My mother is sitting on the sofa, watching TV, with two wine bottles for company. One half-drunk, one empty.

'Mum,' I say.

There's no answer, so I try again, and this time my mother responds. 'I'm watching something.'

I look at the TV. A man is attempting to hook a giant inflatable duck, to great cheers from a studio audience.

'Yes,' I say. 'It's just . . .'

'"Yes" was enough,' my mother replies. The man gets the duck out of the pool, but drops it before reaching the bucket. The audience groans.

'I'll leave you alone in a moment. It's just . . . I need a letter. For school tomorrow.'

'And you think this is the time to ask?' My mother continues to watch the screen as she speaks. The man is being comforted by a woman in a leopard-print dress. 'The night before you need it?'

'I didn't know I'd need it.'

'Then perhaps you should plan better.'

'But—'

'The answer's no.'

I lace my hands across my stomach. 'It's just—'

'I'm sorry. I can't deal with this right now.'

'But—'

There's a loud crack as my mother hurls a bottle at the skirting board. 'What is it about "no" you don't understand?'

I stare at the skirting board, at the line of red that is leaking from bottle to carpet. It occurs to me that I'll need to put some stain remover on it. Then I look at the back of my mother's head, at the sheet of hair falling from scalp to shoulder: greasy at the top and dry at the bottom. I open my mouth – think about telling my mother to buy better shampoo – but say nothing. I think about Aurelie, at her friend's house, and our father, away for work, and wonder whether anyone would notice if I were to open the front door and start walking. If I were to walk in a straight line until I reached the sea.

But then the carpet would definitely stain.

I go into my parents' bedroom and sit down at the desk, which is piled with books, bills and Post-it notes. I search for an example of my mother's handwriting and find it in the form of a shopping list. Apples, Mince, Toilet cleaner. Bran flakes, Grapes, Honey. *Most of the alphabet covered in thick, looping letters. Next: a signature, which I find on a cheque for Aurelie's flute lessons. Finally, I need a blank sheet of paper. I sift through torn envelopes and under books before finding one being used as a place marker in a tome called* How to Be a Happy, Harmonious Woman.

I almost laugh, but the title also gives me resolve. If my mother can pretend to be someone she isn't, then so can I. I practise a few letters in the style of my mother's handwriting on the back of an envelope, before turning to the blank sheet.

Dear Miss Garnett, *I write, with special attention to the curl of the capital 'G'.* I regret to inform you that Stephanie will not be swimming today.

◆ ◆ ◆

There is a noise, a hard, clipped, human sound. Footsteps. Looking back at the path to the hotel, I can see a solitary figure in the wild-flower meadow, but they are too far away to identify. I return my knife to my bag and my heart beats faster – my wrist too – as I realise it is almost certainly one of two people. Either my mother, sticking to the schedule, or Sarah, arriving early.

The figure draws closer, and I can see they have broad shoulders, a substantive body.

Not my mother. Nor Sarah.

I hear their breath, heavy from their exertions, as they draw yet closer. And then their outfit comes into view: a swathe of pink material from shoulder to knee, and a hat, disc-shaped, set at an angle to their head.

Aunt Jane.

SATURDAY, 9 P.M.

'Stephanie!' she calls uncertainly as she comes to the edge of the meadow. 'Stephanie?'

She steps on to the lake path and walks in my direction, her shoes clomping upon the hard earth. When she reaches the jetty, illuminated by two lines of bollards, I stand up.

'Good God!' She clasps a hand to her chest. 'Are you trying to give me a heart attack?'

I keep my injured hand behind me. 'What are you doing here?'

'I might well ask you the same question!' She places her hands on her hips, puffs a bit. 'First you run away from me, and now you and your mother are playing silly buggers, wandering around the gardens in the dead of night. And on your sister's wedding day too!'

'Is my mother here?'

'She's in the rose garden. I can't see you properly, Stephanie.'

But I can see you. I run my fingers along the line on my left wrist and look out at the lake. Its surface is dark, smooth, with only the faintest of ripples from the breeze.

'She said you were supposed to be taking her but you'd run off somewhere, and weren't answering her calls, so she asked me to take her instead.'

I automatically reach into my bag for my phone, before remembering it's in my room. Secreted under the duvet. 'We never agreed to go to the rose garden.'

'No, I didn't mean the rose garden specifically!' She puffs a bit more. 'Your mother said you were going to bring her up here, for some lakeside air. Said it would be good for her lungs. But, if I'm honest, her lungs don't really seem up to the task of getting her here in the first place. So much coughing and wheezing! She's resting in the rose garden at the moment, but she asked me to come and find you. To tell you she's on her way. So there: I've told you. Even though I can't see you, and, to be frank, I think it's a terrible idea.'

I say nothing to this, just watch her squinting in my direction, one hand above her eyes to shield them from the glare of the bollards.

'She's not in a state for gallivanting, you know.'

It's strange, I realise, how terrifying darkness can be when you're wandering into it, and how the opposite is true when you're cocooned at its centre, looking out.

'Particularly as she's not been holding back on the booze. I mean, I'm the first to appreciate the power of a good tipple, but then it's fair to say I don't have your mother's . . . *history*.'

She's only an arm's length away from the edge of the jetty. One firm push, and she'd be in the water. I imagine her falling backwards, limbs flailing. Pink fabric swirling around her like an explosion in a tutu factory.

'You should come back to the hotel with me. I understand you're upset about Mike, but hiding away out here is ridiculous. It's your sister's wedding day!' She pauses. 'There are guests!' When even this statement has no impact, she sighs. 'I did say to your mother that perhaps it wasn't the right day to tell you, but she had some misguided notion it would reunite you all.'

243

'We're long past the point of Happy Families.' My mind returns to the stormy night at Loch Ness, when our father made the decision to walk away. And I think of the photos of Peter: the chubby toddler; the gawky teenager; the boy on the brink of a manhood which never came to pass. How Kirsty can't shut her eyes without seeing his face. How she leaves flowers every month on the banks of Loch Ness: a gathering of daisies; a bunch of gypsophila.

Two families died that night, and perhaps it's time we acknowledged it.

'I know, I know, but your mother's never had the best judgement. She's too swayed by her emotions; her moods go up and down faster than your Uncle Grant's sciatica. That's what got her into this mess in the first place, of course.'

'Grant's sciatica?'

'No! Don't be facetious. Her overwrought emotions. She thought she was in love.'

I can't believe my mother has ever been in love. Or, at least, not a genuine, selfless love, the sort where you'd sacrifice yourself for another. For her, love has always been a matter of possession, a case of holding too tightly and proclaiming *this is mine*. 'But he can't have been much older than a teenager.'

'He was nineteen. But then she was only sixteen. Both of them young and foolish.'

I point out that I was talking about my mother and Mike.

'So was I.' She folds her arms across her chest.

'When my mother was sixteen, Mike wasn't even born.'

'He was, actually.'

I don't have time for this. 'Maybe so, but he'd have been a baby or a toddler. Not old enough for sex.'

Jane's eyes widen and she puts a hand to her neck. 'You . . . what . . . you . . . how . . . no!'

'Would you prefer a euphemism?' I say. 'Not old enough to churn the butter? Daub the brush? Bury the bishop?' I'm sure my father could add many more.

'No, no!' She runs her hand across the beads of her necklace. 'I mean, yes, your mother . . . no . . .'

I've never seen Jane so lost for words. It's disquieting – an upset of the natural order. Like a lull in the Earth's rotation.

'She wasn't Mike's lover,' she manages eventually. 'You've got the wrong end of the stick *completely*.'

And we're spinning again. 'Lover, fuck buddy, whatever,' I say. 'They're all much of a muchness.'

'Except she wasn't any of those.'

'So what was she, then?'

'The same thing she still is to Mike.' Jane looks at the lake and then back to me. 'The same thing she always will be, however much anyone wishes otherwise. His mother.'

SATURDAY, 9.05 P.M.

The lake no longer seems real. It appears superimposed on the land-scape, a painter's rendition of a lake. Everything two-dimensional, scribbled lines amid daubs of colour. I try to process what Jane has just told me, but her words slip around inside my head.

'Stephanie?'

The scale is wrong, I think; the jetty is too large. The hide on the opposite bank looks closer than the reeds in front of it.

'Stephanie? Did you hear what I said? Mike is your mother's son.'

Your mother's son. There is something convoluted about it. Like saying 'not nothing' instead of 'something'.

'Stephanie!'

'Mike's my brother.' I speak without thinking, and as I do the world expands back into three dimensions. I stand up, walk toward Jane.

'Your half-brother, yes.'

I lean against one of the jetty's bollards, run my hand across the uneven stone. 'I don't understand.'

'He was born in 1985, when your mother was only sixteen.' Jane pulls a face at this: half grimace, half smile. 'She went off the rails a bit after your grandmother died, went through some-thing of a wild-child phase. I think she was trying to get your grandfather's attention but that was a lost cause – the only thing that got his attention was the bottom of a whisky bottle – and so she'd go out with these . . . men . . . and some of them were truly dreadful! Very rough-looking – one was a Communist! Well, of course, that turned out to be a lost cause too – but then William came along, and I have to say he was an improvement on the others, but still so *young*, and clearly not that clued-up on contraception. He—'

'William?'

'Mike's father. He was from Scotland, but he was studying in Bristol when your mother met him. She was still at school, and became infatuated. And then, soon after, pregnant.' She sighs. 'The oldest story in the book.'

I can't wrap my head around it: that my mother gave birth to another child, in the days before me; before Aurelie; before our father. When she was just a teenager. And yet, at the same time, it makes perfect sense. All those stupid rules about not spending time alone with a member of the opposite sex. Not wearing a skirt above the knee. 'But she didn't want the baby?'

'No, she did.' Jane straightens the neckline of her dress. 'But she wasn't being practical. I think she had this idea of a doll-like creature, all sweetness and cuddles and gurgling in a high chair, but she didn't think of how she was going to *afford* a baby, how she was going to look after him while finishing school, what would happen when he screamed in the night and our father got annoyed with the noise. And William, well, he was a nice enough chap, but he wasn't exactly brimming with common sense either, so I did the necessary thing and got his parents involved, and they agreed to take him, to raise him as their own, up in—'

'Mike's grandparents raised him?'

'Yes, in a large house on Culloden Moor.'

Culloden Moor. Only sixty miles from Ullapool, and just up the road from Inverness. I've even been there once, on a rare tourist day out. I don't normally like tourist venues, with their swarms of cheery people and mug-flogging gift shops, but I made an exception for Culloden, with its windswept death fields. The site of the last pitched battle on British soil. 'And my mother didn't mind?'

Jane whistles, a low, breathy sound. 'Oh, she minded, all right. Kicked up the most unholy fuss, which, if I'm honest, only made me all the surer it was the right decision. Babies can't raise babies, whereas Will's parents had time, space, money, *maturity* . . . all things your mother couldn't offer.'

I picture a tiny, mewling infant in my mother's arms. A much younger version of my mother: her face unlined, her body unravaged, her mind un-unhinged. Before my father, before Lucille, before Jennifer. Before we ever went to Loch Ness.

'So those trips to Scotland . . .' I begin.

'Were to see Mike, yes. As well as to have a holiday with you, Aurelie and your father. Two birds with one stone and all that. Although camping – goodness – not my idea of a good time. Especially not in Scotland.'

As she proceeds to tell me about the midges and rain she never experienced, I think back to the North Ness Hotel. To its high ceilings and faded carpets. To the way my mother was so particular about the days and times we visited, and her constant surveillance of the waiters at work. How she always ordered the same thing: a pot of tea to share with our father, and pancakes for me and Aurelie. How she gathered up loose change for weeks beforehand, and counted it out upon the wobbly tables to pay for our treat.

Or, rather, as it turns out, to pay for sight of her son.

◆ ◆ ◆

August 2003

The walk is only supposed to take two hours but ends up taking four. Our mother claims our father has read the map incorrectly – that we've taken a wrong turn – while he claims the path marked on the map doesn't exist. I suggest we return to the last point on the map that definitely does exist and both of them tell me to be quiet. A rare moment of parental unity.

Over an hour later, after struggling through dense vegetation and traversing two electric fences, we finally make it back to an established path, albeit one which is still some distance from the campsite. 'We'll need to hurry,' our mother says. 'If we want to get to the North Ness tonight.'

Our father looks at his watch. 'Perhaps we should go tomorrow instead.'

'Tomorrow's no good.'

'Tomorrow would be better.' He pulls a burr from his sleeve. 'We can go for a slap-up breakfast: pastries, full English, the works.'

'We can't afford that.'

'What?' He comes to a halt without warning, and I nearly trip over the back of his boot. 'If you really think that, then surely we shouldn't go at all.'

'No!' Our mother's voice is adamant. 'Pancakes and a pot of tea this afternoon. It's good and it's affordable. It's what we always have.'

Our father opens his mouth to argue but, seeming to think better of it, walks away. He walks so fast that his figure grows smaller and smaller until, by and by, he is nothing more than a speck on the purpled moor.

◆ ◆ ◆

Jane cocks her head to one side. 'Your father never knew about Mike,' she says. 'It's terrible that she never told him. Such a big thing to keep from your partner. Perhaps that was why he never made her his wife, because he knew she was holding something back. And yet she still dragged him – dragged all of you! – on those trips to Scotland, to that awful campsite and that godforsaken hotel—'

'We liked going there.' For some reason, I feel compelled to defend my mother. Despite her turbulent moods. Despite her lies. Despite everything.

'Really?' She sniffs. 'Well, it takes all sorts to make a world.'

'Did Mike know?' I ask. 'About us?' I run my mind back across the weekend. Mike, staring, as my mother was lowered to the ground, coughing and fighting for breath. The way he scrutinised me so closely during the ceremony, and again in the corridor by the Nightingale Suite. His aggression when Lewis talked about their North Ness days. His comments, during his speech, about being the third wheel to a well-established pair.

The third child. The missing wheel of our shoddy sibling tricycle, steered according to our mother's whims.

Careening out of control.

'Not at first. We'd agreed it was better for him that way. But eventually, when he was an adult, that night your mother went with him to the pub . . . she told him.'

Another event which took place that night. 'And?'

'And?'

'How did he take it?'

'Not well, apparently.' She holds her necklace away from her chest, clasps the beads tightly. 'Not well at all.'

I look down at my feet and notice my laces need tying.

'But then . . .' she says. 'It's got to be one hell of a shock, hasn't it? To discover you have a second family?'

I think of the photo on Grandma's mantelpiece. My father, Lucille and the twins, all sunny and smiling. Not a shock so much as a wrench. The realisation that, in the pitched battle for parental love, I was on the losing side. 'But he was okay to come to the wedding?'

She shrugs. 'He's here, isn't he?'

I bend down and retie my laces. 'I suppose so.'

In the quiet which follows, I start to reassess. The way my mother watched Mike during the speeches. The way she cried when he talked about forgiveness, her shoulders heaving and her philtrum filling with snot.

Is it merely shame that has led her to hide the truth from me and Aurelie all these years? Or is there something more? She was so reluctant to answer my questions about Mike and Sarah's actions on the night before the dress fitting, so adamant it had nothing to do with the letter she wrote six months ago; but I now know that Mike bullied Peter and carried the canoe to the loch, and that Sarah found out about it. And also that Mike is my mother's son. It suddenly all makes sense: Sarah told Aurelie about Mike and the canoe, and my mother overheard, panicked and wrote a letter to me. This whole ridiculous plan about Sarah and bribes and lakes: it's because she wants to protect *him*.

I think of her standing by the sink earlier, telling me how spineless she was. How it was her fault he'd left. *The only reason we're going through all this is because I let him go.* I'd assumed she was talking about my father, ruminating on his affair. But now I realise she was talking about Mike. Her lost son. Her lost son who took us to Scotland and, in so doing, set everything else in motion.

So what now? If the heat is on Mike, can I assume my family is out of the firing line? Or, knowing he's *part* of my family, does that only increase the danger?

251

SATURDAY, 9.10 P.M.

I turn to Jane. 'I need to talk to my mother.'

She nods and agrees. 'Although my advice to you, Stephanie – my *strong* advice – is to pick somewhere indoors. The Nightingale Suite, perhaps, or one of the hotel bedrooms?'

I leave the jetty, head away from the lake into the long grass of the meadow.

'Oh, for goodness' sake, don't go running off again! It's dark; the two of you will miss each other. Here, I'll give her a ring.' She searches through her bag, pulls out and replaces a pair of glasses, a lipstick, a purse, a pen, the glasses again, a set of keys and a charging cable, before finally extracting her phone. And then her glasses for the third time, in order to see her phone, which she says has only one bar of reception. Then no bars. She waves it from side to side and over her head.

I set off through the meadow.

'Stephanie! Aren't you going to wait for me?'

I extend my stride, increase my pace, and she shouts after me, something about ungratefulness and the sacrifices she has made, and something even less coherent about Barbra Streisand and an Amarena cherry.

But the only words that stick in my head are my mother's. *Because I let him go, because I let him go, because I let him go.* That stormy night, in Loch Ness, did my mother actually meet Mike in the pub? Or did she just say she did, to protect him? To protect him from the fact that, while she was alone with her wine, he was out in the rain, carrying a canoe? Something which haunts his sleeping hours even more perniciously than Sarah haunts his waking ones?

The skirt of my dress restricts my stride, so I hitch it up above my knees and run with my elbows sticking out, like a lunatic Victorian washerwoman. I keep running even when I'm panting, find a rhythm of footfall and breath as I reach the far side of the meadow. Until, out of nowhere, there's a cough – a harsh, jagged sound – and I see my mother approaching, acquiring detail as she draws closer. A blue and white dress; a chestnut wig; a face with sunken cheeks.

I feel dizzy. Her proximity is like a blow to the head, stopping me from thinking clearly. The only definite: I can't talk to her. Not yet. So I lie down flat in the grass and wait until she has passed, then crawl to the archway, at which point I stand up and run toward the aviary, but as I approach I see the silhouettes of the scarab beetles with their outstretched wings, like monstrous locusts, and I can't bear them either, so I take the path to the Gargoyle Trail, but that's too close to the hotel, to other people, so I go back the way I have come and see the gap in the hedge leading to the car park and run to it, through it, place my hands upon the bonnet of my car and inhale. A place of refuge at last.

Until a figure with red hair appears out of the darkness.

'Stephanie,' she says. 'I've been waiting for you.'

SATURDAY, 9.20 P.M.

She comes out of the shadows toward me in her dark grey trouser suit, dark grey handbag slung over her shoulder. Although she's short and slight, there's something frightening, almost spider-like, about the way she moves, quick and light across the gravel.

'Where's Alistair?' I ask.

'He's gone back inside.'

Unsure if I believe her, I scan the car park for . . . what? Signs of a struggle? A dead body? I don't know what I'm looking for, but my heart thuds madly as Kirsty's words echo inside my head. *Fiona will get to the truth, you know. Whatever it takes.* But I can only see cars, large and ungainly in the moonlight, and the long line of hedge.

I sense her gaze upon me, studying me. 'Kirsty says you know who I am,' she says.

'Yes.' I turn back toward her. 'I recognised you from the photo in her living room.' *The photo of you and Peter*, I nearly say. But I can't quite bring myself to speak his name.

'Very observant of you.' Her voice is dry. 'So you know I'm not actually here to take photographs.'

'No . . . I mean yes.' I need to get a grip; it won't do me any favours to sound nervous.

'You said you wanted to meet me here?'

Of course. I sent a message to Kirsty earlier. *I know something about what happened that night. Ask Fiona to meet me in the car park.* It seems so long ago now. Before I knew the truth about my mother and Mike. Before I found out he's my half-brother, and that she's trying to protect him.

'I know you want the truth,' I say. 'And the truth is Alistair wasn't alone that night. At Loch Ness.'

Fiona's eyes look grey and filmy in the darkness. Giving nothing away. 'So who was he with?'

'My sister.'

She stares at me, and I do my best not to squirm. 'Then why would he lie?' she asks. 'Why would he claim he was alone?'

'Because of my mother.' I take a step back, knocking into the wing mirror of the car behind me.

She raises her eyebrows and I do my best to explain how difficult my mother was to live with, growing up; how she oscillated between anger and depression, depending on what our father was doing, and how much she drank. How she imposed irrational rules – particularly when it came to spending time with boys, or men – and could spiral into near-mania if we broke them. How Aurelie – beautiful, golden, heterosexual – found this more difficult than I did; how, while I went out of my way not to break the rules, she went out of her way to conceal that she had. Hence lying to everyone about where she'd been that night.

'But this is a young man's death we're talking about.' Fiona's eyes are still upon me. 'Are you really trying to claim that Alistair and your sister lied to the police solely to avoid admitting to your mother that they were together?'

I nod. 'I know it sounds mad, but we panicked. Or, strictly speaking, I panicked; I told the police Aurelie had been in the tent all night. And then, once we'd lied, we panicked about trying to

255

undo the lie, thinking it would make us look suspicious. So we didn't. Undo the lie, I mean.'

'But that doesn't make any sense.'

'I was only fifteen! A lot doesn't make sense when you're fifteen.' Even as I'm saying it, I'm thinking of my mother. Of the fact she gave birth to Mike at a similar age, and had to give him up.

And then I'm thinking of Jennifer. Who, at a similar age, had to give up everything.

◆ ◆ ◆

July 2005

It's the first day of the holidays, and summer stretches out before me like a salt flat: arid, cracked, lifeless. Days composed of hours filled with minutes, with nothing planned except for a week in Scotland with my family.

Everything has changed since the men came to school. Jennifer and her mother have been earmarked for 'administrative removal': a fate which tries to clothe its monstrosity in bureaucratic language but, in so doing, becomes more monstrous still. As if the people involved are mere sheets of paper who can be thrown out with as little compunction as a broken stapler or a wonky office chair. And yet the system lacks the coherence of an office clean-out. Jennifer and Lan have to make regular visits to the immigration reporting centre, but are never given any certainty on the timings for their removal. Never told when they will be detained, or for how long. The sheets of paper simply shuffled and separated and stacked and reshuffled, but never actually sorted.

Such uncertainty has taken its toll upon our friendship. Jennifer has stopped coming to school and has become distant, unwilling to engage. Whenever I ring to speak to her, her mother always answers, says she is busy. That she's studying. But I don't believe her.

A knock, and the creak of the front door opening. Aurelie's voice, bored, calling up the stairs. 'Stephanie. It's for you.'

It's never for me. I come downstairs with careful steps, half expecting a toy snake to uncoil from the banisters. Instead, I see Jennifer standing on the doormat.

My hand rushes to my mouth. 'I thought it was a trick!'

She gives a slight smile. 'I don't do tricks. I don't like them.'

'No, but—'

'I've come to say goodbye.'

I slump on to the bottom step. 'So you're definitely going?'

She nods. 'They've told us this time it's happening.'

'I'm sorry.' I hope Jennifer doesn't ask why, as I wouldn't know where to begin. But I am sorry. I'm sorry people have been cruel. I'm sorry about my sister, and Sarah, and the secrets that haven't been kept. I'm sorry for my own uselessness in the face of it all, and for my country's terrible judgement.

'I'm sorry too.' Jennifer steps toward me. 'For avoiding you these past few weeks. I've wasted what little time we had.'

I shake my head. 'It's my fault. If you hadn't helped Aurelie that night, you and your mother wouldn't have to leave now.'

'You don't know that.'

'I do.' I stand up again, my legs unsteady. 'Aurelie says she and Sarah didn't tell the authorities, but I know they did.'

'We can't ever know anything for sure.'

I look at Jennifer: at her small mouth, with its white, even teeth; at the raised curve of her cheek; at her eyes, watching mine. 'I know I'll miss you.'

'I'll miss you too.'

There's a pause, during which all the unspoken words gather between us like caged birds, until she steps forward and presses her lips to mine.

And the birds fly free.

◆ ◆ ◆

'So,' Fiona says. 'Is that all you wanted to tell me?'

I turn the possibilities over in my mind: I could tell her about Mike, about his nightmare, about the canoe. I could tell her he's my half-brother. I could tell her about Sarah, and Jennifer, and how everything came to a terrible head that summer.

I lean against the bonnet and shut my eyes, clench them together. My counsellor Maggie once told me the best remedy for a floundering mind is to pay attention to each of your senses, one by one. I scoffed at it at the time, saying it made no sense to focus on your senses when you were senseless. But now, with everything unspooling, I have nothing to lose. Or rather, I have everything to lose, and thus sense is irrelevant. So, sound: I can hear faint music, leaves rustling, the susurration of my breath. Smell: the sweet woodiness of the yew, a tinge of diesel. Taste – a lingering of over-seasoned heritage potatoes – and touch. My fingertips against the metal of the car, the warm night on my skin.

Finally, sight. I open my eyes and try to see things on a macro level: the hedge and the sheet of sky above, where grey gives way to star-pierced black. Then I hone in on details: yew needles, small and straight; the grooves of a tyre. The outline of a figure passing by the rose garden on the opposite side of the hedge.

And now all my attempts to calm myself fall away. Because the figure must be Sarah, on her way to meet my mother at the lake.

I've got to leave. Immediately. But I can't just abandon Fiona in the hotel car park, not when she's so desperate for answers. 'Do you believe me?' I ask. 'That Alistair wasn't alone that night?'

She blinks a couple of times. 'I'm not sure what I believe. But Alistair's story does at least match yours.'

'He told you?' I look down at the ground, away from her scrutinising gaze. 'About being with my sister?'

'You're surprised?'

In truth, I am. Only a few hours ago, he was pledging undying loyalty to Aurelie and, by extension, our family. But all it took was one red-haired, spidery woman coming to his wedding, and he caved.

It's each man for himself now, I suppose.

Or each woman.

'There's something I need to do.' I turn toward the gap in the hedge. 'Something I need to find out.'

'Something of interest to me?' she asks.

I pause. 'Possibly.'

'Then perhaps I could come with—'

'No. Sorry. I . . . no. It's best if I'm on my own for this. But . . .' I need to think quickly. 'If you can stay here for a bit, I can come back after? Tell you what I've learned.'

'Fine,' she says.

'You don't mind waiting?'

She gives a terse laugh. 'Kirsty and I have waited twelve years already. We can wait a bit longer.'

SATURDAY, 9.25 P.M.

I dash through the gap in the hedge, past the rose garden in the direction of the stone arches. I can see the figure walking ahead of me, near the kitchen garden, and I run to catch up. Except, as I draw closer, I realise the person I'm chasing is of a middling height, slim, bald.

Not Sarah. My father.

I stop but it's too late; he's heard my footsteps. He turns and comes toward me, his face cast in shadow. 'Stephanie! What are you doing here?'

More crappy timing. I stare at him and he stares back, looks down at my trainers with dark, hooded eyes. 'Are you out for a jog?'

This is not what I need right now.

'Stephanie?'

I stay silent.

'Aren't you going to say anything?' He squeezes his hands together.

I move to go round him and he suddenly stamps his foot on the ground. 'For God's sake! When are you going to grow up and realise the entire world doesn't revolve around you?'

The sheer hypocrisy of his words snaps something inside me. All day I've been so tense, so careful, so busy dealing with the fears and secrets of my fucked-up family, and now this pompous, patronising, perfidious, wank-faced hypocrite has the gall to tell me I'm self-obsessed. I reach inside my bag and close my hand around my knife. Its handle is smooth and comfortingly familiar, like slippers worn until they cleave to the feet.

He shakes his head. 'Aurelie's sent me to look for Alistair. If you've seen him, I'd be grateful if you could let me know. Or, if you really won't talk to me, at least let your sister know. She's worried.'

I look at the first stone arch, try to see through it, beyond it, to the meadow. But the path curves behind a wall. 'He was outside, with the red . . . a photographer.'

'She speaks!'

I tighten my grip on the knife's handle. 'But he should be back inside now.'

'Well, that's a relief.' He smiles tentatively at me. 'I do hope everything's all right between him and Aurelie.'

'Of course it isn't.' I extend the knife's blade inside my bag, run one finger along its side. 'They're married.'

'Ha ha. Still. It's not exactly standard, is it? For the groom to spend a large portion of his wedding alone with a photographer?'

'It's not exactly standard to walk out on your children either.'

'Jesus Christ!' The smile disappears and he slides a hand across his scalp. 'At some point you're going to have to let this go. Accept things don't always work out the way you want. That maybe, just maybe, you'll be happier if you can draw a line under the past and move on.'

I imagine drawing a line through the base of his ribs. Watching as his eyes widen, as the blood begins to gush.

'Stephanie? Are you okay?'

Now I imagine the blood pouring out, his guts spilling on to the ground like uncoiled sausages. 'You seem so angry,' he says, as his heart slithers from his chest and he stuffs it back in without looking. *Let it go, Dad.* 'Sort of wild. And then there's this thing with my will.'

Once perforated, can a person prevent their lungs from collapsing?

'Your mother says you need money urgently, that you're in trouble.'

I press one hand to my chest and note it's heaving. And it occurs to me that perhaps I've got this all wrong, that perhaps *I'm* the one who's been sliced open, who's bleeding, who can no longer gather breath—

'And I'm afraid I can't just give you money. I'm not that wealthy. But I could potentially bring some of your legacy forward, if that would be helpful. Although, if I'm going to do that, I'd really like to know what sort of trouble you're in. And to check nothing's been lost in translation, because your mother won't speak to me directly, so I've only heard this via Aunt Jane—'

'Aunt Jane?' My heart flutters like a strangled bird, and I think back to her whispering with my mother in the lounge. *But he wants to speak to Stephanie first. Before he agrees for definite.* So they were talking about my father, not dancing with Lewis. About my father's money. About *my* share of my father's money. No wonder they leaped apart in panic when I showed up unexpectedly.

'Yes,' my father says. 'She said you need the money soon.'

I'm definitely losing oxygen. I'm inhaling rapidly but my lungs refuse to inflate, and all the while my pulse is accelerating. I don't need money. So why is Aunt Jane telling my father I do? Are she and my mother trying to get hold of my share of my father's money? I think back to my earlier conversation with Jane at the lake, and wonder if it's because of Mike, the secret bloody son who seems to be at the centre of everything this weekend. Perhaps *he* needs money, or perhaps my mother just wants to give him some, to assuage her guilty conscience.

But she's not giving him mine. 'I don't need any money,' I say. 'You don't?'

'No.' I begin to run, past the kitchen garden toward the stone archway, and everything is going too fast: my legs, my breath, my heartbeat.

'Stephanie, wait!' my father shouts. 'I thought you were in trouble?'

I run under the first archway, round the corner, through the other arches and into the meadow. In daylight, I'd be able to see all the way to the lake from here, but now everything is murky: a series of lit bollards and long shadows. I look for a person: at close range to begin with, and then further off.

There is something at the far end of the meadow. A dark mass. I squint to improve my focus; it seems to be moving forward. I try to see if the mass is hunched, shuffling – whether there's any possibility it's my mother, still hobbling to the lake, or Jane, not yet returned – but such detail eludes me. If only I had the eyesight of some of the animals I paint. The eagles, which can spy a rabbit from two miles away, or the deer, which reflect light back inside their eyes to see predators in the darkness.

I run faster. Gain on the mass which, as I come closer, takes on a female outline. Long hair, long legs, spindly shoes.

It's her; it's definitely her.

The person who destroyed my relationship with my sister.

The person who hurt Jennifer, and almost certainly spilled her secrets.

The person my mother wants to silence.

Sarah.

SATURDAY, 9.35 P.M.

She turns as I approach, and I look at her closely, hoping my body will act on an instinctive level. That somewhere, buried deep, I'll know what to do.

But nothing happens: no twitch of the wrist; no leap of the legs; no ululation from within. I stand mute, my breath ragged, observing as her dress flutters in the breeze. As she retrieves a couple of loose strands of hair and secures them with metal grips. 'Hello Stephanie,' she says.

I don't reply.

'Stephanie?' She steps forward and peers at my face. 'Oh gosh, are you all right? You look like you've seen a ghost.'

Perhaps that's it: perhaps she's dead. Perhaps I am too. Lost souls in the purgatory of a Berkshire country garden. Condemned forever to admire the topiary.

Except I don't believe in souls.

'I would offer to accompany you back to the hotel. Only' – she drops her voice to a whisper – 'I'm meeting Mike, at the lake.'

But I do hate topiary.

'I've got butterflies!' She touches a hand to her stomach. 'Which is crazy, when you think about it, because it's not like this is the first time he and I have . . . you know . . . Oh gosh, I'm just going to do it! Seize the day! Wish me luck!'

'No,' I say. A hard syllable of sound.

Her smile falters. 'Pardon?'

'I said, *no.*'

'Fine! You don't have to wish me luck; it's just a saying—'

'You're not going to meet Mike at the lake.'

Her forehead creases. 'No offence, but it's not your decision whether I meet him or not!'

'That's because it's not a decision at all. He's not there.'

'I don't see how you'd know.' She taps her violet fingernails on her bag. 'Whereas I do. He sent me a message.'

'No, he didn't. My mother sent you a message.'

She takes out her phone, clacks her nails against its screen. 'I don't have any messages from your mum. Just from Mike. And a couple from your sister, and from a friend of mine in Antigua—'

'No. I mean, the message from Mike's phone was written by my mother.'

'Oh gosh, Stephanie.' She is blinking rapidly. 'Are you sure you're all right? Because you're acting very strangely. Your mum wouldn't write something like that, particularly not on Mike's phone. And Mike wouldn't give her his phone in the first place—'

It falls to me to point out that she would, and he did. That he gave his phone to her during the speeches to take some photos, and she took advantage of the opportunity to send a message to Sarah, which she scheduled to arrive during dessert to avoid suspicion.

Sarah shakes her head. 'You're wrong.'

'Am I? You said yourself his message seemed a little odd. That you didn't think he'd want to meet you at the lake.'

She falls quiet, and I watch as she pats at her hair, takes it all in. 'But I don't understand!' she says eventually. 'Why would she do that?'

'Because she wants to strike a deal with you.'

'A deal? What sort of deal?'

'Well, money I suppose. In return for your silence.' I explain more fully, speaking quickly and without emotion about the night in Loch Ness. Giving only the barest facts. 'She wants your silence on Mike's nightmares, and the fact he carried the canoe to the loch. She wants you to promise not to go to the police.'

'But why? And why would I?' Her eyes are wide. 'If Mike is innocent, then what does it matter . . .'

'Because he might not *appear* innocent. The fact he didn't tell the police about carrying the canoe before, and that he, Alistair and Lewis didn't have the best relationship with Peter—'

'Didn't they?'

'No. Anyway, the point is, he might come under suspicion, if you go to the police, and so might my sister—'

'Aurelie? What does she have to do with any of this?'

I sigh. 'She – we – lied to the police about where she was that night. We said she was in the tent, but actually she was with Alistair.'

'Oh gosh.'

'She was fucking him in the boathouse.'

'Oh gosh!'

'Anyway, my mother's worried, that it will look bad for her. If you go to the police. And I think she might even be willing to pay you not to say anything.'

'Oh gosh, if your mother's worried about your sister, obviously I'll stay quiet. You don't need to give me cash!'

'Good,' I say. 'Because we're not going to.'

She takes a step back. 'Pardon?'

'We're not going to.'

She pats her hair again. 'But I thought—'

'My mother is willing to. But I'm not. Not after what you did to Jennifer.'

'Who?'

266

This is perhaps the worst thing she could have said. Not *what*, which would have been bad enough, or *when* – which at least would have shown she knew she'd committed multiple offences – but *who*. She made Jennifer's time at school a misery; she upended her entire *life*; and yet she can't even grant her the courtesy of memory. I reach into my bag, seek out the knife once more. 'Jennifer,' I repeat. 'My friend at school. The one who helped Aurelie after you overdosed her.'

'The swotty one?' A note of confusion enters her voice. Or perhaps it's panic. I hope it's panic. 'Is this about the homework? Look, I know I shouldn't have got her to do mine for me, but it was years ago—'

'It's not just the homework—'

'And I didn't overdose your sister. She ate one of Doug's hash brownies—'

'Look, it's not about the homework or the fucking hash brownies!' My voice is too loud, but I can't seem to dampen it. 'It's about you betraying Jennifer's trust!' I press down to extend the knife's blade again. 'It's your fault she was sent away!'

'I had nothing to do with her being sent away.'

'You told the authorities about her mum's job! Working illegally as a taxi driver.'

'No, I didn't! I didn't like Jennifer – I thought she was boring and big-headed – but I didn't tell any authorities anything. Why would I? Her mum could have been a prostitute for all I cared.' She tightens the strap of her dress. 'Maybe she was.'

'How can you be so fucking selfish! Not to care about those lives you upended, those lives you *destroyed*.' My teeth are knocking together, making it hard to speak. 'Perhaps you need to be forced to care.' I grip the knife harder within my bag. 'Perhaps I should slit your fucking throat.'

'Woah.' She takes a step back and raises her hands in the air. 'There's no need for that sort of language.'

'It's not just *language*. You should pay for what you've done.' I turn the knife from side to side in my hand, trying to summon the courage to lift it from my bag. But my arm is heavy and uncooperative.

'Stephanie!' Her voice has become high-pitched. 'You're acting really weirdly. I think you need to sober up a bit—'

'I'm not drunk.' My hand is still inside my bag, but my arm has begun to shake, so I use my left hand to stabilise it. 'I know exactly what I'm saying. You told the authorities about Jennifer's mother, and now you need to pay.'

'Will you stop going on about authorities, and paying!' She folds her arms across her chest, her lips squeezed tight together. 'I'm trying to be patient here, for Aurelie's sake, but you're acting kind of crazy. You need to pull yourself together.'

'What I need is the truth!' I scream this at her, my throat suddenly wide and raw.

She stares at me with something approaching disgust. 'Fine. If you really want to know who turned Jennifer's mum in, you should look a bit closer to home. Instead of accusing innocent people.'

My whole body is beginning to shake now, with hot, destructive anger, and I can't tell whether it's directed at her, for being so cruel, or at myself, for being so weak. I run one fingertip across the knife's blade, let it puncture my skin. 'So Aurelie made the call, but you were still with her,' I say, as my finger grows wet with blood. 'It makes no difference.'

'No, it wasn't Aurelie. It was your mother. I heard her, on the phone. Saying she wanted to report an illegal immigrant.'

'What?' I don't understand Sarah's words but I let myself imagine how it would feel to press my knife against her neck. To detect her pulse beneath the blade, the throb of her jugular vein. To pierce her individual cells, red and white, in their plasma broth.

'You're bleeding,' she says softly, and I realise that she's looking at my wrist, where a line of blood has dried.

'I'm fine,' I say, but she's already backing away.

'You need some help,' she says. 'Just stay here; I'm going to fetch you some help.' Her words are soft and rhythmical, whispering on the breeze as she turns and runs in the direction of the hotel. She enters the long grass, where she melds into the shadows, her heels clicking upon the hard earth. But she quickly grows smaller, fainter, quieter, until soon there is no sign of her at all.

For a couple of minutes, I continue to stare into the empty darkness, into the porous space between life and death. Then, with the knife still clutched in my hand, I wheel around.

And head toward the lake.

SATURDAY, 9.45 P.M.

She's on the jetty when I arrive, just like she planned. Standing with her back to me – a thin, hunched figure, looking out across the water.

'Mum,' I say, and she turns. Her gaze passes over my face for a couple of seconds, before travelling to the path behind me.

'Sarah's not coming,' I tell her.

My mother fiddles with the neckline of her dress. 'Don't worry, I'm sure she'll be here soon.'

'No, she won't.' There's a strange buzzing in my ears. 'I met her just now, in the meadow. And I sent her away.'

'What?' My mother looks puzzled.

'It's over. She's gone.'

'What?' Now she looks alarmed. 'What do you mean, she's gone? What did you say to her?'

I look at the lights illuminating the jetty, and out to the dark lake beyond. So calm and serene. But the buzzing in my ears won't shift. 'I told her not to say anything to the police about that night in Loch Ness. And she said she wouldn't.'

'And that's it?'

'What else do you want?' We're standing close together, but it feels as if there's a great distance between us. As if I'm hearing her through an old-fashioned tinny speaker.

'I want to *believe* her. I want to tie her into something which means she won't go back on what she's said.'

'That something is Aurelie,' I say.

She shakes her head, hitches her dress up. 'I don't understand.'

'She won't tell anyone what she knows because I told her it could harm Aurelie.'

'And you think that's enough?' She closes her eyes for a couple of seconds. 'I know the two of them have been friends for a long time but, even so . . . I'm not sure we can trust her.'

I run a foot across the planks of the jetty, feeling the uneven surface beneath my soles. 'It takes one to know one, I suppose.'

'What's that supposed to mean?'

The buzzing inside my head is getting louder. 'You didn't tell me the truth.'

'About what?'

'That you wanted my money. My inheritance.'

'What are you talking about?' Her eyes are unfocused but her voice is sharp. 'Has your father said something?'

'He said you wanted my money. Money owing to me in his will.'

She slaps her hands against her thighs. 'He's twisted the facts! Look, I'm sorry he said that to you. But it's not as if I'm trying to steal your money! I thought I might have to keep Sarah quiet by paying her, and it's not like I have any money; your father and Lucille saw to that.'

'But why *my* money?'

'Because you're the one in trouble.' She slumps down by a bollard, legs cast to one side. 'But I guess we've lost our chance now to make things better.'

'It depends what you consider "better".'

She flashes a look at me then, a look I can't quite decipher. I turn my face to the sky, to the stars bringing light from the distant past. 'Why did you never tell me I have a brother?'

271

When I look back at her, her face is deathly pale. Just like Mike's when I confronted him earlier. The family connection suddenly obvious. 'How did you—'

I tell her about my conversation with Jane and she thumps her fist upon the jetty. 'It wasn't her place to say! I was trying to tell you, earlier, on the way into the hall, but then the speeches began.' She moves her fist to her leg, tries to thump again, but her hand flops down on to her thigh. 'I wanted to explain my side of the story, to answer your questions. I still do. But my priority has always been to protect our family. And my relationship to Mike doesn't change that.'

'Doesn't it?'

'No.'

'Are you sure?' I press my hands to my head, try to block out the noise inside. 'Sarah said he had a nightmare, about taking the canoe to the loch. About Peter drowning. And I think that's what you overheard, that day at the dress fitting. That's why you sent me your letter—'

'No.' She shakes her head from side to side, like a dog trying to get dry.

But I can't leave it there; I need to know. Whether this has just been about Mike or whether . . . 'Do you deny it?' I ask.

'Look, Mike's too sensitive for his own good.'

'But is that what you overheard Sarah saying? The stuff about Mike and the canoe?'

'Yes.'

The buzzing in my head recedes a little.

'But Mike didn't do anything wrong!' my mother goes on. 'He just lost a bet with Alistair and Lewis, that's all. A bet which meant he agreed to meet Peter, to get the canoe from the boathouse for the two of them. He was strong, physically, even back then. But he didn't drown anyone. He was waiting for Peter, by the loch,

272

early that evening, when I came along. And I was so furious with your father for leaving – for prioritising his affair over our family holiday – that I told Mike the truth, right then and there. That I was his mother.'

'And?'

'And nothing.' She runs one hand across her now-flowerless wig. 'I mean, he kicked the canoe a couple of times, because he was angry, but didn't do any major damage; he can't be held responsible for what came after. I persuaded him to leave the loch, long before Peter appeared. To come to the pub with me, to talk everything through. And then, well, you know what happened next.'

'So you *are* protecting him,' I say. 'That's what your whole plan has been about. Protecting Mike. You roped me in under false pretences, and tried to use my money to keep him safe.'

'Is that honestly what you think is going on?'

And just like that, the buzzing is back, with renewed force. I want to answer, but the words won't quite form.

'Listen, Stephanie,' she says, and I notice her eyes are bright, even in the darkness. 'I *am* protecting Mike, because he was the one who took the canoe to the loch. Maybe he even damaged the canoe. And I'm also protecting Aurelie, because she didn't tell the police the truth. Because she wasn't in the tent when you claimed she was. But the main person I'm protecting isn't either of them. It's you.'

'What?' I'm not sure if I'm speaking, or just hearing the question inside my head. 'I don't—'

'Stop it!' she says. 'Just stop with all your bullshit. For once! I found your wet clothes that night, by the foot of your sleeping bag. Your fleece jacket and pyjamas, all completely saturated. Stained with mud.'

'That doesn't—'

'After the police came to the campsite, I destroyed them. Kept my mouth shut and prayed the whole thing would blow over.

Panicked every time I heard a siren, every time I saw a police car. It took a couple of years before I was able to breathe normally again. But then, just as I thought it was all safely in the past, you end up living next door to the boy's parents, and when Sarah started gossiping about Mike, about that night, I couldn't bear it, couldn't bear the thought of my dying and not being able to protect you.'

'I don't need protecting.'

'For heaven's sake, Stephanie! You can deny the truth to every-one else, including yourself if you must, but you can't deny it to me. I know you were with him.'

'I don't know who—'

'Yes, you do!' My mother's eyes are moist with tears which haven't yet fallen. 'I'm talking about the poor boy who disappeared. About *Peter*. It's time you told me what happened to him.'

◆ ◆ ◆

July 2005

I am all alone. My mother left a couple of hours ago, full of wine and rage, and now Aurelie has gone too, but quietly, has slipped from her sleeping bag and tiptoed out into the night. I considered calling after her but didn't know what to say – whether to plead with her to stay or shout at her for leaving.

Yet she'd have left either way. Everyone always does. My father, my mother, Jennifer. I've come to realise my mother is right: I can't keep people close. I'm a wraith, a phantom, an entity which grazes other people's lives, but never touches them properly.

The wind is picking up now, keening like a mournful dog and snapping at the edges of the tent. I pull my sleeping bag tight but can't get warm. The ground feels harder than usual, and when I try to sleep I can't stop thinking about the friction between my eyes and eyelids, so

I stop trying and unzip my sleeping bag. Pull tracksuit bottoms and a fleece jacket over my pyjamas. Put on socks, trainers and gloves. And now, dressed, it seems pointless to stay in the tent any longer.

It's not as if anyone will miss me.

So I leave too; zip everything up and walk past the other tents, head bowed against the gathering wind, on to the track which leads to the boathouse. Rain mists my skin as I walk, and strands of hair blow into my mouth, make me spit. The moon is full but thick clouds press in upon it like unwanted hands, reaching and smothering, and I wish I'd brought a torch.

The boathouse is a small stone building with a corrugated iron roof, which would be unobtrusive against the stony shore were it not for its doors, which are painted in a shiny icecap blue, almost pearlescent. Usually the doors are padlocked but there's no padlock now, only a gap where the doors should meet in the middle. The right-hand door ever so slightly open. I walk toward its blueness, feet placed noiselessly on the ground, and put my face to the gap.

I can hear them, first: strange moans, like echoes of the intensifying wind, and heavy breathing, grunts, rustling. And then, once my eyes have adjusted to the darkness, I can see them too. Or, more accurately, I can see Alistair's buttocks, bare and pale, bouncing in the gloom. The expanse of his back, clawed by Aurelie's hands, and his shoulders, tensed to support his weight. Their lips seek one another stickily, noisily.

The rain falls harder, magnified by the metal roof into a hammering. Alistair's head moves down Aurelie's body, mapping the contours of her chest with a diligence that makes me flush. When his teeth close round a nipple, I have to look away, turn my attention to the wooden rowing boat which lies beyond the couple, with an old net strewn across its base. With a metal oarlock on either side, and two slabs of wood for seats. There are some life jackets on a shelf above, loosely piled together.

I should go. But as I start to back out, I knock against a metal bucket, which rattles so loudly that I stop where I am, knowing I must

275

have been heard, that my presence is about to be uncovered. But when I return my gaze to the couple, I realise they're still engrossed in one another and haven't noticed me at all. That they're beyond me. That, whatever I do, they'll always be beyond me. That I'm forever condemned to be an outsider, looking in.

I stumble from the boathouse, no longer trying to be quiet. Perhaps this is freedom: the inability to leave an imprint. The rain is coming down thickly now, blowing in sheets, and I begin to run through it, welcoming the way it slaps my cheeks and stings my eyes. I run faster along the path – heart pounding, breath pulled from my lungs – beyond the campsite and down to the shores of the loch, where I stop, panting.

'Hello?' A voice from the wilds. The surface of the loch is roiling from the onslaught of wind and rain.

'Hello?' Louder this time. I turn to see a man watching me. He is young – very young, still practically a boy – with a tall, gangling body and smooth pink cheeks.

So I can be seen after all. Unless this is a trick. Or perhaps the man-boy is also wandering the shadowy realms between the living and the dead. 'What are you doing?' I ask.

'I'm about to look for the monster.' He nods with a mass of wet, wavy hair toward a canoe on the bank. It's old and battered, with a dark green, mud-streaked exterior. A couple of paddles are propped up against the larger of two plastic seats.

'You don't need a canoe to find a monster.'

He rubs his hand across the bridge of his nose. 'But Loch Ness has the best monster. The one everyone is desperate to find.'

'I don't think you can have a best monster. Unless you mean a most monstrous monster. The Platonic ideal of a monster.'

He ignores my comment. 'Did you know that the first written account of the Loch Ness monster dates back to 565 AD?'

'No.'

'But even before then, people made carvings of it. Of a creature with flippers.'

The wind is becoming stronger, the surface of the water choppier. The branches of a nearby tree swing from side to side, scratching at the sky.

'But it's unlikely to actually have flippers. What's more likely is it's some kind of giant eel. People used to think the monster was a plesiosaur, an ancient reptile, but that theory's been discredited by scientists. The sonar studies didn't find anything which fit, and plesiosaurs like warmer water. They've also been extinct for sixty-five million years. But eels . . . they still exist and could, potentially, grow unusually large.'

There was a pause. 'So are you going to go out, then?' The wind is cutting through my wet fleece, biting my skin. 'To find the enormous eel?'

'I don't know. I'm meant to be meeting someone but they're late. And the weather's not looking so good. I think perhaps I'll give it five minutes and, if they don't come, I'll go back to my aunt's house.'

'I'll go with you.' His isn't the company I'd choose, but it's company nonetheless. And there's something appealing in the idea of immersing myself in the storm.

But his eyes have widened. 'You want to come to my aunt's house? I'm not sure she'll—'

'No. I'll come with you in the canoe. To find the monster.'

He brushes his hair away from his forehead. 'I don't know . . . It's getting late and . . . the weather . . .' His hair falls back as soon as he releases it.

'Fine.' But it isn't fine; it's damning. That not even a freakish man-boy wants to spend time with me. 'I'll go myself.' I start to push the canoe into the loch.

'Wait, no! You can't just take the canoe!'

But it seems that I can. I yank off my trainers and socks and clamber in, sit on the central seat and use one of the paddles to lever myself away from the bank. As I gain buoyancy, the man-boy's round face seems to crumple in upon itself – all his features converging upon his nose – until, with a great wobbling of the canoe, he lands behind me. I hand him a paddle, and move up to the smaller seat in the bow so he can take the bigger one at the stern.

'We haven't got life jackets,' he says.

I don't respond, just use my paddle to take long, sweeping strokes. There's something soothing about it, even though the water itself is far from calm; it churns as if we're at sea, causing the canoe to pitch and roll.

'The conditions are rough,' he says.

'All the better for finding monsters,' I reply, as the nose of the canoe hits a wave, soaking me with water. The audacious coldness of it – across my chest, down my legs and between my bare toes – is restorative. I begin to paddle harder, faster, wanting to get away from the shore, into the expanse of the loch proper.

'That's not right.' He has to shout to make himself heard above the wind. 'There have been more sightings in calm conditions than stormy ones. Although that might be because more people are on the water when conditions are good. Also, Loch Ness is prone to mirages in calmer weather.'

He goes on to explain how the temperature of the water varies at different depths, causing illusions, but I stop listening. I can barely hear him anyway, over the sound of rain hitting the loch – water meeting water – and the howls of the wind, whipping this reunion into something frenzied, which slams into the canoe and tips us up, down, sideways, like a wild horse desperate to unseat us. I've read the tales of the water-horses, or kelpies, who lived in Scotland's waterways and were capable of shapeshifting. It's said they adopted beautiful forms, both human and animal, to lure their victims into the deep.

'We should go back.' I don't know when it happened, but the man-boy's voice has switched from flat to urgent. As I try to remember, a bolt *of lightning cracks the sky, illuminating the savage beauty with a brief, dazzling burst of energy that makes me feel I too am elemental. I rise to my feet, hold my paddle aloft and yell into the void.*

'Sit down!' comes the voice from behind me.

I turn but remain standing. My mind is a force, my body a force field. 'You wanted to find the monster,' I remind him.

'Sit down!' He is screaming now: a horrible, grating sound. 'You need to sit down!'

'But we can find it. Can't you feel its presence?'

'You need to sit down!'

I don't understand why he has to shout. The storm is magnificent but his bleating is like a bleed to the brain, ruining the moment. 'Can't you be quiet?' I say.

'Not until you sit down!'

'But just feel it,' I implore him. 'Feel the energy, all around us—'

'What's wrong with you!'

His words come like a gut punch. What's wrong with you, what's wrong with you, what's wrong with you. *Always the same: the words reverberating across the years from the lips of Aunt Jane, Sarah and the other pupils at school. From Aurelie, my father, my mother: the people who were supposed to love me the most. But they don't care, none of them care; they don't want me around but they've sent away the one person who did . . .*

'Be quiet,' I beg him. 'Please. Just be quiet.'

'I don't want to be here!' He starts to cry and the sound is unbearable, even worse than his screaming. 'I don't want to be here!'

'Shut up!' I say.

But he doesn't shut up: he says it again, and a fourth time – snot-filled and choking – and I put my hands over my ears, but I can still hear him, can still hear his pained noises, and I beg him to stop, but he doesn't, and it's never going to end, it's incessant—

'Shut the fuck up!' I spin toward him and smack my paddle into the side of his head. For one brief, perfect second he goes quiet, rolling his head into his hands, but then he is whimpering, and I'm reaching out to hit him again, and the canoe is tipping . . .

And then, an icy darkness. Opaque, spinning: a plunge into Hades. Hands clutching at nothing, limbs heavy, being dragged against their will, eyes unseeing. No smell, no light. No familiar axes, no knowledge of this chasm. No breath, no breath, no breath.

A sudden realisation that this is the end.

Until it isn't. My head comes above water and I drink in the air, before going under again, and up – another breath – and under, and on it goes, breath-water-breath, and as I become oriented I see the banks of the loch are not too distant, are reachable if I swim; and I throw my body into motion, fight as I'm sucked down, keep swimming, kick and kick and kick, pull through the water with my arms, my shoulders burning; and then there's stone under my fingers and I haul myself on to the shore and lie, gasping, deadened but not dead.

When I can move again I sit up, look out across the water. But there's no sign of the man-boy. No sign of the canoe. Nothing but the wind-whipped waves and a line of moonlight across them.

A mirage, I think. I've imagined it all. Except wasn't he the one to tell me of the mirages?

I begin to shiver, just a little at first, and then violently, more spasm than shiver, my teeth knocking together uncontrollably, tearing my tongue. I can taste blood as I stumble back to the tent, my feet block-like and clumsy.

No one is inside. No one to help peel the clothes from my numb body, to assist in distinguishing between fantasy and reality. So I unpeel myself – slowly, laboriously – before dropping my clothes in a heap at the foot of my roll mat and finding others. Warm, dry layers: as many as possible in a desperate bid to stop the shivering.

Encased in multiple tops and trousers, I clamber into my sleeping bag, secure its hood around my head. The storm is still raging – the tent flapping and straining to be free of its poles – and a rapacious coldness sits at my core, devouring any embers of bodily warmth before they can catch and spread. I roll from side to side and rub at my limbs, trying to restore life.

But of course that's beyond me. The preserve of myth, of storytelling. The only place where death can be reversed.

◆ ◆ ◆

So, at last: I have an answer. My mother knows I wasn't in the tent. She knows I went out in the rain and the mud all those years ago. I watch her watching me, tears upon her cheeks. Ever since she sent me her letter, I've been wondering, turning over in my head what she wrote. *You, more than anyone, should understand what's at stake here.* I chose to believe she meant I was more perceptive than other members of our family – but, deep down, I suppose I knew that wasn't the case. Why else would I have dragged myself six hundred miles to Berkshire to endure a weekend with my narcissistic, rotten family, if not for my own, equally rotten, protection?

She is still looking at me, so I decide to confess, tell her everything which happened that fateful night. When I finish, she reaches a hand toward me. 'Why did you never tell me this before?'

'You never asked.'

'Oh, Stephanie. I hate to think of you, carrying that knowledge around, alone. Making everything so much worse for everyone. If we'd gone to the police straight away, it might have been all right. Might have saved us all this anguish.' She lifts the skirt of her dress to her face, wipes it across her eyes. 'It's always better to tell the truth.'

'Says the woman who's made an art form out of lying.'

'That's not fair! I should have told you earlier about Mike, but it was difficult for me, to admit to such a failing. To admit I let Jane talk me out of raising him. But you have to remember how young I was. When I—'

'And how about your other failures? Your other lies?'

'Are you talking about your father's will again? It was for your own—'

'No. Lan's job. Sarah said it was you who told the authorities about it, who got Lan and Jennifer sent away.'

My mother's jaw twitches. 'Sarah says a lot of things—'

'She *heard* you. On the phone.'

'And you believe her?'

Do I believe her? Have I found the second answer I've been seeking? Until this moment I couldn't say, but now, looking at my mother – at the redness in her cheeks, at the way her eyes catch mine, both pleading and defiant – I am gripped by certainty. The registrar's voice sounding loud and clear inside my head. *Do you, at long last, see your mother for who she truly is?*

I do.

Do you accept she twists the truth to ensnare those she claims to love?

I do.

Do you believe she betrayed Jennifer, and tore her from you? That, by taking away the one person who could have made you happy, she sent you into a spiral of despair, culminating in tragedy that summer's night at Loch Ness?

'I do,' I say. 'I totally fucking do.'

SATURDAY, 9.55 P.M.

'Stephanie.' She uses a bollard to haul herself to her feet. Stands crookedly for a couple of seconds before taking a step toward me, one arm extended. I can't tell whether it's a gesture of apology, or a way to maintain her balance. 'I'm sorry. I'm so sorry. If I'd known, about Jennifer, that you loved her, I never would have . . .'

I stand up too. 'What? Never would have what?'

'Reported her mother.'

'So why did you?' I press my hands together, palm to palm, hard enough to hurt. 'Just to wreck a bunch of lives?'

'Of course not!' Her eyes are lit from within. 'I wasn't thinking! I was too caught up in my own issues, didn't think through the consequences. All I can say is I regret it every day, nearly as much as I regret giving up Mike. I'm a weak person, Stephanie – so very, very weak!'

There is a pain at my core, as if something has come unstuck inside me. It sends waves of heat through my body, to my every extremity: my tongue becomes thick and swollen, my fingers twitch and my scalp prickles. My eyes are dry, my legs unsteady.

'But I did it for love!' She turns and hobbles to the end of the jetty, looks out across the lake. 'Love can make all of us weak.'

I blink and swallow, saliva catching in my throat.

'I thought your father was having an affair,' she goes on, turning back toward me.

'He was.' My voice is raspy. 'But that had nothing to do with Lan.'

'Except it did, because I got it all wrong! I thought he was having an affair with her, not Lucille!'

'Jennifer's mother?'

'Yes.'

'Why?'

'Because she was everything I wasn't. Accomplished, pretty, poised.' She is speaking rapidly, flinging out her words. 'I knew something was going on with someone, and he was forever talking about Lan, singing her praises.'

'So . . . you . . .' My scalp is prickling more strongly now, as if my hair itself is crawling. I touch one hand to it, rake my nails across its surface.

'I didn't know what else to do. I desperately wanted your father to stay – for your and Aurelie's sake as well as mine – but knew he wanted to be elsewhere. That someone else had come between us, and was preventing us from being happy. So when you told me about the night of Aurelie's cannabis overdose – that Lan was driving a taxi, illegally – I saw a way out, and I grasped it.'

Scratch. Scratch. If you scratch skin hard enough, you'll draw blood.

I walk toward the end of the jetty. Toward her.

'But I never thought it through. What would happen. And when I realised Lan wasn't the one your father was seeing, I was devastated. I still cry about it now.'

It's not enough. Not for what she's done to Lan, and Jennifer, who gain nothing from her tears. Not enough for what she's done to me.

What I did to Peter.

284

Heat continues to course through my body but more strongly now, as if my very bones are molten.

My mother smiles sadly as I draw closer. 'We're so similar, you and I,' she says.

'No.' The heat is rising through my neck, into my head.

'We are,' she insists. 'Think about it. When we love, we love intensely. Perhaps too intensely, perhaps more fiercely than others love us.'

'No!'

'And it can make us capable of terrible things. Dark acts, and darker secrets.'

I shake my head.

'But it doesn't mean we're bad people. How can it, when we're motivated by love?'

I walk right up to her, stare into the face which threatens to reflect mine. 'I'm nothing like you. I don't set out to destroy other people's lives.'

'You're responsible for Peter's death.'

I shake my head again. The heat is making me dizzy, nauseated. 'I was only fifteen! I had nobody. You all left me—'

'And you left him.'

'It's not the same.'

'It is,' she says, touching a hand to my shoulder. 'But don't worry, I get it. I'm part of you, and you're part of me, and I understand you. Whatever happens, you'll always be my angel.'

The heat ignites and my hand flies forward; shoves her hard, in the very centre of her chest. 'I'm not your fucking angel!'

For the briefest of moments it is she who looks like an angel: her face haloed by the light of the bollard, arms outstretched; a beatific smile upon her face.

But then she is falling, falling, her body folding in upon itself as she tumbles through the air, and her head hits the jetty with a crunch, turns sideways, slumps down behind the rest of her. The water rends itself in two to welcome her in. Swallows her whole, before spitting her back to the surface, face down, wig fanned out like an aurora.

She stays in that position, unmoving, and I watch her, unmoved. We are motionless for what could be seconds, minutes, hours. Time is meaningless now, warped beyond all reckoning. She floats in the water and I float too, beyond myself. Untethered from the world.

Free at last.

SATURDAY, 10 P.M.

It's only when time snaps back, linear and unforgiving, that I real-ise: I have killed my mother.

I let out a full-blown scream and jump into the lake. I am dimly aware of it being cold, of my dress becoming heavy and my trainers filling with water, but none of that matters; I have to reach her. I thrash through the lake to her floating form and flip her over, but her face shows no signs of life. Her eyes are unseeing, her lips faintly blue.

I put an arm around her shoulders and drag her toward the water's edge. But I need my arms to hold her and to swim, so I roll on to my back with my arms around her neck, kick to move us. But my legs become tangled in material, and I get a mouthful of wig.

'Stephanie!'

A voice is calling but I'm unable to look, so I keep swimming, my face slapped by the water, my arms clasped around my mother's neck.

'Stephanie!' There is a splashing now, from behind me, and then another pair of arms – slender, bare, a bracelet round one wrist – grabs hold of my mother too. The help which Sarah must have fetched. 'You can stand here,' the voice says.

I should understand, but I don't.

'You can stand up; it's shallow here.'

I take in a large mouthful of water, begin to splutter.

'Stephanie, stand up!'

This time I get it: I shift into a vertical position and make contact with the bottom of the lake. Straighten my body and stand; feel warm air upon my face and neck.

See my sister beside me, submerged from the waist down. Her veil trailing in the water.

'It's my fault,' I say.

'Shh.' My sister tugs our mother toward her. 'Let's get her to the bank. You take one side and I'll take the other.'

I do as she says. Together, we wade the remaining metres to the water's edge, pulling our mother between us. And then Alistair comes splashing in, hoists our mother over his shoulder and carries her to dry land. Lies her flat. Puts his ear to her chest, tips her head back and starts to perform CPR.

Aurelie walks across to him, places a hand in his hair. 'Ally,' she says.

He looks up at her and she shakes her head.

'Are you sure?' He continues to deliver chest compressions.

'I'm sure. It's what she wants.'

'I've called an ambulance, and they're coming, but they say it will take a while to get here—'

My sister shakes her head again. 'She doesn't want to die in a hospital; she wants to die with us.'

He returns his mouth to our mother's. 'Ally!' Aurelie says, more sharply. 'Please!'

This time, he sits back. Rubs his face and nods. Reaches an arm to Aurelie's legs.

'It's because of me,' I say. 'It's my fault.'

'Don't be ridiculous.' My sister crouches beside our mother, takes one of her hands in her own.

'You weren't there.'

'Shh, Stephanie. This is what she wanted. Here, take her other hand.'

Once again, I do as my sister tells me. My mother's hand already feels cold. I stroke her knuckles and nails, then the pads of her fingers, where I try to trace the whorls.

'Rest in peace, Mum,' Aurelie whispers.

'I'm sorry,' I say. 'I've messed up so badly.'

'No, you haven't.' My sister's voice is firm. 'You're here, when it matters. To say goodbye. Mum loves you, and she knows you love her.'

'I wasn't talking about her.'

'Then what are you talking about?'

'You.'

'What?'

'All this time,' I say. 'I thought it was you and Sarah. Who told the authorities about Lan. Who got Jennifer sent away. But it was her.'

'Don't worry about that at the mo—'

'I refused to believe you when you said you knew nothing about it. Wouldn't speak to you, wouldn't reply to your messages.'

'Stephanie, we can talk about this another—'

'I'm trying to tell you I'm sorry! I'm still angry about the way you treated me at school, but I shouldn't have—'

'Shh. As you say, it's not as if I've acted perfectly, either.' She kneels up to extend her free hand to me, across our mother's body, and I notice the lower part of her dress is stained green-brown from the lake. Just like my fleece was, that night at the loch.

'I've ruined your dress,' I say. 'I've ruined your beautiful dress!'

'Oh Stephanie, I don't care about the bloody dress.'

'But it's silk!' I say, as I take her hand.

And, for the first time in sixteen years, I start to cry.

SATURDAY, AFTER 10 P.M.

After that, the night shatters into fragments: slow pieces which contain multitudes, and others which pass so fast my memory can barely cling to them.

Slow: the smell of lake water and roses. My body shivering as tears run down my cheeks without pause, as I clutch at the ground with numb, splayed fingers. My sister, conferring with Alistair and then leading me to bed. The rough edges of the pills she gives me, which I pretend to swallow, but spit out when she's not looking.

Fast: my getting out of bed again once she's gone. Rinsing my face of its tear stains, pulling on a jumper and running to the car park, thinking I'm too late, that I've missed Fiona. The spasm of dreadful relief as I see her emerge from the shadows.

Slow: the conversation which unfolds. When I say I have information for her but need to leave the hotel to impart it. The scepticism on her face as I gesture to my car. Asking if I'm in a fit state to drive, leading me to think my mother's death is writ large upon me, that I haven't rinsed the tears sufficiently, or am shivering again. The realisation she's talking about whether I'm too drunk to drive. My response that I had one glass of champagne, eight hours ago, and the funny way she looks at me – her features unnaturally still – before she gets into the car. The age it takes for her to close the door and fasten her seat belt.

Slow: our journey out of the car park and along the hotel driveway. The discipline it takes to adhere to the 10mph speed limit, when I know an ambulance could arrive at any moment, snatching this opportunity away.

'So,' she asks. 'What do you want to tell me?'

Fast: the decision on what to divulge. And slow: the matter of divulging it. That Mike had agreed to meet Peter that night. That he carried the canoe out to the loch before leaving, to go to the pub with my mother.

'Why?'

Slow: the explanation of Mike losing a bet with Alistair and Lewis. How the three men had been taunting Peter about hunting the Loch Ness monster, and Mike was the one who had to follow through.

'No,' she says. 'Why did Mike go to the pub with your mother?'

More explanations. More drawn-out words as we creep along the drawn-out driveway. That Mike is my mother's son. That she gave him up as baby, when she was still a teenager, but went on holiday to see him. That she told him the truth that night.

Slow: the silence which follows.

Fast: the fluttering of my pulse. A hummingbird trapped in a fist.

Slow: the wheels turning, as we make it out of the hotel driveway at last, on to the road proper. The night air thick with the opposite of promise.

'So, according to you, your mother was with Mike that night, and your sister was with Alistair?'

I nod.

'And your father?'

'Away with work. Aka cheating on my mother.'

She inclines her head. 'And you?'

Slow, slow, slow. The glance of headlights across the tarmac.

'I was in the tent.'

'All night?'

I nod again – slow – and can sense her looking at me.

'Without an alibi?'

Slow: I stare straight ahead, along the dark, empty road. 'Why would I need an alibi?'

Silence, elongated.

'Stephanie, let me ask you something.' Her voice has grown quiet, more precise. 'Why are you taking time out of your sister's wedding to tell me this?'

Fast: the knowledge that one thread can unravel all the others. 'Because I think you deserve to know the truth.'

'But you don't even know me.'

'I know your sister.'

'Why do you know her?'

Slow: 'I don't know what you mean. I'm part of her artist residency.'

'But why, Stephanie? Why did you choose to do an artist residency with *Kirsty*, the mother of *Peter*?'

There's no good answer to this.

'Stephanie?'

I shrug. 'Fate, I guess.'

'Fate?' Her voice is cold.

'I was drawn to her.'

'By what?'

'By our shared history. By the symmetries.'

'But you don't have a shared history.' Agonisingly slow: the words branding themselves, one by one, across every cell in my body. 'She lost her son, and you've lost . . . what exactly?'

Fast: the assortment of answers I could give, tumbling round and round in my brain like a fruit machine. My best friend (cherry), my mother (cherry), the love of my family (cherry). *Ding, ding, ding: you've won the fucking jackpot!* My innocence. My sanity. My moral compass.

Fast: the cry of a siren in the distance. *Be quiet. Please. Just be quiet.* The speed of the car as I press down upon the accelerator.

Faster: the flicker of blue in the night sky. The crescendo of the siren, to a full-throated scream. The snapshot of fear on Fiona's face as she tells me to slow down, to pull over.

Faster still: the appearance of the ambulance around the corner and the inevitability of my car, hurtling toward it. A swerve, a wall, a crunch.

Terminal velocity.

MARCH 2018

The queue to get through security is long; it winds back and forth in a tight coil, before splitting into six shorter queues at the front. I stand in line with my wheelie case in one hand and my phone and documents in the other, making sure I'm ready. I can't bear it when people queue for an age without readying themselves, only to rummage in their bags for the relevant documents once they reach the desk. Forcing everyone else to wait longer. It's the equivalent of those drivers who insist on changing lanes in stationary traffic, and wonder why no one's going anywhere.

There's a ding on my phone. It's a message from my sister, with a photo attached. A grainy black-and-white image of a kidney bean with a number of protuberances. *It's a boy!* the message reads, and I peer at my screen, try to work out which protuberance has led to this conclusion.

Aurelie and I have been on better terms since her wedding. Which, admittedly, isn't saying much. But it's strange how being in a car accident has rendered me more tolerable in my sister's eyes. How proximity to death has made me more alive to her. Or perhaps it's actual death which is responsible. The weight of our bereavement, coupled with the actions we've had to take. Notifying government departments, making funeral arrangements, getting in touch with utility companies, insurers, banks.

Or maybe I'm simply giving her the benefit of the doubt, because I feel guilty for ruining her wedding. And because she's been surprisingly forgiving about the whole debacle, insisting none of it was my fault. That our mother would have died even if the ambulance hadn't been waylaid by my crash. That what happened was terrible – tragedy layered upon tragedy, a millefeuille of misfortune – but it has made her realise how fleeting and precious life is. How lucky she is to have Alistair and the rest of us, and a baby on the way.

Exciting, I write back now.

The funeral was held at a crematorium a few miles outside Bristol: a squat brick building set in extensive grounds. Lots of green areas but nothing too fancy: a couple of lawns, some trees, a small stream with a Japanese-style footbridge across it. The service itself went smoothly, except for when Aunt Jane insisted on singing 'The Way We Were', her eyes closed in deathly rapture and her black hat quivering. But the wake was more trying, full of people I didn't know, who had clearly only come for the food and gossip. 'We're so sorry for your loss,' one woman mumbled to me, and then, in the same quiche-filled mouthful, trying not to smile or splutter pastry, 'but I hear you have a new brother now!' Others wanted to talk about my broken leg or my mother's last moments: how sad it was; how brave she'd been. 'I admire her enormously,' one elderly man said to me from above a slab of carrot cake. 'It takes great resolve to end things in the way she did, rather than letting the illness take her down.'

The police had found her suicide note the night she died. In an envelope on the desk in her room, written on Goreton Manor notepaper in black ballpoint ink. It was used at the inquest, as evidence of premeditation. Evidence of motive came from her doctor, who confirmed she had stage four lung cancer, and from Aunt Jane, who told the court what our mother had said to her just hours before she died. *It's time to get things settled.*

The post-mortem was consistent with suicide too. Death by drowning, with a trauma to the head that had most likely been caused by falling. There was some bruising around our mother's ribs and shoulders, and some foreign hair, but this matched with the testimonies from me, Aurelie and Alistair, that we had pulled her out of the lake, and Alistair had attempted CPR.

My phone dings again. *He's as big as a banana now!*

I make sure my passport is open at the right page, and switch off my phone.

◆ ◆ ◆

The metal detector beeps as I walk through. I check the pockets of my tracksuit bottoms for keys, coins or other paraphernalia. A security guard scans me, and I worry I might have left my utility knife in the pocket of my hoodie. But she waves me away with a bored grunt.

So on I go, breathing more normally again, into the glare of duty-free. Past the shops with giant teddies and red phone boxes, the empty perfume boutiques, the endless shelves of alcohol, chocolate and cigarettes. I stop to look at a display of designer sunglasses, at the aviators and cat's eyes. When Aurelie and I were children, we liked to compete to find the most expensive item in any given shop, and I think about trying again now, on my own, but am distracted by a pair of bug-like glasses. The type worn by Jackie Onassis and Hollywood stars. And also by my sister, on the day we scattered our mother's ashes.

It was a sunny day, so the glasses weren't a total incongruity. One of those bright autumn days when the usual murk of existence has been peeled from the sky. The trees were honey gold, burnt orange, crimson, their colours made doubly glorious by the water's reflection. As we took it in turns to sprinkle handfuls from the urn – watching the flecks flutter into the loch and shine, like fish scales, among the mirrored leaves and branches – it seemed we were delivering our mother to an underwater forest. A place of enchantment, where kelpies did indeed live and lure. We didn't speak while we scattered, but I played 'Blackbird' on a portable speaker, and passed tissues to Aurelie when her sniffs threatened to overwhelm McCartney's vocals.

Mike didn't come. He didn't come to the funeral either. Aunt Jane disapproved of this, but I understood.

He shares a quarter of my genes, after all.

◆ ◆ ◆

As soon as my gate number is posted, I hurry down the corridors and on to the bank of chairs at the far end. Only three other passengers are already here: a man with a briefcase, and a young couple sharing a jumbo bag of Ready Salted crisps. I gaze out of the window, at planes being filled with luggage, and those taxiing to the runway, readying themselves for take-off.

I've met up with Mike a couple of times since the wedding. Once with Aurelie in London, when I used my crutches to limp to a coffee shop in Paddington, for a 'getting to know you' session. Which was awkward because Aurelie and Mike already knew each other well, but on an entirely different basis. Nearly every time there was an extended silence – and there were many – Aurelie couldn't help but squeal about how weird it was that her husband was best mates with her brother, or that her brother had had sex with her oldest friend. And each time she proceeded to blush, and giggle, and play with the foam on her cappuccino, while I stared into the depths of my glass of milk (and Mike probably wished he'd ordered something larger than a cortado).

The second time was easier, as my leg was no longer in plaster, and Aurelie wasn't there. It was just me and Mike, at a pub in Inverness. I'd returned north to collect my things from White Croft, and messaged him to say I was in the area. At which point he messaged back, suggesting a drink the same evening. I agreed, and promptly wished I hadn't; but when I turned up ten minutes before the allotted time to drink a double gin for courage, I found him already in a booth in the corner, one pint down.

We didn't say much to each other that night, but enjoyed a companionable silence while we drank. What little talking we did do revolved around the Highlands: the tourist hordes at Eilean Donan Castle; the towering cliffs of Skye. The morning light over Ullapool harbour, when the sun cracks through cool mauve clouds to spill across the water.

I never did make it back inside White Croft. I drove there the day after my drinks with Mike, stopped the car on the lane outside to look upon its thick stone walls and square windows. Thought of my canvases propped up in the studio, of my two drawers of clothing, and of Kirsty, unable to sleep.

But then I drove away, thinking of that physics maxim: *For every action in nature there is an equal and opposite reaction.* Because Fiona will never wake up again.

◆ ◆ ◆

September 2017

It turns out forging someone's writing is a lot like riding a bike. A skill which becomes rusty if left unused, but doesn't disappear. I practise in my sketch pad first: rebuild my confidence with looping 'y's and spiky 'k's, both trademarks of my mother's hand. Write out the quick brown fox jumps over the lazy dog *and am pleased with the result, the letters thick and dark.*

I don't have long. The wedding is starting in the Darwin Hall in half an hour, and I haven't yet changed. My green tunic is waiting for me, hanging from my wardrobe door like a corpse on a gibbet. Looking at it, the questions balloon inside my head. Can murder ever be merciful? And isn't premeditation simply the byproduct of a cautious mind, an insurance policy which might never need to be cashed? Why, then, does the law deem it preferable to kill without it? To take a life without thought or purpose?

It's just common sense to be cautious. If my mother knows the truth about Peter's death, it will be better for everyone if she takes it to her grave, instead of spilling it through a lapse into drunkenness or clumsy attempts at protection. And if her grave is already partly dug, then would it be so terrible simply to finish the job? To send her on her way swiftly and cleanly? Might that, perhaps, even be kinder than leaving her to shudder through every last breath?

I turn to the headed notepaper. Write the date a couple of inches below the hotel's name, taking my time on the curves of 'September'. After which I pause, unsure what greeting would be appropriate. To Whom This May Concern? *Too formal.* Hi? *Too far the other way. I turn several options over in my mind, before eventually settling on one which seems to strike the right balance of warmth and gravitas.*

Dear Family . . .

Seat 29A is a good one: by the window, not too close to the toilets, sufficient room to stop my bad leg from seizing up. Not over the wing either, so I should get a decent view. I'm looking forward to seeing the world by night: the constellations of city lights and the voids of uninhabited land. The curve of the Earth's shadow in the sky as we chase the dawn.

As the other passengers file on, I speculate as to who will sit next to me. A woman with a screaming baby stops nearby and I try not to grimace. That could be Aurelie soon, I tell myself. I should be understanding.

Yet no amount of understanding stops me from exhaling in relief when she moves on down the aisle. The flight is eleven hours long, after all.

Eventually, a Chinese couple takes the two seats beside me. They are speaking Mandarin to one another at the moment, which bodes well; I can let their voices wash over me while I read, or sleep, or gaze out at foreign lands.

A short while later, the safety briefing begins. I reach for the in-flight magazine and look at the films and food being offered. Then I leaf through the remaining pages and come upon a full-page photograph of the Oriental Pearl Tower. The accompanying headline: *Shanghai: The City Where Anything Is Possible.*

Of course it's no surprise to see a photograph of Shanghai on a flight to that very city, nor is it strange that the Oriental Pearl Tower – one of its most iconic landmarks – should be featured. And yet I can't help but think of that afternoon, thirteen years ago, when I held Jennifer's fingers in mine and painted our future on her nails. Seeing the tower in my hands again now feels auspicious, as if I'm doing the right thing. As if it's somehow meant to be. As if perhaps, despite having no address or contact details to go on, I might be able to find one person in a country of over a billion.

The money from my father seemed auspicious too. At my mother's funeral, I told him I'd changed my mind, that I was keen for my share of his will to be brought forward after all; and perhaps it was just the shock at my being civil for once, or maybe he was merely keen to get rid of me, but he was only too quick to oblige.

As soon as I had the money, I booked a ticket to China.

A ticket to a new life far away.

Three hours into the flight, and the first meal is over, the trays collected. There is nothing to see from the window at the moment, so I'm watching the map instead: the way the plane symbol is gradually moving across Europe, a yellow line already scored through Germany and Poland.

I've written a short goodbye email to Kirsty. We've spoken just twice since the day of the wedding, and on both occasions she was barely capable of holding a conversation: starting questions only to abandon them halfway through, and mostly failing to answer mine. Obviously I feel bad about how things turned out for her, but equally, she has to take some responsibility herself. *She* was the one who accepted me on to her artist residency programme under false pretences; *she* was the one who mined me mercilessly for information about Alistair and his groomsmen; and *she* was the one who sent her sister, uninvited, to *my* sister's wedding to snoop, spread lies and potentially cause physical harm. Her actions were unhinged – dangerous, even – and sad as it is to say, the world is probably a safer place now she's lapsed into melancholy.

At the wedding, Sarah went and fetched my sister and Alistair after I threatened to cut her throat. But it seems she never mentioned the detail of the threat to them, or anybody else. Unbelievable, really – that a woman notorious for opening her mouth is keeping it shut when she finally has good reason not to. I can only suppose it's out of loyalty to my sister, or continued feelings for Mike, or maybe it's just because she deemed my threat entirely empty and therefore unworthy of her thought.

Or maybe she's changed. Maybe there's a new sympathy within her, a glimmer of kindness. Or maybe I've just learned to see it, now I know she wasn't responsible. Not responsible for Jennifer being sent away and, thus, not responsible for my mind unravelling, and for everything which followed that hot, stormy summer, and beyond.

I like to think we're all capable of change.

An air steward comes down the aisle with a bin bag, asking for rubbish. I reach into my crossbody bag and unzip the small compartment at the back. Extract the Goreton Manor ballpoint pen and my mother's keycard, which have lain there since the wedding. Which I haven't used since that last trip to my mother's room, just before I left for the lake. As the steward draws level with me, I pass them over. Watch as they join the detritus of my fellow passengers, and smile.

This is a fresh start. A chance to create a better future through the reframing of my past. The peace I brought to a boy who was bullied. The mercy I showed to my terminally ill mother, by allowing her to die with her family around her.

And swerving off the road in the face of an oncoming ambulance? One death instead of many. It's a shame, of course, that the front passenger seat bore the brunt of the impact, but that's something I'll just have to live with.

I thank the steward for taking away my rubbish.

And ask for a glass of champagne.

ACKNOWLEDGEMENTS

I want to start by expressing my unending thanks to Sarah, literary agent and author extraordinaire, who took a chance on me from a relatively small sample of work, and has gone on to teach me so much, greatly improve my writing, answer all my newbie questions, and, of course, sell my book. I will be forever grateful for your confidence and support, Sarah.

I am also extremely grateful to Vic, my commissioning editor, for seeing something in my work, and to both her and Mike for their incredible editorial input. I feel very privileged that two such astute and experienced editors gave their time to improve my manuscript, and believe the final book is so much better as a result.

Similarly, I want to thank all the other people who have taken my writing from a messy document on a computer and turned it into a fully fledged book. Gemma, whose meticulous copy-editing picked up errors I hadn't spotted in two years, and Swati, who did her best to lessen my addiction to semicolons. Liron Gilenberg for producing a wonderful cover, and Rebecca Hills, who oversaw the marketing and publicity. Thank you, one and all, for everything you have done.

Thanks are also due to the people and institutions providing support to aspiring writers, including competition organisers and creative writing schools and groups. In my case, specific thanks are owed to the Lucy Cavendish Fiction Prize – which led me to my agent and a whole community of wonderful writers – the Bath Novel Award, the Mslexia Novel Competition and Curtis Brown Creative. The last of these not only improved my writing; it also introduced me to a fantastic – and fantastically supportive – group of writers (a shout-out here to Nichelle, Kim, Keith, Jo L, Jo H, John and Cara). We share thoughts on each other's work, but also congratulations and commiserations on each other's successes and disappointments, which are all part of the writing experience, and all the richer for being shared.

And while on the topic of writerly support, thank you to Nat, my Bedfordshire writing buddy and fellow Lucy Cavendish shortlistee, and to everyone else who read and provided advice on early drafts of this book. Particular thanks to John, Trish, Lorraine, Caitlin and my dad, whose encyclopaedic knowledge of the British Isles knows no bounds.

Thank you, also, to the book community on X, and to the unsung heroes of the book industry who work in libraries and schools, inspiring passion for – and supporting access to – writing and reading. Particular thanks to Mr Malin and Mr Lumsden, two teachers who ignited and fuelled my love of creative writing as a child. Your lessons might have taken place over thirty years ago, but their legacy lives on, and I will always be grateful that you taught me.

Thank you to you, the reader, for picking up this book. It's a privilege to share my words with you.

And, finally, thanks to Mark, Holly and Ethan. For your love and support, always.

ABOUT THE AUTHOR

Photo © 2022 Lisa Jeffries Photography

Born in Washington DC and raised in Derbyshire and Oxfordshire in the UK, Claire studied at Cambridge University and LSE before working for many years as an economist. The quiet of lockdown provided an opportunity to rekindle her passion for creative writing.

When not cold-water swimming or planning her next overseas adventure, Claire is partial to lots of coffee and a good cryptic crossword. She lives in Bedfordshire with her husband and two children.

Follow the Author on Amazon

If you enjoyed this book, follow Claire Ackroyd on Amazon to be notified when the author releases a new book!
To do this, please follow these instructions:

Desktop:

1) Search for the author's name on Amazon or in the Amazon App.
2) Click on the author's name to arrive on their Amazon page.
3) Click the 'Follow' button.

Mobile and Tablet:

1) Search for the author's name on Amazon or in the Amazon App.
2) Click on one of the author's books.
3) Click on the author's name to arrive on their Amazon page.
4) Click the 'Follow' button.

Kindle eReader and Kindle App:

If you enjoyed this book on a Kindle eReader or in the Kindle App, you will find the author 'Follow' button after the last page.